In a closely guarded bastion of evil high in the Swiss Alps ERNST STAVRO BLOFELD, puts the finishing touches to a most fiendish plot involving ten beautiful and ingenuous girls . . . to a most diabolical plot for murder on a mass scale. Only one man can stop him and that man is Blofeld's archenemy— secret agent JAMES BOND.

"The hottest sleuth in the suspense field, James Bond, really tops himself in this new Ian Fleming thriller."
—St. Paul Dispatch

"James Bond, 007, the best-known spy of our times, now by public acclaim one of the master-spies of the cloak-and-dagger fantasy. On Her Majesty's Secret Service is packed with danger, mystery, crime, and wild pursuit, to which the author has added sex in generous proportions."
—Chicago Sunday Tribune

"One of Bond's most ominous and chilling adventures."
—Newsweek

"Solid Fleming."
—New York Herald Tribune

Ian Fleming

ON HER MAJESTY'S SECRET SERVICE

A SIGNET BOOK

SIGNET BOOKS

PUBLISHED BY
THE NEW AMERICAN LIBRARY

First Printing, August, 1964
Second Printing, August, 1964
Third Printing, August, 1964
Fourth Printing, August, 1964

SIGNET TRADEMARK REG. U.S. PAT. OFF. AND FOREIGN COUNTRIES
REGISTERED TRADEMARK—MARCA REGISTRADA
HECHO EN CHICAGO, U.S.A.

SIGNET BOOKS are published by
The New American Library of World Literature, Inc.
501 Madison Avenue, New York, New York 10022

PRINTED IN THE UNITED STATES OF AMERICA

for SABLE BASILISK PURSUIVANT
and HILARY BRAY
who came to the aid of the party

CONTENTS

1 SEASCAPE WITH FIGURES

It was one of those Septembers when it seemed that the summer would never end.

The five-mile promenade of Royale-les-Eaux, backed by trim lawns emblazoned at intervals with tricolour beds of salvia, alyssum and lobelia, was bright with flags and, on the longest beach in the north of France, the gay bathing tents still marched prettily down to the tide-line in big, money-making battalions. Music, one of those lilting accordion waltzes, blared from the loudspeakers around the Olympic-size piscine and, from time to time, echoing above the music, a man's voice announced over the public address system that Phillippe Bertrand, aged seven, was looking for his mother, that Yolande Lefèvre was waiting for her friends below the clock at the entrance, or that a Madame Dufours was demanded on the telephone. From the beach, particularly from the neighbourhood of the three playground enclosures —"Joie de Vivre," "Hélio" and "Azur"—came a twitter of children's cries that waxed and waned with the thrill of their games, and, farther out, on the firm sand left by the now distant sea, the shrill whistle of the physical-fitness instructor marshalled his teen-agers through the last course of the day.

It was one of those beautiful, naïve seaside panoramas for which the Brittany and Picardy beaches have provided the setting—and inspired their recorders, Boudin, Tissot, Monet—ever since the birth of plages and bains de mer more than a hundred years ago.

To James Bond, sitting in one of the concrete shelters

with his face to the setting sun, there was something poignant, ephemeral about it all. It reminded him almost too vividly of childhood—of the velvet feel of the hot powder sand, and the painful grit of wet sand between young toes when the time came for him to put his shoes and socks on, of the precious little pile of sea-shells and interesting wrack on the sill of his bedroom window ("No, we'll have to leave that behind, darling. It'll dirty up your trunk!"), of the small crabs scuttling away from the nervous fingers groping beneath the seaweed in the rock-pools, of the swimming and swimming and swimming through the dancing waves—always in those days, it seemed, lit with sunshine—and then the infuriating, inevitable "time to come out." It was all there, his own childhood, spread out before him to have another look at. What a long time ago they were, those spade-and-bucket days! How far he had come since the freckles and the Cadbury milk-chocolate Flakes and the fizzy lemonade! Impatiently Bond lit a cigarette, pulled his shoulders out of their slouch and slammed the mawkish memories back into their long-closed file. Today he was a grown-up, a man with years of dirty, dangerous memories—a spy. He was not sitting in this concrete hideout to sentimentalize about a pack of scrubby, smelly children on a beach scattered with bottle-tops and lollysticks and fringed by a sea thick with sun-oil and putrid with the main drains of Royale. He was here, he had chosen to be here, to spy. To spy on a woman.

The sun was getting lower. Already one could smell the September chill that all day had lain hidden beneath the heat. The cohorts of bathers were in quick retreat, striking their little camps and filtering up the steps and across the promenade into the shelter of the town where the lights were going up in the cafés. The announcer at the swimming-pool harried his customers: "Allo! Allo! Fermeture en dix minutes! A dix-huit heures, fermeture de la piscine!" Silhouetted in the path of the setting sun, the two Bombard rescue-boats with flags bearing a blue cross on a yellow background were speeding northwards for their distant shelter up-river in the Vieux Port. The last of the gay, giraffe-like sand-yachts fled down the distant water-line towards its corral among the sand dunes, and the three agents cyclistes in charge of the car-parks pedalled away through the melting ranks of cars towards the police station in the centre of the town. In a matter of minutes the vast expanse of sand—the tide, still receding, was already a mile out—would be left to the sea-gulls that would soon be flocking in their hordes to forage for the scraps of food left by the picnickers. Then the orange ball of the sun would hiss down into the sea and the beach would, for a while, be entirely deserted, until, under cover of darkness, the prowling lovers would come to writhe briefly, grittily in the dark corners between the bathing-huts and the seawall.

On the beaten stretch of sand below where James Bond was sitting, two golden girls in exciting bikinis packed up the game of Jokari which they had been so provocatively playing and raced each other up the steps towards Bond's shelter. They flaunted their bodies at him, paused and chattered to see if he would respond, and, when he didn't, linked arms and sauntered on towards the town, leaving Bond wondering why it was that French girls had more prominent navels than any others. Was it that French surgeons sought to add, even in this minute respect, to the future sex-appeal of girl babies?

And now, up and down the beach, the lifeguards gave a final blast on their horns to announce that they were going off duty, the music from the piscine stopped in mid-tune and the great expanse of sand was suddenly deserted.

But not quite! A hundred yards out, lying face downwards on a black and white striped bathing-wrap, on the private patch of firm sand where she had installed herself an hour before, the girl was still there, motionless, spread-eagled in direct line between James Bond and the setting sun that was now turning the left-behind pools and shallow rivulets into blood-red, meandering scrawls across the middle distance. Bond went on watching her—now, in the silence and emptiness, with an ounce more tension. He was waiting for her to do something—for something, he didn't know what, to happen. It would be more true to say that he was watching *over* her. He had an instinct that she was in some sort of danger. Or was it just that there was the smell of danger in the air? He didn't know. He only knew that he mustn't leave her alone, particularly now that everyone else had gone.

James Bond was mistaken. Not everyone else had gone. Behind him, at the Café de la Plage on the other side of the promenade, two men in raincoats and dark caps sat at a secluded table bordering the sidewalk. They had half-empty cups of coffee in front of them and they didn't talk. They sat and watched the blur on the frosted-glass partition of the shelter that was James Bond's head and shoulders. They also watched, but less intently, the distant white blur on the sand that was the girl. Their stillness, and their unseasonable clothes, would have made a disquieting impression on anyone who, in his turn, might have been watching them. But there was no such person, except their waiter who had simply put them in the category of "bad news" and hoped they would soon be on their way.

When the lower rim of the orange sun touched the sea, it was almost as if a signal had sounded for the girl. She slowly got to her feet, ran both hands backwards through her hair and began to walk evenly, purposefully, towards the sun and the far-away froth of the water-line over a mile away. It would be violet dusk by the time she reached the sea and one might have guessed that this was probably the last day of her holiday, the last bathe.

James Bond thought otherwise. He left his shelter, ran down the steps to the sand and began walking out after her at a fast pace. Behind him, across the promenade, the two men in raincoats also seemed to think otherwise. One of them briskly threw down some coins and they both got up and, walking strictly in step, crossed the promenade to the sand and, with a kind of urgent military precision, marched rapidly side by side in Bond's tracks.

Now the strange pattern of figures on the vast expanse of empty, blood-streaked sand was eerily conspicuous. Yet it was surely not one to be interfered with! The pattern had a nasty, a secret smell. The white girl, the bare-headed young man, the two squat, marching pursuers—it had something of a kind of deadly Grandmothers' Steps about it. In the café, the waiter collected the coins and looked after the distant figures, still outlined by the last quarter of the orange sun. It smelt like police business—or the other thing. He would keep it to himself but remember it. He might get his name in the papers.

James Bond was rapidly catching up with the girl. Now he knew that he would get to her just as she reached the water-line. He began to wonder what he would say to her, how he would put it. He couldn't say, "I had a hunch you were going to commit suicide so I came after you to stop you." "I was going for a walk on the beach and I thought I recognized you. Will you have a drink after your swim?" would be childish. He finally decided to say, "Oh, Tracy!" and then, when she turned round, "I was worried about you." Which would at least be inoffensive and, for the matter of that, true.

The sea was now gunmetal below a primrose horizon. A small, westerly offshore breeze, drawing the hot land-air out to sea, had risen and was piling up wavelets that scrolled in whitely as far as the eye could see. Flocks of herring gulls lazily rose and settled again at the girl's approach, and the air was full of their mewing and of the endless lap-lap of the small waves. The soft indigo dusk added a touch of melancholy to the empty solitude of sand and sea, now so far away from the comforting bright lights and holiday bustle of "La Reine de la Côte Opale," as Royale-les-Eaux had splendidly christened herself. Bond looked forward to getting the girl back to those bright lights. He watched the lithe golden figure in the white one-piece bathing-suit and wondered how soon she would be able to hear his voice above the noise of the gulls and the sea. Her pace had slowed a fraction as she approached the water-line and her head, with its bell of heavy fair hair to the shoulders, was slightly bowed, in thought perhaps, or tiredness.

Bond quickened his step until he was only ten paces behind her. "Hey! Tracy!"

The girl didn't start or turn quickly round. Her steps faltered and stopped, and then, as a small wave creamed in and died at her feet, she turned slowly and stood squarely facing him. Her eyes, puffed and wet with tears, looked past him. Then they met his. She said dully, "What is it? What do you want?"

"I was worried about you. What are you doing out here? What's the matter?"

The girl looked past him again. Her clenched right hand went up to her mouth. She said something, something Bond couldn't understand, from behind it. Then a voice, from very close behind Bond, said softly, silkily, "Don't move or you get it back of the knee."

Bond swirled round into a crouch, his gun hand inside his coat. The steady silver eyes of the two automatics sneered at him.

Bond slowly straightened himself. He dropped his hand to his side and the held breath came out between his teeth in a quiet hiss. The two dead-pan, professional faces told him even more than the two silver eyes of the guns. They held no tension, no excitement. The thin half-smiles were relaxed, contented. The eyes were not even wary. They were almost bored. Bond had looked into such faces many times before. This was routine. These men were killers—pro killers.

Bond had no idea who these men were, who they worked for, what this was all about. On the theory that worry is a dividend paid to disaster before it is due, he consciously relaxed his muscles and emptied his mind of questions. He stood and waited.

"Position your hands behind your neck." The silky, patient

voice was from the south, from the Mediterranean. It fitted with the men's faces—tough-skinned, widely pored, yellow-brown. Marseillais perhaps, or Italian. The Mafia? The faces belonged to good secret police or tough crooks. Bond's mind ticked and whirred, selecting cards like an IBM machine. What enemies had he got in those areas? Might it be Blofeld? Had the hare turned upon the hound?

When the odds are hopeless, when all seems to be lost, then is the time to be calm, to make a show of authority—at least of indifference. Bond smiled into the eyes of the man who had spoken. "I don't think your mother would like to know what you are doing this evening. You are a Catholic? So I will do as you ask." The man's eyes glittered. Touché! Bond clasped his hands behind his head.

The man stood aside so as to have a clear field of fire while his Number Two removed Bond's Walther PPK from the soft leather holster inside his trouser belt and ran expert hands down his sides, down his arms to the wrists and down the inside of his thighs. Then Number Two stood back, pocketed the Walther and again took out his own gun.

Bond glanced over his shoulder. The girl had said nothing, expressed neither surprise nor alarm. Now she was standing with her back to the group, looking out to sea, apparently relaxed, unconcerned. What in God's name was it all about? Had she been used as a bait? But for whom? And now what? Was he to be executed, his body left lying to be rolled back inshore by the tide? It seemed the only solution. If it was a question of some kind of a deal, the four of them could not just walk back across the mile of sand to the town and say polite goodbyes on the promenade steps. No. This was the terminal point. Or was it? From the north, through the deep indigo dusk, came the fast, rattling hum of an outboard and, as Bond watched, the cream of a thick bow-wave showed and then the blunt outline of one of the Bombard rescue-craft, the flat-bottomed inflatable rubber boats with a single Johnson engine in the flattened stern. So they had been spotted! By the coast-guards perhaps? And here was rescue! By God, he'd roast these two thugs when they got to the harbour police at the Vieux Port! But what story would he tell about the girl?

Bond turned back to face the men. At once he knew the worst. They had rolled their trousers up to the knees and were waiting, composedly, their shoes in one hand and their guns in the other. This was no rescue. It was just part of the ride. Oh, well! Paying no attention to the men, Bond bent down, rolled up his trousers as they had done and, in the process of fumbling with his socks and shoes, palmed one of his heel knives and, half-turning towards the boat that had now grounded in the shallows, transferred it to his right-hand trouser pocket.

No words were exchanged. The girl climbed aboard first, then Bond, and lastly the two men who helped the engine with a final shove on the stern. The boatman, who looked like any other French deep-sea fisherman, whirled the blunt nose of the Bombard round, changed gears to forward, and they were off northwards through the buffeting waves while the golden hair of the girl streamed back and softly whipped James Bond's cheek.

"Tracy. You're going to catch cold. Here. Take my coat." Bond slipped his coat off. She held out a hand to help him put it on her. In the process her hand found his and pressed it. Now what the hell? Bond edged closer to her. He felt her body respond. Bond glanced at the two men. They sat hunched against the wind, their hands in their pockets, watchful, but somehow uninterested. Behind them the necklace of lights that was Royale receded swiftly until it was only a golden glow on the horizon. James Bond's right hand felt for the comforting knife in his pocket and ran his thumb across the razor-sharp blade.

While he wondered how and when he might have a chance to use it, the rest of his mind ran back over the previous twenty-four hours and panned them for the gold-dust of truth.

2 GRAN TURISMO

Almost exactly twenty-four hours before, James Bond had been nursing his car, the old Continental Bently—the "R" type chassis with the big 6 engine and a 13 : 40 back-axle ratio—that he had now been driving for three years, along that fast but dull stretch of N.1 between Abbeville and Montreuil that takes the English tourist back to his country via Silver City Airways from Le Touquet or by ferry from Boulogne or Calais. He was hurrying safely, at between eighty and ninety, driving by the automatic pilot that is built in to all rally-class drivers, and his mind was totally occupied with drafting his letter of resignation from the Secret Service.

The letter, addressed "Personal for M," had got to the following stage:

Sir,

I have the honour to request that you will accept my resignation from the Service, effective forthwith.

My reasons for this submission, which I put forward with much regret, are the following:

(1) My duties in the Service, until some twelve months ago, have been connected with the Double-0 Section and you, Sir, have been kind enough, from time to time, to express your satisfaction with my performance of those duties, which I, for my part, have enjoyed. To my chagrin, [Bond had been pleased with this fine word] however, on the successful completion of Operation "Thunderball," I received personal instructions from you to concentrate all my efforts, without a terminal date, [another felicitous phrase!] on the pursuit of Ernst Stavro Bolfeld and on his apprehension, together with any members of SPECTRE—otherwise "The Special Executive for Counter-Intelligence, Revenge and Extortion"—if that organization had been re-created since its destruction at the climax of Operation "Thunderball."

(2) I accepted the assignment with, if you will recall, reluctance. It seemed to me, and I so expressed myself at the time, that this was purely an investigatory matter which could well have been handled, using straightforward police methods, by other sections of the Service—local Stations, allied foreign secret services and Interpol. My objections were overruled, and for close on twelve months I have been engaged all over the world in routine detective work which, in the case of every scrap of rumour, every lead, has proved abortive. I have found no trace of this man nor of a revived SPECTRE, if such exists.

(3) My many appeals to be relieved of this wearisome and fruitless assignment, even when addressed to you personally, Sir, have been ignored or, on occasion, curtly dismissed, and my frequent animadversions [another good one!] to the effect that Blofeld is dead have been treated with a courtesy that I can only describe as scant. [Neat, that! Perhaps a bit too neat!]

(4) The above unhappy circumstances have recently achieved their climax in my undercover mission (Ref. Station R'S PX 437/007) to Palermo, in pursuit of a hare of quite outrageous falsity. This animal took the shape of one "Blauenfelder," a perfectly respectable

German citizen engaged in viniculture—specifically the grafting of Moselle grapes on to the Sicilian strains to enhance the sugar content of the latter which, for your passing information, [Steady on, old chap! Better redraft all this!] are inclined to sourness. My investigations into this individual brought me to the attention of the Mafia and my departure from Sicily was, to say the least, ignominious.

(5) Having regard, Sir, to the above and, specifically, to the continued misuse of the qualities, modest though they may be, that have previously fitted me for the more arduous, and, to me, more rewarding, duties associated with the work of the Double-0 Section, I beg leave to submit my resignation from the Service.

I am, Sir,
Your Obedient Servant,
007

Of course, reflected Bond, as he nursed the long bonnet of his car through a built-up S-bend, he would have to rewrite a lot of it. Some of it was a bit pompous and there were one or two cracks that would have to be ironed out or toned down. But that was the gist of what he would dictate to his secretary when he got back to the office the day after tomorrow. And if she burst into tears, to hell with her! He meant it. By God he did. He was fed to the teeth with chasing the ghost of Blofeld. And the same went for SPECTRE. The thing had been smashed. Even a man of Blofeld's genius, in the impossible event that he still existed, could never get a machine of that calibre running again.

It was then, on a ten-mile straight cut through a forest, that it happened. Triple wind-horns screamed their banshee discord in his ear, and a low, white two-seater, a Lancia Flaminia Zagato Spyder with its hood down, tore past him, cut in cheekily across his bonnet and pulled away, the sexy boom of its twin exhausts echoing back from the border of trees. And it was a girl driving, a girl with a shocking pink scarf tied round her hair, leaving a brief pink tail that the wind blew horizontal behind her.

If there was one thing that set James Bond really moving in life, with the exception of gun-play, it was being passed at speed by a pretty girl; and it was his experience that girls who drove competitively like that were always pretty—and exciting. The shock of the windhorn's scream had automatically cut out "George," emptied Bond's head of all other thought and brought his car back under manual control.

Now, with a tight-lipped smile, he stamped his foot into the floorboard, held the wheel firmly at a quarter to three and went after her.

100, 110, 115, and he still wasn't gaining. Bond reached forward to the dashboard and flicked up a red switch. The thin high whine of machinery on the brink of torment tore at his eardrums and the Bentley gave an almost perceptible kick forward. 120, 125. He was definitely gaining. Fifty yards, 40, 30! Now he could just see her eyes in her rear mirror. But the good road was running out. One of those exclamation marks that the French use to denote danger flashed by on his right. And now, over a rise, there was a church spire, the clustered houses of a small village at the bottom of a steepish hill, the snake sign of another S-bend. Both cars slowed down—90, 80, 70. Bond watched her tail-lights briefly blaze, saw her right hand reach down to the floor stick, almost simultaneously with his own, and change down. Then they were in the S-bend, on cobbles, and he had to brake as he enviously watched the way her de Dion axle married her rear wheels to the rough going, which his own live axle hopped and skittered as he wrenched at the wheel. And then it was the end of the village, and, with a brief wag of her tail as she came out of the S, she was off like a bat out of hell up the long straight rise and he had lost fifty yards.

And so the race went on, Bond gaining a little on the straights but losing it all to the famous Lancia road-holding through the villages—and, he had to admit, to her wonderful, nerveless driving. And now a big Michelin sign said "Montreuil 5, Royale-les-Eaux 10, Le Touquet Paris-Plage 15," and he wondered about her destination and debated with himself whether he shouldn't forget about Royale and the night he had promised himself at its famous casino and just follow where she went, wherever it was, and find out who this devil of a girl was.

The decision was taken out of his hands. Montreuil is a dangerous town with cobbled, twisting streets and much farm traffic. Bond was fifty yards behind her at the outskirts, but, with his big car, he couldn't follow her fast slalom through the hazards and, by the time he was out of the town and over the Etaples-Paris level-crossing, she had vanished. The left-hand turn for Royale came up. Was there a little dust hanging in the bend? Bond took the turn, somehow knowing that he was going to see her again.

He leaned forward and flicked down the red switch. The moan of the blower died away and there was silence in the car as he motored along, easing his tense muscles. He wondered if the supercharger had damaged the engine. Against the solemn warnings of Rolls-Royce, he had had fitted, by his pet expert at the Headquarters' motor pool, an Arnott supercharger controlled by a magnetic clutch. Rolls-Royce had said the crank-shaft bearings wouldn't take the extra load and, when he confessed to them what he had done, they regretfully but firmly withdrew their guarantees and washed their hands of their bastardized child. This was the first time he had notched 125 and the rev. counter had hovered dangerously over the red line at 4500. But the temperature and oil were O.K. and there were no expensive noises. And, by God, it had been fun!

James Bond idled through the pretty approaches to Royale, through the young beeches and the heavy-scented pines, looking forward to the evening and remembering his other annual pilgrimages to this place and, particularly, the great battle across the baize he had had with Le Chiffre so many years ago. He had come a long way since then, dodged many bullets and much death and loved many girls, but there had been a drama and a poignancy about that particular adventure that every year drew him back to Royale and its casino and to the small granite cross in the little churchyard that simply said "Vesper Lynd. R.I.P."

And now what was the place holding for him on this beautiful September evening? A big win? A painful loss? A beautiful girl—that beautiful girl?

To think first of the game. This was the week-end of the "clôture annuelle." Tonight, this very Saturday night, the Casino Royale was holding its last night of the season. It was always a big event and there would be pilgrims even from Belgium and Holland, as well as the rich regulars from Paris and Lille. In addition, the "Syndicat d'Initiative et des Bains de Mer de Royale" traditionally threw open its doors to all its local contractors and suppliers, and there was free champagne and a great groaning buffet to reward the town people for their work during the season. It was a tremendous carouse that rarely finished before breakfast time. The tables would be packed and there would be a very high game indeed.

Bond had one million francs of private capital—Old Francs, of course—about seven hundred pounds' worth. He always reckoned his private funds in Old Francs. It made him feel so rich. On the other hand, he made out his official expenses in New Francs because that made them look smaller—but probably not to the Chief Accountant at Headquarters! One million francs! For that evening he was a millionaire! Might he so remain by tomorrow morning!

And now he was coming into the promenade des Anglais and there was the bastard Empire frontage of the Hotel Splendide. And there, by God, on the gravel sweep alongside its steps, stood the little white Lancia and, at this moment, a bagagiste, in a striped waistcoat and green apron, was carrying two Vuitton suitcases up the steps to the entrance!

So!

James Bond slid his car into the million-pound line of cars in the car park, told the same bagagiste, who was now taking rich, small stuff out of the Lancia, to bring up his bags, and went in to the reception-desk. The manager impressively took over from the clerk and greeted Bond with golden-toothed effusion, while making a mental note to earn a good mark with the Chef de Police by reporting Bond's arrival, so that the Chef could, in his turn, make a good mark with the Deuxième and the SDT by putting the news on the teleprinter to Paris.

Bond said; "By the way, Monsieur Maurice. Who is the lady who has just driven up in the white Lancia? She is staying here?"

"Yes, indeed, mon Commandant." Bond received an extra two teeth in the enthusiastic smile. "The lady is a good friend of the house. The father is a very big industrial from the South. She is La Comtesse Teresa di Vicenzo. Monsieur must surely have read of her in the papers. Madame la Comtesse is a lady—how shall I put it?"—the smile became secret, between men—"a lady, shall we say, who lives life to the full."

"Ah, yes. Thank you. And how has the season been?"

The small talk continued as the manager personally took Bond up in the lift and showed him into one of the handsome grey and white Directoire rooms with the deep rose coverlet on the bed that Bond remembered so well. Then, with a final exchange of courtesies, James Bond was alone.

Bond was faintly disappointed. She sounded a bit grand for him, and he didn't happen to like girls, film stars for instance, who were in any way public property. He liked private girls, girls he could discover himself and make his own. Perhaps, he admitted, there was inverted snobbery in this. Perhaps, even less worthily, it was that the famous ones were less easy to get.

His two battered suitcases came and he unpacked leisurely and then ordered from Room Service a bottle of the Taittinger Blanc de Blancs that he had made his traditional drink at Royale. When the bottle, in its frosted silver bucket, came, he drank a quarter of it rather fast and then went into the bathroom and had an ice-cold shower and washed his hair with Pinaud Elixir, that prince among shampoos, to get the dust of the roads out of it. Then he slipped on his dark-blue tropical worsted trousers, white sea-island cotton shirt, socks and black casual shoes (he abhorred shoe-laces), and went and sat by the window and looked out across the promenade to the sea and wondered where he would have dinner and what he would choose to eat.

James Bond was not a gourmet. In England he lived on grilled soles, œufs cocotte and cold roast beef with potato salad. But when travelling abroad, generally by himself, meals were a welcome break in the day, something to look forward to, something to break the tension of fast driving, with its risks taken or avoided, the narrow squeaks, the permanent background of concern for the fitness of his machine. In fact, at this moment, after covering the long stretch from the Italian frontier at Ventimiglia in a comfortable three days (God knew there was no reason to hurry back to Headquarters!), he was fed to the teeth with the sucker-traps for gourmandizing tourists. The "Hostelleries," the "Vieilles Auberges," the "Relais Fleuris"—he had had the lot. He had had their "Bonnes Tables," and their "Fines Bouteilles." He had had their "Spécialités du Chef"—generally a rich sauce of cream and wine and a few button mushrooms concealing poor quality meat or fish. He had had the whole lip-smacking ritual of winemanship and foodmanship and, incidentally, he had had quite enough of the Bisodol that went with it!

The French belly-religion had delivered its final kick at him the night before. Wishing to avoid Orléans, he had stopped south of this uninspiring city and had chosen a mock-Breton auberge on the south bank of the Loire, despite its profusion of window-boxes and sham beams, ignoring the china cat pursuing the china bird across its gabled roof, because it was right on the edge of the Loire—perhaps Bond's favourite river in the world. He had stoically accepted the hammered copper warming pans, brass cooking utensils and other antique bogosities that cluttered the walls of the entrance hall, had left his bag in his room and had gone for an agreeable walk along the softly running, swallow-skimmed river. The dining-room, in which he was one of a small handful of tourists, had sounded the alarm. Above a fire-place of electric logs and over-polished fire-irons there had hung a coloured plaster escutcheon bearing the dread device: ICY DOULCE FRANCE. All the plates, of some hideous local ware, bore the jingle, irritatingly inscrutable, "Jamais en Vain, Toujours en Vin," and the surly waiter, stale with "fin de saison," had served him with the fly-walk of the Pâté Maison (sent back for a new slice) and a Poularde à la crème that was the only genuine antique in the place. Bond had moodily washed down this sleazy provender with a bottle of instant Pouilly-Fuissé and was finally insulted the next morning by a bill for the meal in excess of five pounds.

It was to efface all these dyspeptic memories that Bond now sat at his window, sipped his Taittinger and weighed up the pros and cons of the local eating places and wondered what dishes it would be best to gamble on. He finally chose one of his favourite restaurants in France, a modest establishment, unpromisingly placed exactly opposite the railway station of Etaples, rang up his old friend Monsieur Bécaud for a table and, two hours later, was motoring back to the Casino with Turbot poché, sauce mousseline, and half the best roast partridge he had eaten in his life, under his belt.

Greatly encouraged, and further stimulated by half a bottle of Mouton Rothschild '53 and a glass of ten-year-old Calvados with his three cups of coffee, he went cheerfully up the thronged steps of the Casino with the absolute certitude that this was going to be a night to remember.

3 THE GAMBIT OF SHAME

(The bombard had now beaten round the dolefully clanging bell-buoy and was hammering slowly up the River Royale against the current. The gay lights of the little marina, haven of cross-channel yachtsmen, showed way up on the right bank, and it crossed Bond's mind to wait until they were slightly above it and then plunge his knife into the side and bottom of the rubber Bombard and swim for it. But he already heard in his mind the boom of the guns and heard the zwip and splash of the bullets round his head until, probably, there came the bright burst of light and the final flash of knowledge that he had at last had it. And anyway, how well could the girl swim, and in this current? Bond was now very cold. He leant closer against her and went back to remembering the night before and combing his memories for clues.)

After the long walk across the Salle d'Entrée, past the vitrines of Van Cleef, Lanvin, Hermès and the rest, there came the brief pause for identification at the long desk backed by the tiers of filing cabinets, the payment for the Carte d'Entrée pour les Salles de Jeux, the quick, comptometer survey of the physiognomiste at the entrance, the bow and flourish of the garishly uniformed huissier at the door and James Bond was inside the belly of the handsome, scented machine.

He paused for a moment by the caisse, his nostrils flaring at the smell of the crowded, electric, elegant scene, then he walked slowly across to the top chemin de fer table beside the entrance to the luxuriously appointed bar, and caught the eye of Monsieur Pol, the Chef de Jeu of the high game. Monsieur Pol spoke to a huissier and Bond was shown to Number Seven, reserved by a counter from the huissier's pocket. The huissier gave a quick brush to the baize inside the line—that famous line that had been the bone of contention in the Tranby Croft case involving King Edward VII—polished an ash-tray and pulled out the chair for Bond. Bond sat down. The shoe was at the other end of the table, at Number Three. Cheerful and relaxed, Bond examined the faces of the other players while the Changeur changed his notes for a hundred thousand into ten blood-red counters of ten thousand each. Bond stacked them in a neat pile in front of him and watched the play which, he saw from the notice hanging between the green-shaded lights over the table, was for a minimum of one hundred New Francs, or ten thousand of the old. But he noted that the game was being opened by each banker for up to five hundred New Francs—serious money—say forty pounds as a starter.

The players were the usual international mixture—three Lille textile tycoons in over-padded dinner-jackets, a couple of heavy women in diamonds who might be Belgian, a rather Agatha Christie-style little English-woman who played quietly and successfully and might be a villa owner, two middle-aged Americans in dark suits who appeared cheerful and slightly drunk, probably down from Paris, and Bond. Watchers and casual punters were two-deep round the table. No girl!

The game was cold. The shoe went slowly round the table, each banker in turn going down on that dread third coup which, for some reason, is the sound barrier at chemin de fer which must be broken if you are to have a run. Each time, when it came to Bond's turn, he debated whether to bow to the pattern and pass his bank after the second coup. Each time, for nearly an hour of play, he obstinately told himself that the pattern would break, and why not with him? That the cards have no memory and that it was time for them to run. And each time, as did the other players, he went down on the third coup. The shoe came to an end. Bond left his money on the table and wandered off among the other tables, visiting the roulette, the trente et quarante and the baccarat table, to see if he could find the girl. When she had passed him that evening in the Lancia, he had only caught a glimple of fair hair and of a pure, rather authoritative profile. But he knew that he would recognize her at once, if only by the cord of animal magnetism that had bound them together during the race. But there was no sign of her.

Bond went back to the table. The croupier was marshalling the six packs into the oblong block that would soon be slipped into the waiting shoe. Since Bond was beside him, the croupier offered him the neutral, plain red card to cut the pack with. Bond rubbed the card between his fingers and, with amused deliberation, slipped it as nearly half-way down the block of cards as he could estimate. The croupier smiled at him and at his deliberation, went through the legerdemain that would in due course bring the red stop card into the tongue of the shoe and stop the game just seven cards before the end of the shoe, packed the long block of cards into the shoe, slid in the metal tongue that held them prisoner and announced, loud and clear: "Messieurs [the "mesdames" are traditionally not mentioned; since Victorian days it has been assumed that ladies do not gamble], les jeux sont faits. Numéro six à la main." The Chef de Jeu, on his throne behind the croupier, took up the cry, the huissiers shepherded distant stragglers back to their places, and the game began again.

James Bond confidently bancoed the Lille tycoon on his left, won, made up the cagnotte with a few small counters and doubled the stake to two thousand New Francs—two hundred thousand of the old.

He won that, and the next. Now for the hurdle of the third coup and he was off to the races! He won it with a natural nine! Eight hundred thousand in the bank (as Bond reckoned it!) Again he won, with difficulty this time—his six against a five. Then he decided to play it safe and pile up some capital. Of the one million six, he asked for the six hundred to be put "en garage," removed from the stake, leaving a bank of one million. Again he won. Now he put a million "en garage." Once more a bank of a million, and now he would have a fat cushion of one million six coming to him anyway! But it was getting difficult to make up his stake. The table was becoming wary of this dark Englishman who played so quietly, wary of the half-smile of certitude on his rather cruel mouth. Who was he? Where did he come from? What did he do? There was a murmur of excited speculation round the table. So far a run of six. Would the Englishman pocket his small fortune and pass the bank? Or would he continue to run it? Surely the cards must change! But James Bond's mind was made up. The cards have no memory in defeat. They also have no memory in victory. He ran the bank three more times, adding each time a million to his "garage," and then the little old English lady, who had so far left the running to the others, stepped in and bancoed him at the tenth turn, and Bond smiled across at her, knowing that she was going to win. And she did, ignominiously, with a one against Bond's "bûche"—three kings, making zero.

There was a sigh of relief round the table. The spell had been broken! And a whisper of envy as the heavy, mother-of-pearl plaques piled nearly a foot high, four million, six hundred thousand francs' worth, well over three thousand pounds, were shunted across to Bond with the flat of the croupier's spatula. Bond tossed a plaque for a thousand New Francs to the croupier, received the traditional "Merci, monsieur! Pour le personnel!" and the game went on.

James Bond lit a cigarette and paid little attention as the shoe went shunting round the table away from him. He had made a packet, dammit! A bloody packet! Now he must be careful. Sit on it. But not too careful, not sit on all of it! This was a glorious evening. It was barely past midnight. He didn't want to go home yet. So be it! He would run his bank when it came to him, but do no bancoing of the others—absolutely none. The cards had got hot. His run had shown that. There would be other runs now, and he could easily burn his fingers chasing them.

Bond was right. When the shoe got to Number Five, to one of the Lille tycoons two places to the left of Bond, an ill-mannered, loud-mouthed player who smoked a cigar out of an amber-and-gold holder and who tore at the cards with heavily manicured, spatulate fingers and slapped them down like a German tarot player, he quickly got through the third coup and was off. Bond, in accordance with his plan, left him severely alone and now, at the sixth coup, the bank stood at twenty thousand New Francs—two million of the old, and the table had got wary again. Everyone was sitting on his money.

The croupier and the Chef de Jeu made their loud calls, "Un banco de vingt mille! Faites vos jeux, messieurs. Il reste à compléter! Un banco de vingt mille!"

And then there she was! She had come from nowhere

and was standing beside the croupier, and Bond had no time to take in more than golden arms, a beautiful golden face with brilliant blue eyes and shocking pink lips, some kind of a plain white dress, a bell of golden hair down to her shoulders, and then it came. "Banco!"

Everyone looked at her and there was a moment's silence. And then "Le banco est fait" from the croupier, and the monster from Lille (as Bond now saw him) was tearing the cards out of the shoe, and hers were on their way over to her on the croupier's spatula.

She bent down and there was a moment of discrete cleavage in the white V of her neckline.

"Une carte."

Bond's heart sank. She certainly hadn't anything better than a five. The monster turned his up. Seven. And now he scrabbled out a card for her and flicked it contemptuously across. A simpering queen!

The croupier delicately faced her other two cards with the tip of his spatula. A four! She had lost!

Bond groaned inwardly and looked across to see how she had taken it.

What he saw was not reassuring. The girl was whispering urgently to the Chef de Jeu. He was shaking his head, sweat was beading on his cheeks. In the silence that had fallen round the table, the silence that licks its lips at the strong smell of scandal, which was now electric in the air, Bond heard the Chef de Jeu say firmly, "Mais c'est impossible. Je regrette, madame. Il faut vous arranger à la caisse."

And now that most awful of all whispers in a casino was running among the watchers and the players like a slithering reptile: "Le coup du déshonneur! C'est le coup du déshonneur! Quelle honte! Quelle honte!"

Oh, my God! thought Bond. She's done it! She hasn't got the money! And for some reason she can't get any credit at the caisse!

The monster from Lille was making the most of the situation. He knew that the casino would pay in the case of a default. He sat back with lowered eyes, puffing at his cigar, the injured party.

But Bond knew of the stigma the girl would carry for the rest of her life. The casinos of France are a strong trade union. They have to be. Tomorrow the telegrams would go out: "Madame la Comtesse Teresa di Vicenzo, passport number X, is to be put on the black list." That would be the end of her casino life in France, in Italy, probably also in Germany, Egypt and, today, England. It was like being declared a bad risk at Lloyd's or with the City security firm of Dun and Bradstreet. In American gambling circles, she might even have been liquidated. In Europe, for her, the fate would be almost as severe. In the circles in which, presumably, she moved, she would be bad news, unclean. The "coup du déshonneur" simply wasn't done. It was social ostracism.

Not caring about the social ostracism, thinking only about the wonderful girl who had outdriven him, shown him her tail, between Abbeville and Montreuil, James Bond leant slightly forward. He tossed two of the precious pearly plaques into the centre of the table. He said, with a slightly bored, slightly puzzled intonation, "Forgive me. Madame has forgotten that we agreed to play in partnership this evening." And, not looking at the girl, but speaking with authority to the Chef de Jeu, "I beg your pardon. My mind was elsewhere. Let the game continue."

The tension round the table relaxed. Or rather it changed to another target, away from the girl. Was it true what this Englishman had said? But it must be! One does not pay two million francs for a girl. But previously there had been no relationship between them—so far as one could see. They had been at opposite sides of the table. No signs of complicity had been exchanged. And the girl? She had shown no emotion. She had looked at the man, once, with directness. Then she had quietly moved away from the table, towards the bar. There was certainly something odd here—something one did not understand. But the game was proceeding. The Chef De Jeu had surreptitiously wiped a handkerchief across his face. The croupier had raised his head, which, previously, had seemed to be bowed under some kind of emotional guillotine. And now the old pattern had re-established itself. "La partie continue. Un banco de quarante mille!"

James Bond glanced down at the still formidable pile of counters between his curved, relaxed arms. It would be nice to get that two million francs back. It might be hours before a banco of equal size offered the chance. After all, he was playing with the casino's money! His profits represented "found" money and, if he lost, he could still go away with a small profit—enough and to spare to pay for his night at Royale. And he had taken a dislike to the monster from Lille. It would be amusing to reverse the old fable—first to rescue the girl, then to slay the monster. And it was time for the man's run of luck to end. After all, the cards have no memory!

James Bond had not enough funds to take the whole banco, only half of it, what is known as "avec la table," meaning that the other players could make up the remaining half if they wanted to. Bond, forgetting the conservative strategy he had sworn himself to only half an hour before, leant slightly forward and said, "Avec la table," and pushed twenty thousand New Francs over the line.

Money followed his on to the table. Was this not the Englishman with the green fingers? And Bond was pleased to note that the little old Agatha Christie Englishwoman supported him with one thousand. That was a good omen! He looked at the banker, the man from Lille. His cigar had gone out in its holder and his lips, where they gripped the holder, were white. He was sweating profusely. He was debating whether to pass the hand and take his fat profits or have one more go. The sharp, pig-like eyes darted round the table, estimating if his four million was covered.

The croupier wanted to hurry the play. He said firmly, "C'est plus que fait, monsieur."

The man from Lille made up his mind. He gave the shoe a fat slap, wiped his hand on the baize and forced out a card. Then one for himself, another for Bond, the fourth for him. Bond did not reach across Number Six for the cards. He waited for them to be nudged towards him by the croupier's spatula. He raised them just off the table, slid them far enough apart between his hands to see the count, edged them together again and laid them softly face down again on the table. He had a five! That dubious jade on which one can either draw or not! The chances of improving your hand towards or away from a nine are equal. He said "Non," quietly, and looked across at the two anonymous pink backs of the cards in front of the banker. The man tore them up, disgustedly tossed them out on to the table. Two knaves. A "bûche"! Zero!

Now there were only four cards that could beat Bond and only one, the five, that could equal him. Bond's heart thumped. The man scrabbled at the shoe, snatched out the card, faced it. A nine, the nine of diamonds! The curse of Scotland! The best!

It was a mere formality to turn over and reveal Bond's miserable five. But there was a groan round the table. "Il fallait tirer," said someone. But if he had, Bond would have drawn the nine and disimproved down to a four. It all depended on what the next card, its pink tongue now hiding its secret in the mouth of the shoe, might have been. Bond didn't wait to see. He smiled a thin, rueful smile round the table to apologize to his fellow losers, shovelled the rest of his chips into his coat pocket, tipped the huissier who had been so busy emptying his ash-tray over the hours of play, and slipped away from the table towards the bar, while the croupier triumphantly announced, "Un banco de quatre-vingts mille francs! Faites vos jeux, messieurs! Un banco de quatre-vingts mille Nouveaux Francs." To hell with it! thought Bond. Half an hour before he had had a small fortune in his pocket. Now, through a mixture of romantic quixotry and sheer folly he had lost it. Well, he shrugged, he had asked for a night to remember. That was the first half of it. What would be the second?

The girl was sitting by herself, with half a bottle of Bollinger in front of her, staring moodily at nothing. She barely looked up when Bond slipped into the chair next to hers and said, "Well, I'm afraid our syndicate lost again. I tried to get it back. I went 'avec.' I should have left that brute alone. I stood on a five and he had a 'bûche' and then drew a nine."

She said dully, "You should have drawn on the five. I always do." She reflected. "But then you would have had a four. What was the next card?"

"I didn't wait to see. I came to look for you."

She gave him a sideways, appraising glance. "Why did you rescue me when I made the 'coup du déshonneur'?"

Bond shrugged. "Beautiful girl in distress. Besides, we made friends between Abbeville and Montreuil this evening. You drive like an angel." He smiled. "But I don't think you'd have passed me if I'd been paying attention. I was doing about ninety and not bothering to keep an eye on the mirror. And I was thinking of other things."

The gambit succeeded. Vivacity came into her face and voice. "Oh, yes. I'd have beaten you anyway. I'd have passed you in the villages. Besides"—there was an edge of bitterness in her voice—"I would always be able to beat you. You want to stay alive."

Oh, lord! thought Bond. One of those! A girl with a wing, perhaps two wings, down. He chose to let the remark lie. The half-bottle of Krug he had ordered came. After the huissier had half filled the glass, Bond topped it to the brim. He held it towards her without exaggeration. "My name is Bond, James Bond. Please stay alive, at any rate for tonight." He drank the glass down at one long gulp and filled it again.

She looked at him gravely, considering him. Then she also drank. She said, "My name is Tracy. That is short for all the names you were told at the reception in the hotel. Teresa was a saint. I am not a saint. The manager is perhaps a romantic. He told me of your inquiries. So shall we go now? I am not interested in conversation. And you have earned your reward."

She rose abruptly. So did Bond, confused. "No. I will go alone. You can come later. The number is forty-five. There, if you wish, you can make the most expensive piece of love of your life. It will have cost you four million francs. I hope it will be worth it."

4 ALL CATS ARE GREY

She was waiting in the big double bed, a single sheet pulled up to her chin. The fair hair was spread out like golden wings under the single reading light that was the only light in the room, and the blue eyes blazed with a fervour that, in other girls, in other beds, James Bond would have interpreted. But this one was in the grip of stresses he could not even guess at. He locked the door behind him and came over and sat on the edge of her bed and put one hand firmly on the little hill that was her left breast. "Now listen, Tracy," he began, meaning to ask at least one or two questions, find out something about this wonderful girl who did hysterical things like gambling without the money to meet her debts, driving like a potential suicide, hinting that she had had enough of life.

But the girl reached up a swift hand that smelt of Guerlain's "Ode" and put it across his lips. "I said 'no conversation.' Take off those clothes. Make love to me. You are handsome and strong. I want to remember what it can be like. Do anything you like. And tell me what you like and what you would like from me. Be rough with me. Treat me like the lowest whore in creation. Forget everything else. No questions. Take me."

An hour later, James Bond slipped out of bed without waking her, dressed by the light of the promenade lights filtering between the curtains, and went back to his room.

He showered and got in between the cool, rough French sheets of his own bed and switched off his thinking about her. All he remembered, before sleep took him, was that she had said when it was all over, "That was heaven, James. Will you please come back when you wake up. I must have it once more." Then she had turned over on her side away from him and, without answering his last endearments, had gone to sleep—but not before he had heard that she was crying.

What the hell? All cats are grey in the dark.

True or false?

Bond slept.

At eight o'clock he woke her and it was the same glorious thing again. But this time he thought that she held him to her more tenderly, kissed him not only with passion but with affection. But, after, when they should have been making plans about the day, about where to have lunch, when to bathe, she was at first evasive and then, when he pressed her, childishly abusive.

"Get to hell away from me! Do you hear? You've had what you wanted. Now get out!"

"Wasn't it what you wanted too?"

"No. You're a lousy goddam lover. Get out!"

Bond recognized the edge of hysteria, at least of desperation. He dressed slowly, waiting for the tears to come, for the sheet that now covered her totally to shake with sobs. But the tears didn't come. That was bad! In some way this girl had come to the end of her tether, of too many tethers. Bond felt a wave of affection for her, a sweeping urge to protect her, to solve her problems, make her happy. With his hand on the door-knob he said softly, "Tracy. Let me help you. You've got some troubles. That's not the end of the world. So have I. So has everyone else."

The dull clichés fell into the silent, sun-barred room, like clinker in a grate.

"Go to hell!"

In the instant of opening and closing the door, Bond debated whether to bang it shut, to shake her out of her mood, or to close it softly. He closed it softly. Harshness would do no good with this girl. She had had it, somehow, somewhere—too much of it. He went off down the corridor, feeling, for the first time in his life, totally inadequate.

(The Bombard thrashed on up river. It had passed the marina and, with the narrowing banks, the current was stronger. The two thugs in the stern still kept their quiet eyes on Bond. In the bow, the girl still held her proud profile into the wind like the figure-head on a sailing ship. In Bond, the only warmth was in his contact with her back and his hand on the haft of his knife. Yet, in a curious way, he felt closer to her, far closer, than in the transports of the night before. Somehow he felt that she was as much a prisoner as he was. How? Why? Way ahead the lights of the Vieux Port, once close to the sea, but now left behind by some quirk of the Channel currents that had built up the approaches to the river, shone sparsely. Before many years they would go out and a new harbour, nearer the mouth of the river, would be built for the deep-sea trawlers that served Royale with their soles and lobsters and crabs and prawns. On this side of the lights were occasional gaunt jetties built out into the river by private yacht-owners. Behind them were villas that would have names like "Rosalie," "Toi et Moi," "Nid Azur" and "Nouvelle Vague." James Bond nursed the knife and smelt the "Ode" that came to him above the stink of mud and seaweed from the river banks. His teeth had never chattered before. Now they chattered. He stopped them and went back to his memories.)

Normally, breakfast was an important part of Bond's day, but today he had barely noticed what he was eating, hurried through the meal and sat gazing out of his window and across the promenade, chain-smoking and wondering about the girl. He knew nothing positive about her, not even her nationality. The Mediterranean was in her name, yet she was surely neither Italian nor Spanish. Her English was faultless and her clothes and the way she wore them were the products of expensive surroundings—perhaps a Swiss finishing school. She didn't smoke, seemed to drink only sparingly and there was no sign of drug-taking. There had not even been sleeping pills beside the bed or in her bathroom. She could only be about twenty-five, yet she made love with the fervour and expertness of a girl who, in the American phrase, had "gone the route." She hadn't laughed once, had hardly smiled. She seemed in the grip of some deep melancholy, some form of spiritual accidie that made life, on her own admission, no longer worth living. And yet there were none of those signs that one associates with the hysteria of female neurotics—the unkempt hair and sloppy make-up, the atmosphere of disarray and chaos they create around them. On the contrary, she seemed to possess an ice-cold will, authority over herself and an exact idea of what she wanted and where she was going. And where was that? In Bond's book she had desperate intentions, most likely suicide, and last night had been the last fling.

He looked down at the little white car that was now not far from his in the parking lot. Somehow he must stick close to her, watch over her, at least until he was satisfied that his deadly conclusions were wrong. As a first step, he rang down to the concierge and ordered a drive-yourself Simca Aronde. Yes, it should be delivered at once and left in the parking lot. He would bring his international driving licence and green insurance card down to the concierge who would kindly complete the formalities.

Bond shaved and dressed and took the papers down and returned to his room. He stayed there, watching the entrance and the little white car until 4.30 in the afternoon. Then, at last, she appeared, in the black and white striped bathing-wrap, and Bond ran down the corridor to the lift. It was not difficult to follow her as she drove along the promenade and left her car in one of the parking lots, and it was also no problem for the little anonymous 2CV Citroën that followed Bond.

And then had been set up the train of the watchers and the watched which was now drawing to its mysterious climax as the little Bombard thrashed its way up the River Royale under the stars.

What to make of it all? Had she been a witting or unwitting bait? Was this a kidnapping? If so, of one or of both? Was it blackmail? The revenge of a husband or another lover? Or was it to be murder?

Bond was still raking his mind for clues when the helmsman turned the Bombard in a wide curve across the current towards a battered, skeletal jetty that projected from the muddy bank into the stream. He pulled up under its lee, a powerful flashlight shone down on them out of the darkness, a rope clattered down and the boat was hauled to the foot of muddy wooden steps. One of the thugs climbed out first, followed by the girl, the white bottom of her bathing dress lascivious below Bond's coat, then Bond, then the second thug. Then the Bombard backed quickly away and continued up river, presumably, thought Bond, to its legitimate mooring in the Vieux Port.

There were two more men, of much the same build as the others, on the jetty. No words were spoken as, surrounded, the girl and Bond were escorted up the small dust road that led away from the jetty through the sand dunes. A hundred yards from the river, tucked away in a gully between tall dunes, there was a glimmer of light. When Bond got nearer he saw that it came from one of those giant corrugated aluminium transport trucks that, behind an articulated driver's cabin, roar down the arterial routes of France belching diesel smoke and hissing angrily with their hydraulic brakes as they snake through the towns and villages. This one was a glinting, polished affair. It looked new, but might be just well cared for. As they approached, the man with the flashlight gave some signal, and an oblong of yellow light promptly blazed as the caravan-like door in the rear was thrown open. Bond fingered his knife. Were the odds in any way within reason? They were not. Before he climbed up the steps into the interior, he glanced down at the number-plate. The commercial licence said, "Marseille-Rôhne. M. Draco. Appareils électriques. 397694." So! One more riddle!

Inside it was, thank God, warm. A passage-way led between stacked rows of cartons marked with the famous names of television manufacturers. Dummies? There were also folded chairs and the signs of a disturbed game of cards. This was presumably used as the guard-room. Then, on both sides, the doors of cabins. Tracy was waiting at one of the doors. She held out his coat to him, said an expressionless "Thank you" and closed the door after Bond had caught a brief glimpse of a luxurious interior. Bond took his time putting on his coat. The single man with the gun who was following him said impatiently, "Allez!" Bond wondered whether to jump him. But, behind, the other three men stood watching. Bond contented himself with a mild "Merde à vous!" and went ahead to the aluminium door that presumably sealed off the third and forward compartment in this strange vehicle. Behind this door lay the answer. It was probably one man—the leader. This might be the only chance. Bond's right hand was already grasping the hilt of his knife in his trouser pocket. Now he put out his left hand and, in one swirl of motion, leaped through, kicked the door shut behind him and crouched, the knife held for throwing.

Behind him he felt the guard throw himself at the door, but Bond had his back to it and it held. The man, ten feet away behind the desk, within easy range for the knife, called out something, an order, a cheerful, gay order in some language Bond had never heard. The pressure on the door ceased. The man smiled a wide, a charming smile that cracked his creased walnut of a face in two. He got to his feet and slowly raised his hands. "I surrender. And I am now a much bigger target. But do not kill me, I beg of you. At least not until we have had a stiff whisky and soda and a talk. Then I will give you the choice again. O.K.?"

Bond rose to his full height. He smiled back. He couldn't help it. The man had such a delightful face, so lit with humour and mischief and magnetism that, at least in the man's present role, Bond could no more have killed him than he could have killed, well, Tracy.

There was a calendar hanging on the wall beside the man. Bond wanted to let off steam against something, anything. He said, "September the sixteenth," and jerked his right hand forward in the underhand throw. The knife flashed across the room, missed the man by about a yard, and stuck, quivering, half-way down the page of the calendar.

The man turned and looked inquisitively at the calendar. He laughed out loud. "Actually the fifteenth. But quite respectable. I must set you against my men one of these days. And I might even bet on you. It would teach them a lesson."

He came out from behind his desk, a smallish, middleaged man with a brown, crinkled face. He was dressed in the sort of comfortable dark blue suit Bond himself wore. The chest and the arms bulged with muscle. Bond noticed the fullness of the cut of the coat under the arm-pits. Built for guns? The man held out a hand. It was warm and firm and dry. "Marc-Ange Draco is my name. You have heard of it?"

"No."

"Aha! But I have heard of yours. It is Commander James Bond. You have a decoration called the C.M.G. You are a member, an important member, of Her Majesty's Secret Service. You have been taken off your usual duties and you are on temporary assignment abroad." The impish face creased with delight. "Yes?"

James Bond, to cover his confusion, walked across to the calendar, verified that he had in fact pierced the fifteenth, pulled out the knife and slipped it back in his trouser pocket. He turned and said, "What makes you think so?"

The man didn't answer. He said, "Come. Come and sit down. I have much to talk to you about. But first the whisky and soda. Yes?" He indicated a comfortable armchair across the desk from his own, put in front of it a large silver box containing various kinds of cigarettes, and went to a metal filing cabinet against the wall and opened it. It contained no files. It was a complete and compact bar. With efficient, housekeeperly movements he took out a bottle of Pinchbottle Haig & Haig, another of I.W. Harper bourbon, two pint glasses that looked like Waterford, a bucket of ice cubes, a siphon of soda and a flagon of iced water. One by one he placed these on the desk between his chair and Bond's. Then while Bond poured himself a stiff bourbon and water with plenty of ice, he went and sat down across the desk from Bond, reached for the Haig & Haig and said, looking Bond very directly in the eye, "I learned who you are from a good friend in the Deuxième in Paris. He is paid to give me such information when I want it. I learned it very early this morning. I am in the opposite camp to yourself—not directly opposite. Let us say at a tangent on the field." He paused. He lifted his glass. He said with much seriousness,

"I am now going to establish confidence with you. By the only means. I am going once again to place my life in your hands."

He drank. So did Bond. In the filing cabinet, in its icebox, the hum of the generator broke in on what Bond suddenly knew was going to be an important moment of truth. He didn't know what the truth was going to be. He didn't think it was going to be bad. But he had an instinct that, somehow, perhaps because he had conceived respect and affection for this man, it was going to mean deep involvement for himself.

The generator stopped.

The eyes in the walnut face held his.

"I am the head of the Union Corse."

5 THE CAPU

The Union Corse! Now at least some of the mystery was explained. Bond looked across the desk into the brown eyes that were now shrewdly watching his reactions while his mind flicked through the file that bore the innocent title, "The Union Corse," more deadly and perhaps even older than the Unione Siciliano, the Mafia. He knew that it controlled most organized crime throughout metropolitan France and her colonies—protection rackets, smuggling, prostitution and the suppression of rival gangs. Only a few months ago a certain Rossi had been shot dead in a bar in Nice. A year before that, a Jean Giudicelli had been liquidated after several previous attempts had failed. Both these men had been known pretenders to the throne of Capu—the ebullient, cheerful man who now sat so peacefully across the table from Bond. Then there was this mysterious business of Rommel's treasure, supposed to be hidden beneath the sea somewhere off Bastia. In 1948 a Czech diver called Fleigh, who had been in the Abwehr, and had got on the track of it, was warned off by the Union and then vanished off the face of the earth. Quite recently the body of a young French diver, André Mattei, was found riddled with bullets by the roadside near Bastia. He had foolishly boasted in the local bars that he knew the whereabouts of the treasure and had come to dive for it. Did Marc-Ange know the secret of this treasure? Had he been responsible for the killing of these two divers? The little village of Calenzana in the Balagne boasted of having produced more gangsters than any other village in Corsica and of being in consequence one of the most prosperous. The local mayor had held office for fifty-six years—the longest reigning mayor in France. Marc-Ange would surely be a son of that little community, know the secrets of that famous mayor, know, for instance, of that big American gangster who had just returned to discreet retirement in the village after a highly profitable career in the States.

It would be fun to drop some of these names casually in this quiet little room—fun to tell Marc-Ange that Bond knew of the old abandoned jetty called the Port of Crovani near the village of Galeria, and of the ancient silver mine called Argentella in the hills behind, whose maze of underground tunnels accommodates one of the great world junctions in the heroin traffic. Yes, it would be fun to frighten his captor in exchange for the fright he had given Bond. But better keep this ammunition in reserve until more had been revealed! For the time being it was interesting to note that this was Marc-Ange Draco's travelling headquarters. His contact in the Deuxième Bureau would be an essential tip-off man. Bond and the girl had been "sent for" for some purpose that was still to be announced. The "borrowing" of the Bombard rescue-boat would have been a simple matter of finance in the right quarter, perhaps accompanied by a "pot de vin" for the coastguards to look the other way. The guards were Corsicans. On reflection, that was anyway what they looked like. The whole operation was simple for an organization as powerful as the Union—as simple in France as it would have been for the Mafia in most of Italy. And now for more veils to be lifted! James Bond sipped his drink and watched the other man's face with respect. This was one of the great professionals of the world!

[How typical of Corsica, Bond thought, that their top bandit should bear the name of an angel! He remembered that two other famous Corsical gangsters had been called "Gracieux" and "Toussaint"—"All-Saints."] Marc-Ange spoke. He spoke excellent but occasionally rather clumsy English, as if he had been well taught but had little occasion to use the language. He said, "My dear Commander, everything I am going to discuss with you will please remain behind your Herkos Odonton. You know the expression? No?" The wide smile lit up his face. "Then, if I may say so, your education was incomplete. It is from the classical Greek. It means literally 'the hedge of the teeth.' It was the Greek equivalent of your 'top secret.' Is that agreed?"

Bond shrugged. "If you tell me secrets that affect my profession, I'm afraid I shall have to pass them on."

"That I fully comprehend. What I wish to discuss is

a personal matter. It concerns my daughter, Teresa."

Good God! The plot was indeed thickening! Bond concealed his surprise. He said, "Then I agree." He smiled. " 'Herkos Odonton' it is."

"Thank you. You are a man to trust. You would have to be, in your profession, but I see it also in your face. Now then." He lit a Caporal and sat back in his chair. He gazed at a point on the aluminium wall above Bond's head, only occasionally looking into Bond's eyes when he wished to emphasize a point. "I was married once only, to an English girl, an English governess. She was a romantic. She had come to Corsica to look for bandits"—he smiled—"rather like some English women adventure into the desert to look for sheiks. She explained to me later that she must have been possessed by a subconcious desire to be raped. Well"—this time he didn't smile—"she found me in the mountains and she was raped—by me. The police were after me at the time, they have been for most of my life, and the girl was a grave encumbrance. But for some reason she refused to leave me. There was a wildness in her, a love of the unconventional, and, for God knows what reason, she liked the months of being chased from cave to cave, of getting food by robbery at night. She even learned to skin and cook a moufflon, those are our mountain sheep, and even eat the animal, which is tough as shoe leather and about as palatable. And in those crazy months, I came to love this girl and I smuggled her away from the island to Marseilles and married her." He paused and looked at Bond. "The result, my dear Commander, was Teresa, my only child."

So, thought Bond. That explained the curious mixture the girl was—the kind of wild "lady" that was so puzzling in her. What a complex of bloods and temperaments! Corsican English. No wonder he hadn't been able to define her nationality.

"My wife died ten years ago"—Marc-Ange held up his hand, not wanting sympathy—"and I had the girl's education finished in Switzerland. I was already rich and at that time I was elected Capu, that is chief, of the Union, and became infinitely richer—by means, my dear Commander, which you can guess but need not inquire into. The girl was—how do you say?—that charming expression, 'the apple of my eye,' and I gave her all she wanted. But she was a wild one, a wild bird, without a proper home, or, since I was always on the move, without proper supervision. Through her school in Switzerland, she entered the fast international set that one reads of in the newspapers—the South American millionaires, the Indian princelings, the Paris English and Americans, the playboys of Cannes and Gstaad. She was always getting in and out of scrapes and scandals, and when I remonstrated with her, cut off her allowance, she would commit some even grosser folly—to spite me, I suppose." He paused and looked at Bond and now there was a terrible misery in the happy face. "And yet all the while, behind her bravado, the mother's side of her blood was making her hate herself, despise herself more and more, and as I now see it, the worm of self-destruction had somehow got a hold inside her and, behind the wild, playgirl façade, was eating away what I can only describe as her soul." He looked at Bond. "You know that this can happen, my friend—to men and to women. They burn the heart out of themselves by living too greedily, and suddenly they examine their lives and see that they are worthless. They have had everything, eaten all the sweets of life at one great banquet, and there is nothing left. She made what I now see was a desperate attempt to get back on the rails, so to speak. She went off, without telling me, and married, perhaps with the idea of settling down. But the man, a worthless Italian called Vicenzo, Count Giulio di Vicenzo, took as much of her money as he could lay his hands on and deserted her, leaving her with a girl child. I purchased a divorce and bought a small château for my daughter in the Dordogne and installed her there, and for once, with the baby and a pretty garden to look after, she seemed almost a peace. And then, my friend, six months ago, the baby died—died of that most terrible of all children's ailments, spinal meningitis."

There was silence in the little metal room. Bond thought of the girl a few yards away down the corridor. Yes. He had been near the truth. He had seen some of this tragic story in the calm desperation of the girl. She had indeed come to the end of the road!

Marc-Ange got slowly up from his chair and came round and poured out more whisky for himself and for Bond. He said, "Forgive me. I am a poor host. But the telling of this story, which I have always kept locked up inside me, to another man, has been a great relief." He put a hand on Bond's shoulder. "You understand that?"

"Yes. I understand that. But she is a fine girl. She still has nearly all her life to live. Have you thought of psychoanalysis? Of her church? Is she a Catholic?"

"No. Her mother would not have it. She is Presbyterian.

But wait while I finish the story." He went back to his chair and sat down heavily. "After the tragedy, she disappeared. She took her jewels and went off in that little car of hers, and I heard occasional news of her, selling the jewels and living furiously all over Europe, with her old set. Naturally I followed her, had her watched when I could, but she avoided all my attempts to meet her and talk to her. Then I heard from one of my agents that she had reserved a room here, at the Splendide, for last night, and I hurried down from Paris"—he waved a hand—"In this, because I had a presentiment of tragedy. You see, this was where we had spent the summers in her childhood and she had always loved it. She is a wonderful swimmer and she was almost literally in love with the sea. And, when I got the news, I suddenly had a dreadful memory, the memory of a day when she had been naughty and had been locked in her room all afternoon instead of going bathing. That night she had said to her mother, quite calmly, 'You made me very unhappy keeping me away from the sea. One day, if I get really unhappy, I shall swim out into the sea, down the path of the moon or the sun, and go on swimming until I sink. So there!' Her mother told me the story and we laughed over it together, at the childish tantrum. But now I suddenly remembered again the occasion and it seemed to me that the childish fantasy might well have stayed with her, locked away deep down, and that now, wanting to put an end to herself, she had resurrected it and was going to act on it. And so, my dear friend, I had her closely watched from the moment she arrived. Your gentlemanly conduct in the casino, for which"—he looked across at Bond—"I now deeply thank you, was reported to me, as of course were your later movements together." He held up his hand as Bond shifted with embarrassment. "There is nothing to be ashamed of, to apologize for, in what you did last night. A man is a man and, who knows?—but I shall come to that later. What you did, the way you behaved in general, may have been the beginning of some kind of therapy."

Bond remembered how, in the Bombard, she had yielded when he leaned against her. It had been a tiny reaction, but it had held more affection, more warmth, than all the physical ecstasies of the night. Now, suddenly he had an inkling of why he might be here, where the root of the mystery lay, and he gave an involuntary shudder, as if someone had walked over his grave.

Marc-Ange continued, "So I put in my inquiry to my friend from the Deuxième, at six o'clock this morning. At eight o'clock he went to his office and to the central files and by nine o'clock he had reported to me fully about you—by radio. I have a high-powered station in this vehicle." He smiled. "And that is another of my secrets that I deliver into your hands. The report, if I may say so, was entirely to your credit, both as an officer in your Service, and, more important, as a man—a man, that is, in the terms that I understand the word. So I reflected. I reflected all through this morning. And, in the end, I gave orders that you were both to be brought to me here." He made a throw-away gesture with his right hand. "I need not tell you the details of my instructions. You yourself saw them in operation. You have been inconvenienced. I apologize. You have perhaps thought yourself in danger. Forgive me. I only trust that my men behaved with correctness, with finesse."

Bond smiled. "I am very glad to have met you. If the introduction had to be effected at the point of two automatics, that will only make it all the more memorable. The whole affair was certainly executed with neatness and expedition."

Marc-Ange's expression was rueful. "Now you are being sarcastic. But believe me, my friend, drastic measures were necessary. I knew they were." He reached to the top drawer of his desk, took out a sheet of writing-paper and passed it over to Bond. "And now, if you read that, you will agree with me. That letter was handed in to the concierge of the Splendide at 4.30 this afternoon for posting to me in Marseilles, when Teresa went out and you followed her. You suspected something? You also feared for her? Read it, please."

Bond took the letter. He said, "Yes. I was worried about her. She is a girl worth worrying about." He held up the letter. It contained only a few words written clearly, with decision.

Dear Papa,

I am sorry, but I have had enough. It is only sad because tonight I met a man who might have changed my mind. He is an Englishman called James Bond. Please find him and pay him 20,000 New Francs which I owe him. And thank him from me.

This is nobody's fault but my own.

Goodbye and forgive me.

Tracy

Bond didn't look at the man who had received this letter.

He slid it back to him across the desk. He took a deep drink of the whisky and reached for the bottle. He said, "Yes, I see."

"She likes to call herself Tracy. She thinks Teresa sounds too grand."

"Yes."

"Commander Bond." There was now a terrible urgency in the man's voice—urgency, authority and appeal. "My friend, you have heard the whole story and now you have seen the evidence. Will you help me? Will you help me save this girl? It is my only chance, that you will give her hope. That you will give her a reason to live. Will you?"

Bond kept his eyes on the desk in front of him. He dared not look up and see the expression on this man's face. So he had been right, right to fear that he was going to become involved in all this private trouble! He cursed under his breath. The idea appalled him. He was no Good Samaritan. He was no doctor for wounded birds. What she needed, he said fiercely to himself, was the psychiatrist's couch. All right, so she had taken a passing fancy to him and he to her. Now he was going to be asked, he knew it, to pick her up and carry her perhaps for the rest of his life, haunted by the knowledge, the unspoken blackmail, that, if he dropped her, it would almost certainly be to kill her. He said glumly, "I do not see that I can help. What is it you have in mind?" He picked up his glass and looked into it. He drank, to give him courage to look across the desk into Marc-Ange's face.

The man's soft brown eyes glittered with tension. The creased dark skin round the mouth had sunk into deeper folds. He said, holding Bond's eyes, "I wish you to pay court to my daughter and marry her. On the day of the marriage, I will give you a personal dowry of one million pounds in gold."

James Bond exploded angrily. "What you ask is utterly impossible. The girl is sick. What she needs is a psychiatrist. Not me. And I do not want to marry, not anyone. Nor do I want a million pounds. I have enough money for my needs. I have my profession." (Is that true? What about that letter of resignation? Bond ignored the private voice.) "You must understand all this." Suddenly he could not bear the hurt in the man's face. He said, softly, "She is a wonderful girl. I will do all I can for her. But only when she is well again. Then I would certainly like to see her again—very much. But, if she thinks so well of me, if you do, then she must first get well of her own accord. That is the only way. Any doctor would tell you so. She must go to some clinic, the best there is, in Switzerland probably, and bury her past. She must want to live again. Then, only then, would there be any point in our meeting again." He pleaded with Marc-Ange. "You do understand, don't you, Marc-Ange? I am a ruthless man. I admit it. And I have not got the patience to act as anyone's nurse, man or woman. Your idea of a cure might only drive her into deeper despair. You must see that I cannot take the responsibility, however much I am attracted by your daughter." Bond ended lamely, "Which I am."

The man said resignedly, "I understand you, my friend. And I will not importune you with further arguments. I will try and act in the way you suggest. But will you please do one further favour for me? It is now nine o'clock. Will you please take her out to dinner tonight? Talk to her as you please, but show her that she is wanted, that you have affection for her. Her car is here and her clothes. I have had them brought. If only you can persuade her that you would like to see her again, I think I may be able to do the rest. Will you do this for me?"

Bond thought, God, what an evening! But he smiled with all the warmth he could summon. "But of course. I would love to do that. But I am booked on the first morning flight from Le Touquet tomorrow morning. Will you be responsible for her from then?"

"Certainly, my friend. Of course I will do that." Marc-Ange brusquely wiped a hand across his eyes. "Forgive me. But you have given me hope at the end of a long night." He straightened his shoulders and suddenly leaned across the desk and put his hands decisively down. "I will not thank you. I cannot, but tell me, my dear friend, is there anything in this world that I can do for you, now at this moment? I have great resources, great knowledge, great power. They are all yours. Is there nothing I can do for you?"

Bond had a flash of inspiration. He smiled broadly. "There is a piece of information I want. There is a man called Blofeld, Ernst Stavro Blofeld. You will have heard of him. I wish to know if he is alive and where he is to be found."

Marc-Ange's face underwent a remarkable change. Now the bandit, cold, cruel, avenging, looked out through the eyes that had suddenly gone as hard as brown opals. "Aha!" he said thoughtfully. "The Blofeld. Yes, he is certainly alive. Only recently he suborned three of my men, bribed them away from the Union. He has done this to me before. Three of the members of the old SPECTRE were taken from the Union. Come, let us find out what we can."

There was a single black telephone on the desk. He picked up the receiver and at once Bond heard the soft crackle of the operator responding. *"Dammi u commandu."* Marc-Ange put the receiver back. "I have asked for my local headquarters in Ajaccio. We will have them in five minutes. But I must speak fast. The police may know my frequency, though I change it every week. But the Corsican dialect helps." The telephone burred. When Marc-Ange picked up the receiver, Bond could hear the zing and crackle he knew so well. Marc-Ange spoke, in a voice of rasping authority. *"Ecco u Capu. Avette nuttizie di Bloefeld, Ernst Stavro? Duve sta?"* A voice crackled thinly. *"Site sigura? Ma no ezzatu indirizzu?"* More crackle. *"Buon. Sara tutto."*

Marc-Ange put back the receiver. He spread his hands apologetically. "All we know is that he is in Switzerland. We have no exact address for him. Will that help? Surely your men there can find him—if the Swiss Sécurité will help. But they are difficult brutes when it comes to the privacy of a resident, particularly if he is rich."

Bond's pulse had quickened with triumph. Got you, you bastard! He said enthusiastically, "That's wonderful, Marc-Ange. The rest shouldn't be difficult. We have good friends in Switzerland."

Marc-Ange smiled happily at Bond's reaction. He said seriously, "But if things go wrong for you, on this case or in any other way, you will come at once to me. Yes?" He pulled open a drawer and handed a sheet of notepaper over to Bond. "This is my open address. Telephone or cable to me, but put your request or your news in terms that would be used in connection with electrical appliances. A consignment of radios is faulty. You will meet my representative at such and such a place, on such and such a date. Yes? You understand these tricks, and anyway"—he smiled slyly—"I believe you are connected with an international export firm. 'Universal Export,' isn't it?"

Bond smiled. How did the old devil know these things? Should he warn Security? No. This man had become a friend. And anyway, all this was Herkos Odonton!

Marc-Ange said diffidently, "And now may I bring in Teresa? She does not know what we have been discussing. Let us say it is about one of the South of France jewel robberies. You represent the insurance company. I have been making a private deal with you. You can manage that? Good." He got up and came over to Bond and put his hand on Bond's shoulder. "And thank you. Thank you for everything." Then he went out of the door.

Oh, my God! thought Bond. Now for my side of the bargain.

6 BOND OF BOND STREET?

It was two months later, in London, and James Bond was driving lazily up from his Chelsea flat to his headquarters.

It was nine-thirty in the morning of yet another beautiful day of this beautiful year, but, in Hyde Park, the fragrance of burning leaves meant that winter was only just round the corner. Bond had nothing on his mind except the frustration of waiting for Station Z somehow to penetrate the reserves of the Swiss Sécurité and come up with the exact address of Blofeld. But their "friends" in Zürich were continuing to prove obtuse, or, more probably, obstinate. There was no trace of any man, either tourist or resident, called Blofeld in the whole of Switzerland. Nor was there any evidence of the existence of a reborn SPECTRE on Swiss soil. Yes, they fully realized that Blofeld was still urgently "wanted" by the governments of the NATO alliance. They had carefully filed all the circulars devoted to the apprehension of this man, and for the past year he had been constantly reconfirmed on their "watch" lists at all frontier posts. They were very sorry, but unless the SIS could come up with further information or evidence about this man, they must assume that the SIS was acting on mistaken evidence. Station Z had asked for an examination of the secret lists at the banks, a search through those anonymous "numbered" accounts which conceal the owners of most of the fugitive money in the world. This request had been peremptorily refused. Blofeld was certainly a very great criminal, but the Sécurité must point out that such information could only be legally obtained if the criminal in question was guilty of some crime committed on Federal soil and indictable under the Federal Code. It was true that this Blofeld had held up Britain and America to ransom by his illegal possession of atomic weapons. But this could not be considered a crime under the laws of Switzerland, and particularly not having regard to Article 47B of the banking laws. So that was that! The Holy Franc, and the funds which backed it, wherever they came from, must remain untouchable. Wir bitten höflichst um Entschuldigung!

Bond wondered if he should get in touch with Marc-Ange.

So far, in his report, he had revealed only a lead into the Union Corse, whom he gave, corporately, as the source of his information. But he shied away from this course of action, which would surely have, as one consequence, the reopening with Marc-Ange of the case of Tracy. And that corner of his life, of his heart, he wanted to leave undisturbed for the time being. Their last evening together had passed quietly, almost as if they had been old friends, old lovers. Bond had said that Universal Export was sending him abroad for some time. They would certainly meet when he returned to Europe. The girl had accepted this arrangement. She herself had decided to go away for a rest. She had been doing too much. She had been on the verge of a nervous breakdown. She would wait for him. Perhaps they could go skiing together around Christmas time? Bond had been enthusiastic. That night, after a wonderful dinner at Bond's little restaurant, they had made love, happily, and this time without desperation, without tears. Bond was satisfied that the cure had really begun. He felt deeply protective towards her. But he knew that their relationship, and her equanimity, rested on a knife-edge which must not be disturbed.

It was at this moment in his reflections that the syncraphone in his trouser pocket began to bleep. Bond accelerated out of the park and drew up beside the public telephone booth at Marble Arch. The syncraphone had recently been introduced and was carried by all officers attached to Headquarters. It was a light plastic radio receiver about the size of a pocket watch. When an officer was somewhere in London, within a range of ten miles of Headquarters, he could be bleeped on the receiver. When this happened, it was his duty to go at once to the nearest telephone and contact his office. He was urgently needed.

Bond rang his exchange on the only outside number he was allowed to use, said "007 reporting," and was at once put through to his secretary. She was a new one. Loelia Ponsonby had at last left to marry a dull, but worthy and rich member of the Baltic Exchange, and confined her contacts with her old job to rather yearning Christmas and birthday cards to the members of the Double-O Section. But the new one, Mary Goodnight, an ex-Wren with blue-black hair, blue eyes and 37-22-35, was a honey and there was a private five-pound sweep in the Section as to who would get her first. Bond had been lying equal favourite with the ex-Royal Marine Commando who was 006 but, since Tracy, had dropped out of the field and now regarded himself as a rank outsider, though he still, rather bitchily, flirted with her. Now he said to her, "Good morning, Goodnight. What can I do for you? Is it war or peace?"

She giggled unprofessionally. "It sounds fairly peaceful, as peaceful as a hurry message from upstairs can be. You're to go at once to the College of Arms and ask for Griffon Or."

"Or what?"

"Just Or. Oh, and he's Pursuivant as well, whatever that means. He's one of the Heralds. Apparently they've got some kind of a line on 'Bedlam.' "

"Bedlam" was the code name for the pursuit of Blofeld. Bond said respectfully, "Have they indeed? Then I'd better get cracking. Goodbye, Goodnight." He heard her giggle before he put the receiver down.

Now what the hell? Bond got back into his car, that had mercifully not yet attracted the police or the traffic wardens, and motored fast across London. This was a queer one. How the hell did the College of Arms, of which he knew very little except that they hunted up people's family trees, allotted coats of arms, and organized various royal ceremonies, get into the act?

The College of Arms is in Queen Victoria Street on the fringe of the City. It is a pleasant little Queen Anne backwater in ancient red brick with white sashed windows and a convenient cobbled courtyard, where Bond parked his car. There are horseshoe-shaped stone stairs leading up to an impressive entrance, over which, that day, there hung a banner showing a splended heraldic beast, half animal and half bird, in gold against a pale blue background. Griffon, thought Bond. Made of Or. He went through the door into a large gloomy hall whose dark panelling was lined with the musty portraits of proud-looking gentlemen in ruffs and lace, and from whose cornice hung the banners of the commonwealth. The porter, a kindly, soft-spoken man in a cherry-coloured uniform with brass buttons, asked Bond what he could do for him. Bond asked for the Griffon Or and confirmed that he had an appointment.

"Ah yes sir," said the porter mysteriously. "Griffon Or is in waiting this week. That is why his banner is flying outside. This way please, sir."

Bond followed the porter along a passage hung with gleaming coats of arms in carved wood, up a dank, cobwebby staircase and round a corner to a heavy door over which was written in gold "Griffon Or Pursuivant" under a representation of the said golden griffon. The porter knocked, opened the door and announced Bond, and left him facing, across an unkempt study littered with books, papers and important-looking inscribed parchments, the top of a bald, round pink head fringed with grizzled curls. The room smelt like the crypt of a church. Bond walked down the narrow lane of carpet left between the piles of litter and stood beside the single chair that faced the man behind the books on the desk. He cleared his throat. The man looked up and the Pickwickian, pince-nez'd face broke into an absent smile. He got to his feet and made a little bow. "Bond," he said in a voice that creaked like the lid of an old chest. "Commander James Bond. Now then, Bond, Bond, Bond. I think I've got you here." He had kept his finger at the open page of a vast tome. He now sat down and Bond followed suit. "Yes, yes, yes. Very interesting indeed. Very. But I fear I have to disappoint you, my dear sir. The title is extinct. Actually it's a baronetcy. Most desirable. But no doubt we can establish a relationship through a collateral branch. Now then"—he put his pince-nez very close to the page—"we have some ten different families of Bonds. The important one ended with Sir Thomas Bond, a most distinguished gentleman. He resided in Peckham. He had, alas, no issue"—the pince-nez gleamed encouragingly at Bond—"no legitimate issue that is. Of course in those days, ahem, morals were inclined to be laxer. Now if we could establish some connection with Peckham . . ."

"I have no connection with Peckham. Now, I . . ."

Griffon Or held up his hand. He said severely, "Where did your parents come from, if I may ask? That, my dear fellow, is the first step in the chain. Then we can go back from there—Somerset House, parish records, old tombstones. No doubt, with a good old English name like yours we will get somewhere in the end."

"My father was a Scot and my mother was Swiss. But the point is . . ."

"Quite, quite. You are wondering about the cost of the research. That, my dear fellow, we can leave until later. But, now tell me. From whereabouts in Scotland did your father come? That is important. The Scottish records are of course less fully documented than those from the south. In those days I am forced to admit that our cousins across the border were little more than savages." Griffon Or bobbed his head politely. He have a fleeting and, to Bond's eye, rather false smile. "Very pleasant savages, of course, very brave and all that. But alas, very weak at keeping up their records. More useful with the sword than with the pen, if I may say so. But perhaps your grandparents and their forebears came from the south?"

"My father came from the Highlands, from near Glencoe. But look here . . ."

But Griffon Or was not to be diverted from the scent. He pulled another thick book towards him. His finger ran down the page of small print. "Hum. Hum. Hum. Yes, yes. Not very encouraging, I fear. *Burke's General Armory* gives more than ten different families bearing your name. But, alas, nothing in Scotland. Not that that means there is no Scottish branch. Now, perhaps you have other relatives living. So often in these matters there is some distant cousin . . ." Griffon Or reached into the pocket of the purple-flowered silk waistcoat that buttoned almost up to his neat bow tie, fished out a small silver snuff-box, offered it to Bond and then himself took two tremendous sniffs. He exploded twice into an ornate bandana handkerchief.

Bond took his opportunity. He leaned forward and said distinctly and forcibly, "I didn't come here to talk about myself. It's about Blofeld."

"What's that?" Griffon Or looked at him in astonishment. "You are not interested in your line of descent?" He held up an admonishing finger. "Do you realize, my dear fellow, that if we are successful, you may be able to claim direct"—he hesitated—"or at any rate collateral descent from an ancient baronetcy founded"—he went back to his first volume and peered at it—"in the year 1658! Does it not excite you that a possible ancestor of yours was responsible for the name of one of the most famous streets in the world—I refer of course to Bond Street? That was the Sir Thomas Bond, Baronet of Peckham in the County of Surrey, who, as you are no doubt aware, was Comptroller of the household of the Queen Mother, Henrietta Maria. The street was built in 1686 and its associations with famous British folk are, of course, well known. The first Duke of St Albans, son of Nell Gwynn, lived there, as did Laurence Sterne. Boswell's famous dinner party took place there, with Johnson, Reynolds, Goldsmith and Garrick being present. Dean Swift and Canning were residents at different times, and it is intriguing to recall that while Lord Nelson lived at number 141, Lady Hamilton lived at number 145. And this, my dear sir, is the great thoroughfare of which you bear the name! Do you still wish to establish no claim to this vastly distinguished connection? No?" The bushy eyebrows, raised in astonishment, were now lowered in further admonishment. "This is the very warp and woof of history, my dear Commander Bond." He reached for another volume that lay open on his desk and that he had obviously prepared for Bond's delectation. "The coat of arms, for instance. Surely that must concern you, be at least of profound interest to your family, to your own children? Yes, here we are. 'Argent on a chevron sable three bezants.' " He held up the book so that Bond could see. "A bezant is a golden ball, as I am sure you know. Three balls."

Bond commented drily, "That is certainly a valuable bonus"—the irony was lost on Griffon Or—"but I'm afraid I am still not interested. And I have no relatives and no children. Now about this man . . ."

Griffon Or broke in excitedly, "And this charming motto of the line, 'The World is not Enough.' You do not wish to have the right to it?"

"It is an excellent motto which I shall certainly adopt," said Bond curtly. He looked pointedly at his watch. "Now, I'm afraid we really must get down to business. I have to report back to my Ministry."

Griffon Or Pursuivant looked genuinely affronted. "And here is a name going back to at least to Norman le Bond in 1180! A fine old English name, though one perhaps originally of lowly origin. The *Dictionary of British Surnames* suggests that the meaning is clearly 'husbandman, peasant, churl.' " Was there an edge of malice in the Griffon's watery eye? He added with resignation, "But, if you are not interested in your ancestry, in the womb of your family, then, my dear sir, in what can I be of service?"

At last! James Bond let out a sigh of relief. He said patiently, "I came here to inquire about a certain Blofeld, Ernst Stavro Blofeld. It seems that your organization has some information about this man."

Griffon Or's eyes were suddenly suspicious. "But you represented yourself as a Commander James Bond. And now the name is Blofeld. How does this come about?"

Bond said icily, "I am from the Ministry of Defence. Somewhere in this building is information about a man called Blofeld. Where can I find it?"

Griffon Or ran a puzzled hand round his halo of curls. "Blofeld, is it? Well, well." He looked accusingly at Bond. "Forgive me, but you certainly have wasted plenty of my, of the College's time, Commander Bond. It is a mystery to me why you did not mention this man's name before. Now let me see, Blofeld, Blofeld. Seem to recall that it came up at one of our Chapter meetings the other day. Now who had the case? Ah, yes." He reached for a telephone among the nest of books and papers. "Give me Sable Basilisk."

7 THE HAIRY HEEL OF ACHILLES

James Bond's heart was still in his boots as he was conducted again through the musty corridors. Sable Basilisk indeed! What kind of a besotted old fogy would this be?

There came another heavy door with the name in gold and this time with a nightmare black monster, with a vicious beak, above it. But now Bond was shown into a light, clean, pleasantly furnished room with attractive prints on the walls and meticulous order among its books. There was a faint smell of Turkish tobacco. A young man, a few years younger than Bond, got up and came across the room to meet him. He was rapier-slim, with a fine thin, studious face that was saved from seriousness by wry lines at the edges of the mouth and an ironical glint in the level eyes.

"Commander Bond?" The handshake was brief and firm. "I'd been expecting you. How did you get into the claws of our dear Griffon? He's a bit of an enthusiast, I'm afraid. We all are here, of course. But he's getting on. Nice chap, but he's a bit dedicated if you know what I mean."

It was indeed like a college, this place, reflected Bond. Much of the atmosphere one associates with the Senior Common Room at a University. No doubt Griffon Or mentally put down Sable Basilisk as a young dilettante who was too big for his boots. He said, "He seemed very anxious to establish a connection between me and Bond Street. It took some time to persuade him that I'm perfectly content to be an ordinary Bond, which, by the way, he, rather churlishly I thought said meant 'a churl.' "

Sable Basilisk laughed. He sat down behind his desk, pulled a file towards him and gestured Bond to a chair beside him. "Well, then. Let's get down to business. First of all"—he looked Bond very straight in the eye—"I gather, I guess that is, that this is an Intelligence matter of some kind. I did my national service with Intelligence in BAOR, so please don't worry about security. Secondly, we have in this building probably as many secrets as a government department—and nastier ones at that. One of our jobs is to suggest titles to people who've been ennobled in the Honours Lists. Sometimes we're asked to establish ownership to a title that has become lost or defunct. Snobbery and vanity positively sprawl through our files. Before my time, a certain gentleman who had come up from nowhere, made millions in some light industry or another and had been given a peerage 'for political and public services'—i.e., charities and the party funds—suggested that he should take the title of Lord Bentley Royal, after the village in Essex. We explained that the word Royal could not be used except by the reigning family, but, rather naughtily I fear, we said that 'Lord Bentley Common' was vacant." He smiled. "See what I mean? If that got about, this man would become the laughingstock of the country. Then sometimes we have to chase up lost fortunes. So-and-so thinks he's the rightful Duke of Blank and ought to have his money. His name happens to be Blank and his ancestors migrated to America or Australia or somewhere. So avarice and greed come to join snobbery and vanity in these rooms. Of course," he added, putting the record straight, "that's only the submerged tenth of our job. The rest is mostly official stuff for governments and embassies—problems of precedence and protocol, the Garter ceremonies and others. We've been doing it for around five hundred years so I suppose it's got its place in the scheme of things."

"Of course it has," said Bond staunchly. "And certainly, so far as security is concerned, I'm sure we can be open with each other. Now this man Blofeld. Truth of the matter is he's probably the biggest crook in the world. Remember that Thunderball affair about a year ago? Only some of it leaked into the papers, but I can tell you that this Blofeld was at the bottom of it all. Now, how did you come to hear of him? Every detail, please. Everything about him is important."

Sable Basilisk turned back to the first letter on the file. "Yes," he said thoughtfully, "I thought this might be the same chap when I got a lot of urgent calls from the Foreign Office and the Ministry of Defence yesterday. Hadn't occurred to me before, I'm afraid, that this is a case where our secrets have to come second, or I'd have done something about it earlier. Now then, in June last, the tenth, we got this confidential letter from a firm of respectable Zürich solicitors, dated the day before. I'll read it out:

"Honoured Sirs,

"We have a valued client by the name of Ernst Stravro Blofeld. This gentleman styles himself Monsieur le Comte Balthazar de Bleuville in the belief that he is the rightful heir to this title which we understand to be extinct. His belief is based on stories he heard from his parents in childhood to the effect that his family fled France at the time of the Revolution, settled in Germany under the adopted name of Blofeld, assumed in order to evade the Revolutionary authorities and safeguard their fortune which they had sequestered in Augsburg, and subsequently, in the 1850's, migrated to Poland.

"Our client is now anxious to have these facts established in order legally to obtain right to the de Bleuville title supported by an Acte de Notoriété which would in due course receive the stamp of approval of the Ministère de la Justice in Paris.

"In the meantime, our client proposes to continue to adopt, albeit provisionally, the title of Comte de Bleuville together with the family arms which he informs us are 'Argent four fusils in fesse gules' and the de Bleuville motto which, in English, is 'For Hearth and Home.' "

"That's a good one!" interjected Bond. Sable Basilisk smiled and continued:

"We understand that you, honoured Sirs, are the only body in the world who is capable of undertaking this research work and we have been instructed to get in touch with you *under the strictest conditions of confidence,* which, in view of the social aspects involved, we think we have the right to request.

"The financial standing of our client is impeccable and expense is no object in this matter. As a preliminary honorarium and upon acceptance of this commission, we propose a payment of one thousand pounds sterling to your account in such bank as you may designate.

"Awaiting the favour of an early reply, we remain, honoured sirs etc. etc.,

Gebrüder Gumpold-Moosbrugger, Advokaten,
16 bis, Bahnhofstrasse, Zürich."

Sable Basilik looked up. James Bond's eyes were glittering with excitement. Sable Basilisk smiled. "We were even more interested than you seem to be. You see, to let you in on a secret, our salaries are extremely modest. So we all have private means which we supplement from fees received for special work like this. These fees rarely go above fifty guineas for a piece of pretty tough research and all the leg work at Somerset House and in parish records and graveyards that is usually involved in tracking a man's ancestry. So this looked like a real challenge for the College, and as I was 'in waiting' the day the letter came in, sort of 'officer of the watch,' the job fell into my lap."

Bond said urgently, "So what happened? Have you kept the contact?"

"Oh, yes, but rather tenuously, I'm afraid. Of course I wrote at once accepting the commission and agreeing to the vow of secrecy which"—he smiled—"you now force me to break presumably by invoking the Official Secrets Act. That is so, isn't it? I am acting under force majeure?"

"You are indeed," said Bond emphatically.

Sable Basilisk made a careful note on the top paper in the file and continued. "Of course the first thing I had to ask for was the man's birth certificate and, after a delay, I was told that it had been lost and that I was on no account to worry about it. The Count had in fact been born in Gdynia of a Polish father and a Greek mother—I have the names here—on May 28th, 1908. Could I not pursue my researches backwards from the de Bleuville end? I replied temporizing, but by this time I had indeed established from our library that there had been a family of de Bleuvilles, at least as lately as the seventeenth century, at a place called Blonville-sur-Mer, Calvados, and that their arms and motto were as claimed by Blofeld." Sable Basilisk paused. "This of course he must have known for himself. There would have been no purpose in inventing a family of de Bleuvilles and trying to stuff them down our throats. I told the lawyers of my discovery and, in my summer holidays—the North of France is more or less my private heraldic beat, so to speak, and very rich it is too in connections with England—I motored down there and sniffed around. But meanwhile I had, as a matter of routine, written to our Ambassador in Warsaw and asked him to contact our Consul in Gdynia and request him to employ a lawyer to make the simple researches with the Registrar and the various churches where Blofeld might have been baptized. The reply, early in September, was, but is no longer, surprising. The pages containing the record of Blofeld's birth had been neatly cut out. I kept this information to myself, that is to say I did not pass it on to the Swiss lawyers because I had been expressly instructed to make no inquiries in Poland. Meanwhile I had carried out similar inquiries through a lawyer in Augsburg. There, there was indeed a record of Blofelds, but of a profusion of them, for it is a fairly common German name, and in any case nothing to link any of them with the de Bleuvilles from Calvados. So I was stumped, but no more than I have been before, and I wrote a neutral report to the Swiss lawyers and said that I was continuing my researches. And there"—Sable Basilisk slapped the file shut—"until my telephone began ringing yesterday, presumably because someone in the Northern Department of the Foreign Office was checking the file copies from Warsaw and the name Blofeld rang a bell, and you appeared looking very impatient from the cave of my friend the Griffon, the case rests."

Bond scratched his head thoughtfully. "But the ball's still in play?"

"Oh, yes, definitely."

"Can you keep it in play? I take it you haven't got Blofeld's present address?" Sable Basilisk shook his head. "Then would there be any conceivable excuse for an envoy from you?" Bond smiled. "Me, for example, to be sent out from the College to have an interview with Blofeld—some tricky point that cannot be cleared up by correspondence, something that needs a personal inquiry from Blofeld?"

"Well, yes, there is in a way." Sable Basilisk looked rather dubious. "You see, in some families there is a strong physical characteristic that goes on inevitably from generation to generation. The Habsburg lip is a case in point. So is the tendency to haemophilia amongst descendants of the Bourbons. The hawk nose of the Medici is another. A certain royal family have minute, vestigial tails. The original maharajahs of Mysore were born with six fingers on each hand. I could go on indefinitely, but those are the most famous cases. Now, when I was scratching around in the crypt of the chapel at Blonville, having a look at the old Bleuville tombs, my flashlight, moving over the stone faces, picked out a curious fact that I tucked away in my mind but that your question has brought to the surface. None of the de Bleuvilles, as far as I could tell, and certainly not through a hundred and fifty years, had lobes to their ears."

"Ah," said Bond, running over in his mind the Identicast picture of Blofeld and the complete, printed physiognometry of the man in Records. "So he shouldn't by rights have lobes to his ears. Or at any rate it would be a strong piece of evidence for his case if he hadn't?"

"That's right."

"Well, he *has* got lobes," said Bond, annoyed. "Rather pronounced lobes as a matter of fact. Where does that get us?"

"To begin with, added to what I know anyway, that makes him probably not a de Bleuville. But after all"—Sable Basilisk looked sly—"there's no reason why he should know what physical characteristic we're looking for in this interview."

"You think we could set one up?"

"Don't see why not. But"—Sable Basilisk was apologetic—"would you mind if I got clearance from Garter King of Arms? He's my boss, so to speak, under the Duke of Norfolk that is, the Earl Marshal, and I can't remember that we've ever been mixed up in this sort of cloak-and-dagger stuff before. Actually"—Sable Basilisk waved a deprecating hand—"we are, we have to be, damned meticulous. You do see that, don't you?"

"Naturally. And I'm sure there'd be no objection. But, even if Blofeld agreed to see me, how in hell could I play the part? This stuff is all double Dutch to me." He smiled. "I don't know the difference between a gule and a bezant and I've never been able to make out what a baronet is. What's my story to Blofeld? Who am I exactly?"

Sable Basilisk was getting enthusiastic. He said cheerfully, "Oh, that'll be all right. I'll coach you in all the dope about the de Bleuvilles. You can easily mug up a few popular books on heraldry. It's not difficult to be impressive on the subject. Very few people know anything about it."

"Maybe. But this Blofeld is a pretty smart animal. He'll want the hell of a lot of credentials before he sees anyone but his lawyer and his banker. Who exactly am I?"

"You think Blofeld's smart because you've seen the smart side of him," said Sable Basilisk sapiently. "I've seen hundreds of smart people from the City, industry, politics—famous people I've been quite frightened to meet when they walked into this room. But when it comes to snobbery, to buying respectability, so to speak, whether it's the title they're going to choose or just a coat of arms to hang over their fire-places in Surbiton, they dwindle and dwindle in front of you"—he made a downward motion over his desk with his hand—"until they're no bigger than homunculi. And the women are even worse. The idea of suddenly becoming a "lady" in their small community is so intoxicating that the way they bare their souls is positively obscene. It's as if"—Sable Basilisk furrowed his high, pale brow, seeking for a simile—"these fundamentally good citizens, these Smiths and Browns and Joneses and"—he smiled across the desk—"Bonds, regarded the process of ennoblement as a sort of laying-on of hands, a way of ridding themselves of all the drabness of their lives, of all their, so the speak, essential meagreness, their basic inferiority. Don't worry about Blofeld. He has already swallowed the bait. He may be a tremendous gangster, and he must be from what I remember of the case. He may be tough and ruthless in his corner of human behaviour. But if he is trying to prove that he is the Comte de Bleuville, you can be sure of various things. He wants to change his name. That is obvious. He wants to become a new, a respectable personality. That is obvious too. But above all he wants to become a count." Sable Basilisk brought his hand flat down on his desk for emphasis. "That, Mr. Bond, is tremendously significant. He is a rich and successful man in his line of business—no matter what it is. He no longer admires the material things, riches and power. He is now 54, as I reckon it. He wants a new skin. I can assure you, Mr. Bond, that he will receive you, if we play our cards right that is, as if he were consulting his doctor about"—Sable Basilisk's aristocratic face took on an expression of distaste—"as if he were consulting his doctor after contracting V.D." Sable Basilisk's eyes were now compelling. He sat back in his chair and lit his first cigarette. The smell of Turkish tobacco drifted across to Bond. "That's it," he said with certitude. "This man knows he is unclean, a social pariah. Which of course he is. Now he has thought up this way of buying himself a new identity. If you ask me, we must help the hair to grow and flourish on his heel of Achilles until it is so luxuriant that he trips on it."

8 FANCY COVER

And who the hell are *you* supposed to be?

M more or less repeated Bond's question when, that evening, he looked up from the last page of the report that Bond had spent the afternoon dictating to Mary Goodnight. M's face was just outside the pool of yellow light cast by the green-shaded reading lamp on his desk, but Bond knew that the lined, sailor's face was reflecting, in varying degrees, scepticism, irritation and impatience. The "hell" told him so. M rarely swore and when he did it was nearly always at stupidity. M obviously regarded Bond's plan as stupid, and now, away from the dedicated, minutely focused world of the Heralds, Bond wasn't sure that M wasn't right.

"I'm to be an emissary from the College of Arms, sir. This Basilisk chap recommended that I should have some kind of a title, the sort of rather highfalutin one that would impress a man with this kind of bee in his bonnet. And Blofeld's obviously got this bee or he wouldn't have revealed his existence, even to such a presumably secure and—er—sort of remote corner of the world as the College of Arms. I've put down there the arguments of this chap and they make a lot of sense to me. Snobbery's a real Achilles heel with people. Blofeld's obviously got the bug badly. I think we can get to him through it."

"Well, I think it's all a pack of nonsense," said M testily.

(Not many years before, M had been awarded the K.C.M.G. for his services, and Miss Moneypenny, his desirable secretary, had revealed in a moment of candour to Bond that M had not replied to a single one of the notes and letters of congratulation. After a while he had refused even to read them and had told Miss Moneypenny not to show him any more but to throw them in the wastepaper basket.) "All right then, what's this ridiculous title to be? And what happens next?"

If Bond had been able to blush, he would have blushed. He said, "Er—well, sir, it seems there's a chap called Sir Hilary Bray. Friend of Sable Basilisk's. About my age and not unlike me to look at. His family came from some place in Normandy. Family tree as long as your arm. William the Conqueror and all that. And a coat of arms that looks like a mixture between a jigsaw puzzle and Piccadilly Circus at night. Well, Sable Basilisk says he can fix it with him. This man's got a good war record and sounds a reliable sort of chap. He lives in some remote glen in the Highlands, watching birds and climbing the hills with bare feet. Never sees a soul. No reason why anyone in Switzerland should have heard of him." Bond's voice became defensive, stubborn. "Well, sir, the idea is that I should be him. Rather fancy cover, but I think it makes sense."

"Sir Hilary Bray, eh?" M tried to conceal his scorn. "And then what do you do? Run around the Alps waving this famous banner of his?"

Bond said patiently, obstinately, refusing to be brow-beaten. "First I'll get Passport Control to fix up a good passport. Then I mug up Bray's family tree until I'm word-perfect on the thing. Then I swot away at the rudiments of this heraldry business. Then, if Blofeld takes the bait, I go out to Switzerland with all the right books and suggest that I work out his de Bleuville pedigree with him."

"Then what?"

"Then I try and winkle him out of Switzerland, get him over the frontier to somewhere where we can do a kidnap job on him, rather like the Israelis did with Eichmann. But I haven't worked out all the details yet, sir. Had to get your approval and then Sable Basilisk has got to make up a damned attractive fly and throw it over these Zürich solicitors."

"Why not try putting pressure on the Zürich solicitors and winkle Blofeld's address out of them? Then we might think of doing some kind of a commando job."

"You know the Swiss, sir. God knows what kind of a retainer these lawyers have from Blofeld. But it's bound to be millionaire size. We might eventually get the address, but they'd be bound to tip off Blofeld if only to lay their hands on their fees before he vamoosed. Money's the religion of Switzerland."

"I don't need a lecture of the qualities of the Swiss, thank you, 007. At least they keep their trains clean and cope with the beatnik problem [two very rampant bees in M's bonnet!], but I daresay there's some truth in what you say. Oh, well." M wearily pushed the file over to Bond. "Take it away. It's a messy-looking bird's-nest of a plan. But I suppose it had better go ahead." M shook his head sceptically. "Sir Hilary Bray! Oh, well, tell the Chief of Staff I approve. But reluctantly. Tell him you can have the facilities. Keep me informed." M reached for the Cabinet telephone. His voice was deeply disgruntled. "Suppose I'll have to tell the P.M. we've got a line on the chap. The kind of tangle it is, I'll keep to myself. That's all, 007."

"Thank you, sir. Good night." As Bond went across to the door he heard M say into the green receiver, "M speaking. I want the Prime Minister personally, please." He might have been asking for the mortuary. Bond went out and softly closed the door behind him.

So, as November blustered its way into December, James Bond went unwillingly back to school, swotting up heraldry at his desk instead of top-secret reports, picking up scraps of medieval French and English, steeping himself in fusty lore and myth, picking the brains of Sable Basilisk and occasionally learning interesting facts, such as that the founders of Gamages came from the de Gamaches in Normandy and that Walt Disney was remotely descended from the D'Isignys of the same part of France. But these were nuggets in a wasteland of archaisms, and when, one day, Mary Goodnight, in reply to some sally of his, addressed him as "Sir Hilary" he nearly bit her head off.

Meanwhile the highly delicate correspondence between Sable Basilisk and the Gebrüder Moosbrugger proceeded haltingly and at a snail's pace. They, or rather Blofeld behind them, posed countless irritating but, Sable Basilisk admitted, erudite queries, each one of which had to be countered with this or that degree of heraldic obfuscation. Then there were minute questions about this emissary, Sir Hilary Bray. Photographs were asked for, and, suitably doctored, were provided. His whole career since his schooldays had to be detailed and was sent down from Scotland with a highly amused covering note from the real man. To test the market, more funds were asked for by Sable Basilisk and, with encouraging promptitude, were forthcoming in the shape of a further thousand pounds. When the cheque arrived on December 15th Sable Basilisk telephoned Bond delightedly. "We've got him," he said. "He's hooked!" And, sure enough, the next day came a letter from Zürich to say that their client agreed to a meeting with Sir Hilary. Would Sir Hilary please arrive at Zürich Central Airport by Swissair flight Number 105, due at Zürich at 1300 hours on December 21st. On Bond's prompting, Sable Basilisk wrote back that the date was not convenient to Sir Hilary owing to a prior engagement with the Canadian High Commissioner regarding a detail in the Arms of the Hudson's Bay Company. Sir Hilary could, however, manage the 22nd. By return came a cable agreeing and, to Bond, confirming that the fish had not only swallowed the hook but the line and sinker as well.

The last few days were spent in a flurry of meetings, with the Chief of Staff presiding, at Headquarters. The main decisions were that Bond should go to the meeting with Blofeld absolutely "clean." He would carry no weapons, no secret gear of any kind, and he would not be watched or followed by the Service in any way. He would communicate only with Sable Basilisk, getting across such information as he could by using heraldic double-talk (Sable Basilisk had been cleared by M.I.5 immediately after Bond's first meeting with him), and Sable Basilisk, who vaguely thought that Bond was employed by the Ministry of Defence, would be given a cut-out at the ministry who would be his go-between with the Service. This was all assuming that Bond managed to stay close to Blofeld for at least a matter of days. And that was to be his basic stratagem. It was essential to find out as much as possible about Blofeld, his activities and his associates, in order to proceed with planning the next step, his abduction from Switzerland. Physical action might not be necessary. Bond might be able to trick the man into a visit to Germany, as a result of a report which Sable Basilisk had prepared of certain Blofeld family documents at the Augsburg Zentral Archiv, which would need Blofeld's personal identification. Security precautions would include keeping Station Z completely in the dark about Bond's mission to Switzerland and a closure of the "Bedlam" file at Headquarters which would be announced in the routine "Orders of the Day." Instead, a new code-word for the operation, known only to an essential handful of senior officers, would be issued. It would be "Corona."

Finally, the personal dangers to Bond himself were discussed. There was total respect for Blofeld at Headquarters.

Nobody questioned his abilities or his ruthlessness. If Bond's true identity somehow became known to Blofeld, Bond would of course instantly be liquidated. A more dangerous and likely event would be that, once Blofeld had probed Bond's heraldic gen to its rather shallow bottom and it had been proved that he was or was not the Comte de Bleuville, Sir Hilary Bray, his usefulness expended, might "meet with an accident." Bond would just have to face up to these hazards and watch out particularly for the latter. He, and Sable Basilisk behind him, would have to keep some tricks up their sleeves, tricks that would somehow make Sir Hilary Bray's continued existence important to Blofeld. In conclusion, the Chief of Staff said he considered the whole operation "a lot of bezants" and that "Bezants" would have been a better code-word than "Corona." However, he wished Bond the best of luck and said, cold-heartedly, that he would instruct the Technical Section to proceed forthwith with the devising of a consignment of explosive snowballs for Bond's protection.

It was on this cheery note that Bond, on the evening of December 21st, returned to his office for a last run-through of his documentation with Mary Goodnight.

He sat sideways to his desk, looking out over the triste winter twilight of Regent's Park under snow, while she sat opposite him and ran through the items: "*Burke's Extinct and Dormant Baronetage*, property of the College of Heralds. Stamped 'Not to be removed from the Library.' The printed *Visitations in the College of Arms*, stamped ditto. *Genealogist's Guide*, by G. W. Marshall, with Hatchard's receipted bill to Sable Basilisk inserted. *Burke's General Armory*, stamped 'Property of the London Library,' wrapped and franked December 10th. Passport in the name of Sir Hilary Bray, containing various recently dated frontier stamps in and out of France, Germany and the Low Countries, fairly well used and dog-eared. One large file of correspondence with Augsburg and Zürich on College of Arms writing-paper and the writing-paper of the addressees. And that's the lot. You've fixed your laundry tags and so on?"

"Yes," said Bond dully. "I've fixed all that. And I've got two new suits with cuffs and double vents at the back and four buttons down the front. Also a gold watch and chain with the Bray seal. Quite the little baronet." Bond turned and looked across the desk at Mary Goodnight. "What do you think of this caper, Mary? Think it'll come off?"

"Well, it should do," she said staunchly. "With all the trouble that's been taken. But"—she hesitated—"I don't like you taking this man on without a gun." She waved a hand at the pile on the floor. "And all these stupid books about heraldry! It's just not *you*. You will take care, won't you?"

"Oh, I'll do that all right," said Bond reassuringly. "Now, be a good girl and get a radio taxi to the Universal Export entrance. And put all that junk inside it, would you? I'll be down in a minute. I'll be at the flat all this evening"—he smiled sourly—"packing my silk shirts with the crests on them." He got up. "So long, Mary. Or rather good night, Goodnight. And keep out of trouble till I get back."

She said, "You do that yourself." She bent and picked up the books and papers from the floor and, keeping her face hidden from Bond, went to the door and kicked it shut behind her with her heel. A moment or two later she opened the door again. Her eyes were bright. "I'm sorry, James. Good luck! And Happy Christmas!" She closed the door softly behind her.

Bond looked at the blank face of the Office of Works cream door. What a dear girl Mary was! But now there was Tracy. He would be near her in Switzerland. It was time to make contact again. He had been missing her, wondering about her. There had been three noncommittal but cheerful postcards from the Clinique de l'Aube at Davos. Bond had made inquiries and had ascertained that this was run by a Professor Auguste Kommer, President of the Société Psychiatrique et Psychologique Suisse. Over the telephone, Sir James Molony, the nerve specialist by appointment to the Service, had told Bond that Kommer was one of the top men in the world at his job. Bond had written affectionately and encouragingly to Tracy and had had the letters posted from America. He had said he would be home soon and would be in touch with her. Would he? And what would he do then? Bond had a luxurious moment feeling sorry for himself, for the miscellaneous burdens he was carrying alone. He then crushed out his cigarette and, banging doors behind him, got the hell out of his office and down in the lift to the discreet side-entrance that said "Universal Export."

The taxi was waiting. It was seven o'clock. As the taxi got under way, Bond made his plan for the evening. He would first do an extremely careful packing job of his single suitcase, the one that had no tricks to it, have two double vodkas and tonics with a dash of Angostura, eat a large dish of May's speciality—scrambled eggs fines herbes—have two more vodkas and tonics, and then, slightly drunk, go to bed with half a grain of seconal.

Encouraged by the prospect of this cosy self-anaesthesia, Bond brusquely kicked his problems under the carpet of his consciousness.

9 IRMA LA NOT SO DOUCE

The next day, at London Airport, James Bond, bowler hat, rolled umbrella, neatly folded *Times* and all, felt faintly ridiculous. He felt totally so when he was treated with the deference due to his title and shown into the V.I.P. lounge before take-off. At the ticket desk, when he had been addressed as Sir Hilary, he had looked behind him to see who the girl was talking to. He really must pull himself together and damn well *be* Sir Hilary Bray!

Bond had a double brandy and ginger ale and stood aloof from the handful of other privileged passengers in the gracious lounge, trying to *feel* like a baronet. Then he remembered the real Sir Hilary Bray, perhaps now gralloching a hind with his bare hands somewhere up in the Glens. There was nothing of the baronet about him! He really must get rid of the inverted snobbery that, with its opposite, is ingrained in so many of the English! He must stop acting a part, being a stage nobleman! He would just be himself and, if he gave the appearance of being rather a rough-hewn baronet, the easy-going kind, well, that at least was like the real one up in Scotland. Bond threw down the *Times* that he had been carrying as an extra badge of Top Peopleship, picked up the *Daily Express* and asked for another brandy and ginger ale.

Then, with its twin jets whispering far back of the first-class cabin, the Swissair Caravelle was airborne and Bond's mind was reaching forward to the rendezvous that had been so briefly detailed by the Zürich solicitors. Sir Hilary would be met at the airport by one of the Comte de Bleuville's secretaries. He would be seeing the Count that day or the next. Bond had a moment of panic. How should he address the man when he met him? Count? Monsieur le Comte? No, he would call him nothing—perhaps an occasional patronizing "my dear sir" in context. What would Blofeld look like? Would he have changed his appearance much? Probably, or the fox wouldn't have kept ahead of the hounds so efficiently. Bond's excitement mounted as he consumed a delicious lunch served by a delicious stewardess, and the winter-brown chequerboard of France fled backwards distantly below. Now there was scattered snow and barren trees as they crossed the tiny hillocks of the Vosges, then permanent snow and ice-floes on the Rhine, a short stop at Basle, and then the black crisscross of Zürich Airport and "fasten your lap-straps" in three languages, and they were planing down, a slight bump, the roar of jet deflection, and then they were taxying up to the apron in front of the imposing, very European-looking buildings decked with the gay flags of the nations.

At the Swissair desk inside the door, a woman was standing beside the reception counter. As soon as Bond appeared in the entrance she came forward. "Sair Hilary Bray?"

"Yes."

"I am Fräulein Irma Bunt. Personal secretary to the Count. Good afternoon. I hope you had a happy flight."

She looked like a very sunburnt female wardress. She had a square, brutal face with hard yellow eyes. Her smile was an oblong hole without humour or welcome, and there were sunburn blisters at the left corner of her mouth which she licked from time to time with the tip of a pale tongue. Wisps of brownish grey hair, with a tight, neat bun at the back, showed from under a skiing hat with a yellow talc visor that had straps which met under her chin. Her strong, short body was dressed in unbecomingly tight vorlage trousers topped by a grey wind-jacket ornamented over the left breast with a large red G topped by a coronet. Irma La not so Douce, thought Bond. He said, "Yes. It was very pleasant."

"You have your baggage check? Will you follow me, please? And first your passport. This way."

Bond followed her through the Passport Control and out into the customs hall. There were a few standers-by. Bond noticed her head nod casually. A man with a brief-case under his arm, hanging about, moved away. Bond studiously examined his baggage check. Beyond the scrap of cardboard, he noticed the man slip into one of the row of telephone booths in the main hall outside the customs area.

"You speak German?" The tongue flicked out and licked the blisters.

"No, I'm afraid not."

"French perhaps?"

"A little. Enough for my work."

"Ah, yes. That is important, yes?"

Bond's suitcase was unloaded off the trolley on to the barrier. The woman flashed some kind of a pass at the customs officer. It was very quickly done, but Bond caught a glimpse of her photograph and the heading "Bundespolizei." So! Blofeld had got the fix in!

The officer said deferentially, "Bitte sehr," and chalked his symbol in the colour of the day, yellow, on Bond's suitcase. A porter took it and they walked across to the entrance. When they came out on the steps, an anonymous black Mercedes 300 SE saloon pulled smartly out of the parking area and slid to a stop beside them. Next to the chauffeur sat the man who had gone to the telephone. Bond's suitcase was put in the boot and they moved off fast in the direction of Zürich. A few hundred yards down the wide road, the man beside the driver, who, Bond noticed, had been surreptitiously watching in the twin driving-mirror, said softly, "Is' gut," and the car turned right-handed up a side road which was marked "Eingang Verboten! Mit Ausnahme von Eigentümer und Personell von Privatflugzeugen."

Bond was amused as he ticked off the little precautions. It was obvious that he was still very much on probation.

The car came up with the hangars to the left of the main building, drove slowly between them and pulled up beside a bright orange Alouette helicopter, adapted by Sud Aviation for mountain rescue work. But this one had the red G with the coronet on its fuselage. So! He was going to be taken for a flight rather than a ride!

"You have travelled in one of these machines before? No? It is very pleasant. One obtains a fine view of the Alps." Fräulein Bunt's eyes were blank with disinterest. They climbed up the aluminium ladder. "Mind your head, please!" Bond's suitcase was handed up by the chauffeur.

It was a six-seater, luxurious in red leather. Above and in front of them under his Perspex canopy the pilot lifted a thumb. The ground staff pulled away the chocks and the big blades began to move. As they accelerated, the men on the ground drew away, shielding their faces against the whirling snow. There was a slight jolt and then they were climbing fast, and the crackle of radio from the control tower went silent.

Irma Bunt was across the passage-way from Bond. The extra man was in the rear, hidden behind the *Züricher Zeitung*. Bond leaned sideways and said loudly, against the rattle of the machine, "Where are we heading for?"

She pretended not to hear. Bond repeated his question, shouting it.

"Into the Alps. Into the high Alps," shouted the woman. She waved towards the window. "It is very beautiful. You like the mountains, isn't it?"

"I love them," shouted Bond. "Just like Scotland." He leaned back in his seat, lit a cigarette and looked out of the window. Yes, there was the Zürichersee to port. Their course was more or less east-south-east. They were flying at about 2,000 feet. And now there was the Wallensee. Bond, apparently uninterested, took the *Daily Express* out of his brief-case and turned to the sports pages. He read the paper from last page to first, meticulously, every now and then casting a bored glance out of the window. The big range to port would be the Rhätikon Alps. That would be the railway junction of Landquart below them. They held their course up the valley of the Prätigau. Would they keep on at Klosters or veer to starboard? Starboard it was. So! Up the Davos Valley! In a few minutes he would be flying over Tracy! A casual glance. Yes, there was Davos under its thin canopy of evening mist and smoke, while, above her, he was still in bright sunshine. At least she seemed to have had plenty of snow. Bond remembered the tremendous run down the Parsenn. Those had been the days! And now back on the old course again and giant peaks to right and left. This must be the Engadine. The Silvretta Group away to starboard, to port Piz Languard and, ahead, the Bernina range diving down, like a vast ski-jump, into Italy. That forest of lights away to starboard must be St Moritz! Now where? Bond buried himself in his paper. A slight veer to port. More lights. Pontresina? And now the radio began to crackle and the "Seat belts" sign went up. Bond thought it time to express open interest. He gazed out. Below, the ground was mostly in darkness, but ahead the giant peaks were still golden in the dying sun. They were making straight for one of them, for a small plateau near its summit. There was a group of buildings from which golden wires swooped down into the darkness of the valley. A cable car, spangled in the sun, was creeping down. Now it had been swallowed up in the murk. The helicopter was still charging the side of the peak that towered above them. Now it was only a hundred feet up above the slope, coming in to the plateau and the buildings. The pilot's arms moved on his joy stick. The machine pitched a little and slowed. The rotor arms swung languidly and then accelerated as the machine hovered and settled. There came a slight bump as the inflated rubber "floats" met the snow, a dying whirr from the rotor and they were there.

Where? Bond knew. They were in the Languard range, somewhere above Pontresina in the Engadine and their altitude would be about 10,000 feet. He buttoned up his raincoat and prepared for the rasping dagger of the cold air on his lungs when the door was opened.

Irma Bunt gave her box-like smile. "We have arrived," she said unnecessarily.

The door, with a clatter of falling ice particles, was wrenched open. The last rays of the sun shone into the cabin. They caught the woman's yellow sun visor and shone through, turning her face Chinese. The eyes gave out a false blaze, like the glass eyes of a toy animal, under the light. "Mind your head." She bent low, her tight, squat behind inviting an enormous kick, and went down the ladder.

James Bond followed her, holding his breath against the searing impact of the Arctic, oxygenless air. There were one or two men standing around dressed like ski guides. They looked at Bond with curiosity, but there was no greeting. Bond went on across the hard-trodden snow in the wake of the woman, the extra man following with his suitcase. He heard the engine stutter and roar, and a blizzard of snow particles stung the right side of his face. Then the iron grasshopper rose into the air and rattled off into the dusk.

It was perhaps fifty yards from where the helicopter had landed to the group of buildings. Bond dawdled, getting preliminary bearings. Ahead was a long, low building, now ablaze with lights. To the right, and perhaps another fifty yards away, were the outlines of the typical modern cable railhead, a box-like structure, with a thick flat roof canted upwards from close to the ground. As Bond examined it, its lights went out. Presumably the last car had reached the valley and the line was closed for the night. To the right of this was a large, bogus-chalet type structure with a vast veranda, sparsely lit, that would be for the mass tourist trade—again a typical piece of high-Alpine architecture. Down to the left, beneath the slope of the plateau, lights shone from a fourth building that, except for its flat roof, was out of sight.

Bond was now only a few yards from the building that was obviously his destination. An oblong of yellow opened invitingly as the woman went in and held the door for him. The light illuminated a big sign with the red G surmounted by the coronet. It said GLORIA KLUB. 3605 METRES. PRIVAT! NUR FUR MITGLIEDER. Below in smaller letters it said "Alpenberghaus und Restaurant Piz Gloria," and the drooping index finger of the traditional hand pointed to the right, towards the building near the cable-head.

So! Piz Gloria! Bond walked into the inviting yellow oblong. The door, released by the woman, closed with a pneumatic hiss.

Inside it was deliciously warm, almost hot. They were in a small reception room, and a youngish man with a very pale crew-cut and shrewd eyes got to his feet from behind a desk and made a slight bob in their direction. "Sir Hilary is in Number Two."

"Weiss schon," said the woman curtly and, only just more politely, to Bond, "Follow me, please." She went through a facing door and down a thickly piled, red-carpeted passage. The left-hand wall was only occasionally broken by windows interspersed with fine skiing and mountain photographs. On the right were at first the doors of the club rooms, marked Bar, Restaurant and Toiletten. Then came what were obviously the doors of bedrooms. Bond was shown into Number Two. It was an extremely comfortable, chintzy room in the American motel style with a bathroom leading off. The broad picture window was now curtained, but Bond knew that it must offer a tremendous view over the valley to the Suvretta group above St Moritz. Bond threw his brief-case on the double bed and gratefully disposed of his bowler hat and umbrella. The extra man appeared with his suitcase, placed it on the luggage stand without looking at Bond and withdrew, closing the door behind him. The woman stayed where she was. "This is to your satisfaction?" The yellow eyes were indifferent to his enthusiastic reply. She had more to say. "That is good. Now perhaps I should explain some things, convey to you some laws of the club, isn't it?"

Bond lit a cigarette. "That would certainly be helpful." He put a politely interested expression on his face. "Where are we, for instance?"

"In the Alps. In the high Alps," said the woman vaguely. "This Alp, Piz Gloria, is the property of the Count. Together with the Gemeinde, the local authorities, he constructed the Seilbahn. You have seen the cables, yes? This is the first year it is opened. It is very popular and brings in much money. There are some fine ski runs. The Gloria Abfahrt is already famous. There is also a bob-sleigh run that is much greater than the Cresta at St Moritz. You have heard of that? You ski perhaps? Or make the bob-sleigh?"

The yellow eyes were watchful. Bond thought he would continue to answer no to all questions. Instinct told him to. He said apologetically. "I'm afraid not. Never got around to it, you know. Too much bound up with my books, perhaps."

He smiled ruefully, self-critically.

"Schade! That is a pity." But the eyes registered satisfaction. "These installations bring good income for the Count. That is important. It helps to support his life's work, the Institut."

Bond raised his eyebrows a polite fraction.

"The Institut für physiologische Forschung. It is for scientific research. The Count is a leader in the field of allergies—you understand? This is like the hay fever, the unableness to eat shellfish, yes?"

"Oh really? Can't say I suffer from any myself."

"No? The laboratories are in a separate building. There the Count also lives. In this building, where we are, live the patients. He asks that you will not disturb them with too many questions. These treatments are very delicate. You understand?"

"Yes, of course. And when may I see the Count? I'm afraid I am a very busy man, Fräulein Bunt. There are matters awaiting my attention in London." Bond spoke impressively. "The new African states. Much work has to be done on their flags, the design of their currency, their stamps, their medals. We are very short-handed at the College. I hope the Count understands that his personal problem, interesting and important though it is, must take second place to the problems of government."

Bond had got through. Now she was all eagerness, reassurance. "But of course, my dear Sair Hilary. The Count asks to be excused tonight, but he would much like to receive you at eleven o'clock tomorrow morning. That is suitable?"

"Certainly, certainly. That will give me time to marshal my documents, my books. Perhaps"—Bond waved to the small writing desk near the window—"I could have an extra table to lay these things out. I'm afraid"—Bond smiled deprecatingly—"we bookworms need a lot of space."

"Of course, Sair Hilary. It will be done at once." She moved to the door and pressed a bell-button. She gestured downwards, now definitely embarrassed. "You will have noticed that there is no door handle on this side?" (Bond had done so. He said he hadn't.) "You will ring when you wish to leave the room. Yes? It is on account of the patients. It is necessary that they have quiet. It is difficult to prevent them visiting each other for the sake of gossiping. It is for their good. You understand? Bedtime is at ten o'clock. But there is a night staff in case you should need any service. And the doors are of course not locked. You may re-enter your room at any time. Yes? We meet for cocktails in the bar at six. It is—how do you say?—the rest-pause of the day." The box-like smile made its brief appearance. "My girls are much looking forward to meeting you."

The door opened. It was one of the men dressed as guides, a swarthy, bull-necked man with brown Mediterranean eyes. One of Marc-Ange's Corsican defectors? In rapid, bad French, the woman said that another table was desired. This was to be furnished during dinner. The man said "Entendu." She held the door before he could close it and he went off down the passage to the right. Guards' quarters at the end of the passage? Bond's mind went on clicking up the clues.

"Then that is all for the present, Sair Hilary? The post leaves at midday. We have radio-telephone communications if you wish to use them. May I convey any message to the Count?"

"Please say that I look forward greatly to meeting him tomorrow. Until six o'clock then." Bond suddenly wanted to be alone with his thoughts. He gestured towards his suitcase. "I must get myself unpacked."

"Of course, of course, Sair Hilary. Forgive me for detaining you." And, on this gracious note, Irma Bunt closed the door, with its decisive click, behind her.

Bond stood still in the middle of the room. He let out his breath with a quiet hiss. What the hell of a kettle of fish! He would have liked to kick one of the dainty bits of furniture very hard indeed. But he had noticed that, of the four electric light prisms in the ceiling, one was a blank, protruding eyeball. Closed-circuit television? If so, what would be its range? Not much more than a wide circle covering the centre of the room. Microphones? Probably the whole expanse of ceiling was one. That was the war-time gimmick. He must, he simply must assume that he was under constant supervision.

James Bond, his thoughts racing, proceeded to unpack, take a shower and make himself presentable for "my girls."

10 TEN GORGEOUS GIRLS

It was one of those leather-padded bars, bogus-masculine, and still, because of its newness, smelling like the inside of a new motor-car. It was made to look like a Tyrolean Stube by a big stone fire-place with a roaring log fire and cartwheel chandeliers with red-stemmed electric "candles." There were many wrought-iron gimmicks—wall-light brackets, ashtrays, table lamps—and the bar itself was "gay" with small flags and miniature liqueur bottles. Attractive zither music tripped out from a hidden loud speaker. It was not, Bond decided, a place to get seriously drunk in.

When he closed the leather-padded, brass-studded door behind him, there was a moment's hush, then a mounting of decibels to hide the covert glances, the swift summing-up. Bond got a fleeting impression of one of the most beautiful groups of girls he had ever seen, when Irma Bunt, hideous in some kind of homemade, homespun "après-ski," in which orange and black predominated, waddled out from among the galaxy and took him in charge. "Sair Hilary." She grasped his hand with a dry, monkey grip. "How delightful, isn't it? Come please, and meet my girls."

It was tremendously hot in the room and Bond felt the sweat bead on his forehead as he was led from table to table and shook this cool, this warm, this languid hand. Names like Ruby, Violet, Pearl, Anne, Elizabeth, Beryl, sounded in his ears, but all he saw was a sea of beautiful, sunburned faces and a succession of splendid, sweatered young bosoms. It was like being at home to the Tiller or the Bluebell Girls. At last he got to the seat that had been kept for him, between Irma Bunt and a gorgeous, bosomy blond with large blue eyes. He sat down, overcome. The barman hovered. Bond pulled himself together. "Whisky and soda, please," he said, and heard his voice from far away. He took some time lighting a cigarette while sham, stage conversation broke out among the four tables in the semicircular embrasure that must, during the day, be the great lookout point. Ten girls and Irma. All English. No surnames. No other man. Girls in their twenties. Working girls probably. Sort of air-hostess type. Excited at having a man amongst them—a personable man and a baronet to boot—if that was what one did to a baronet. Pleased with his private joke, Bond turned to the blonde. "I'm terribly sorry, but I didn't catch your name."

"I'm Ruby." The voice was friendly but refined. "It must be quite an ordeal being the only chap—amongst all us girls, I mean."

"Well, it was rather a surprise. But a very pleasant one. It's going to be difficult getting all your names right." He lowered his voice conspiratorially. "Be an angel and run through the field, so to speak."

Bond's drink came and he was glad to find it strong. He took a long but discreet pull at it. He had noticed that the girls were drinking colas and squashes with a sprinkling of feminine cocktails—orange blossoms, daiquiris. Ruby was one of the ones with a daiquiri. It was apparently O.K. to drink, but he would be careful to show a gentlemanly moderation.

Ruby seemed pleased to be able to break the ice. "Well, I'll start on your right. That's Miss Bunt, the sort of matron, so to speak. You've met her. Then, in the violet camelot sweater, well, that's Violet of course. Then at the next table. The one in the green and gold Pucci shirt is Anne and next to her in green is Pearl. She's my sort of best friend here." And so it went on, from one glorious golden girl to the next. Bond heard scraps of their conversation. "Fritz says I'm not getting enough Voreage. My skis keep on running away from me." "It's the same with me"—a giggle—"my sit-upon's black and blue." "The Count says I'm getting on very well. Won't it be awful when we have to go?" "I wonder how Polly's doing? She's been out a month now." "I think Skol's the only stuff for sunburn. All those oils and creams are nothing but frying-fat." And so on—mostly the chatter you would expect from a group of cheerful, healthy girls learning to ski, except for the occasional rather awed reference to the Count and the covert glances at Irma Bunt and Bond to make sure that they were behaving properly, not making too much noise.

While Ruby continued her discreet roll-call, Bond tried to fix the names to the faces and otherwise add to his comprehension of this lovely but bizarre group locked up on top of a very high Alp indeed. The girls all seemed to share a certain basic, girl-guidish simplicity of manners and language, the sort of girls who, in an English pub, you would find sitting demurely with a boy friend sipping a Babycham, puffing rather clumsily at a cigarette and occasionally saying "pardon." Good girls, girls who, if you made a pass at them, would say, "Please don't spoil it all," "Men only want one thing" or, huffily, "Please take your hand away." And there were traces of many accents, accents from all over Britain—the broad vowels of Lancashire, the lilt of Wales, the burr of Scotland, the adenoids of refined Cockney.

Yours truly foxed, concluded Bond as Ruby finished with "And that's Beryl in the pearls and twin-set. Now do you think you've got us all straight?"

Bond looked into the round blue eyes that now held a spark of animation. "Frankly no. And I feel like one of those comic film stars who get snarled up in a girls' school. You know. Sort of St Trinian's."

She giggled. (Bond was to discover that she was a chronic giggler. She was too "dainty" to open her lovely lips and laugh. He was also to find that she couldn't sneeze like a human, but let out a muffled, demure squeak into her scrap of lace handkerchief, and that she took very small mouthfuls at meals and barely masticated with the tips of her teeth before swallowing with hardly a ripple of her throat. She had been "well brought up.") "Oh but we're not at all like St Trinian's. Those awful girls! How could you ever say such a thing!"

"Just a thought," said Bond airily. "Now then, how about another drink?"

"Oh, thenks awfully."

Bond turned to Fräulein Bunt. "And you, Miss Bunt?"

"Thank you, Sair Hilary. An apple-juice. If you please."

Violet, the fourth at their table, said demurely that she wouldn't have another cola. "They give me wind," she explained.

"Oh, Violet!" Ruby's sense of the proprieties was outraged. "How can you say such a thing!"

"Well, anyway, they do," said Violet obstinately. "They make me hiccup. Nor harm in saying that, is there?"

Good old Manchester, thought Bond. He got up and went to the bar, wondering how he was going to plough on through this and other evenings. He ordered the drinks and had a brain-wave. He would break the ice! By hook or by crook he would become the life and soul of the party! He asked for a tumbler and that its rim should be dipped in water. Then he picked up a paper cocktail napkin and went back to the table. He sat down. "Now," he said as eyes goggled at him, "if we were paying for our drinks, I'll show you how we'd decide who should pay. I learned this in the Army." He placed the tumbler in the middle of the table, opened the paper napkin and spread the centre tightly over the top so that it clung to the moist edge of the glass. He took his small change out of his pocket, selected a five-centime piece and dropped it gently on to the centre of the stretched tissue. "Now then," he announced, remembering that the last time he had played this game had been in the dirtiest bar in Singapore. "Who else smokes? We need three others with lighted cigarettes." Violet was the only one at their table. Irma clapped her hands with authority. "Elizabeth, Beryl, come over here. And come and watch, girls, Sair Hilary is making the joke game." The girls clustered round, chattering happily at the diversion. "What's he doing?" "What's going to happen?" "How do you play?"

"Now then," said Bond, feeling like the games director

on a cruise ship, "this is for who pays for the drinks. One by one, you take a puff at your cigarette, knock off the ash, like this, and touch the top of the paper with the lighted end—just enough to burn a tiny hole, like this." The paper sparkled briefly. "Now Violet, then Elizabeth, then Beryl. The point is, the paper gets like a sort of cobweb with the coin just supported in the middle. The person who burns the last hole and makes the coin drop has to pay for the drinks. See? Now then, Violet."

There were squeaks of excitement. "What a lovely game!" "Oh, Beryl, look out!" Lovely heads craned over Bond. Lovely hair brushed his cheek. Quickly the three girls got the trick of very delicately touching a space that would not collapse the cobweb until Bond, who considered himself an expert at the game, decided to be chivalrous and purposely burned a vital strand. With the chink of the coin falling into the glass there was burst of excited laughter and applause.

"So, you see, girls." It was as if Irma Bunt had invented the game. "Sair Hilary pays, isn't it? A most delightful pastime. And now"—she looked at her mannish wrist-watch—"we must finish our drinks. It is five minutes to suppertime."

There were cries of "Oh, one more game, Miss Bunt!" But Bond politely rose with his whisky in his hand. "We will play again tomorrow. I hope it's not going to start you all off smoking. I'm sure it was invented by the tobacco companies!"

There was laughter. But the girls stood admiringly round Bond. What a sport he was! And they had all expected a stuffed shirt! Bond felt justifiable proud of himself. The ice had been broken. He had got them all minutely on his side. Now they were all chums together. From now on he would be able to get to talk to them without frightening them. Feeling reasonably pleased with his gambit, he followed the tight pants of Irma Bunt into the dining-room next door.

It was seven-thirty. Bond suddenly felt exhausted, exhausted with the prospect of boredom, exhausted with playing the most difficult role of his career, exhausted with the enigma of Blofeld and the Piz Gloria. What in hell was the bastard up to? He sat down on the right of Irma Bunt in the same placing as for drinks, with Ruby on his right and Violet, dark, demure, self-effacing, opposite him, and glumly opened his napkin. Blofeld had certainly spent money on his eyrie. Their three tables, in a remote corner by the long, curved, curtained window, occupied only a fraction of the space in the big, low, luxuriously appointed, mock-German baroque room, ornate with candelabra suspended from the stomachs of flying cherubs, festooned with heavy gilt plasterwork, solemnized by the dark portraits of anonymous noblemen. Blofeld must be pretty certain he was here to stay. What was the investment? Certainly not less than a million sterling, even assuming a fat mortgage from Swiss banks on the cost of the cable railway. To lease an alp, put up a cable railway on mortgage, with the engineers and the local district council participating—that, Bond knew, was one of the latest havens for fugitive funds. If you were successful, if you and the council could bribe or bully the local farmers to allow right-of-way through their pastures, cut swaths through the tree-line for the cable pylons and the ski-runs, the rest was publicity and amenities for the public to eat their sandwiches. Add to that the snob-appeal of a posh, heavily restricted club such as Bond imagined this, during the daytime, to be, the coroneted G, and the mystique of a research institute run by a Count, and you were off to the races. Skiing today, Bond had read, was the most widely practised sport in the world. It sounded unlikely, but then one reckoned the others largely by spectators. Skiers were participants, and bigger spenders on equipment than in other sports. Clothes, boots, skis, bindings and now the whole "après-ski" routine which took care of the day from four o'clock, when the sun went, onwards, were a tremendous industry. If you could lay your hands on a good alp, which Blofeld had somehow managed to do, you really had it good. Mortgages paid off—snow was the joker, but in the Engadine, at this height, you would be all right for that—in three or four years, and then jam for ever! One certainly had to hand it to him!

It was time to make the going again! Resignedly, Bond turned to Fräulein Bunt. "Fräulein Bunt. Please explain to me. What is the difference between a piz and an alp and a berg?"

The yellow eyes gleamed with academic enthusiasm. "Ah, Sair Hilary, but that is an interesting question. It had not occurred to me before. Now let me see." She gazed into the middle distance. "A piz, that is only a local name in this department of Switzerland for a peak. An alp, that one would think would be smaller than a berg—a hill, perhaps, or an upland pasture, as compared with a mountain. But that is not so. These"—she waved her hand—"are all alps and yet they are great mountains. It is the same in Austria, certainly in the Tyrol. But in Germany, in Bavaria for instance, which is my home land, there it is all bergs. No, Sair Hilary"—the box-like smile was switched on and off—"I cannot help you. But why do you ask?"

"In my profession," said Bond prosily, "the exact meaning of words is vital. Now, before we met for cocktails, it amused me to look up your surname, Bunt, in my books of reference. What I found, Fräulein, was most interesting. Bunt, is seems, is German for 'gay,' 'happy.' In England, the name has almost certainly been corrupted into Bounty, perhaps even into Brontë, because the grandfather of the famous literary family by that name had in fact changed his name from the less aristocratic name of Brunty. Now this is most interesting." (Bond knew that it wasn't, that this was all hocus-pocus, but he thought it would do no harm to stretch her heraldic muscles.) "Can you remember if your ancestors had any connection with England? There is the Dukedom of Brontë, you see, which Nelson assumed. It would be interesting to establish a connection."

The penny dropped! A duchess! Irma Bunt, hooked, went off into a dreary chronicle of her forebears, including proudly a distant relationship with a Graf von Bunt. Bond listened politely, prodding her back to the immediate past. She gave the name of her father and mother. Bond filed them away. He now had enough to find out in due course exactly who Irma Bunt was. What a splendid trap snobbery was! How right Sable Basilisk had been! There is a snob in all of us and only through snobbery could Bond have discovered who the parents of this woman were.

Bond finally calmed down the woman's momentary fever, and the head waiter, who had been politely hovering, presented giant menus covered in violet ink. There was everything from caviar down to Double Mokka au whisky irlandais. There were also many "spécialités Gloria"—Poulet Gloria, Homard Gloria, Tournedos Gloria and so on. Bond, despite his forswearing of spécialités, decided to give the chicken a chance. He said so and was surprised by the enthusiasm with which Ruby greeted his choice. "Oh, how right you are, Sir Hilary! I adore chicken too. I absolutely dote on it. Can I have that too, please, Miss Bunt?"

There was such surprising fervour in her voice that Bond watched Irma Bunt's face. What was that matronly gleam in her eye as she gave her approval? It was more than approval for a good appetite among her charges. There was enthusiasm, even triumph there. Odd! And it happened again when Violet stipulated plenty of potatoes with her tournedos. "I simply love potatoes," she explained to Bond, her eyes shining. "Don't you?"

"They're fine," agreed Bond, "When you're taking plenty of exercise, that is."

"Oh they're just darling," enthused Violet. "Aren't they, Miss Bunt?"

"Very good indeed, my dear. Very good for you too. And Fritz, I will just have the mixed salad with some cottage cheese." She gave the caricature of a simper. "Alas"—she spoke to Bond—"I have to watch my figure. These young things take plenty of exercise, while I must stay in my office and do the paper-work, isn't it?"

At the next table Bond heard the girl with the Scottish burr, her voice full of saliva, ask that her Aberdeen Angus steak should be cooked very rare indeed. "Guid and bluidy," she emphasized.

What was this? wondered Bond. A gathering of beautiful ogresses? Or was this a day off from some rigorous diet? He felt completely clueless, out of his depth. Well, he would just go on digging. He turned to Ruby. "You see what I mean about surnames. Fräulein Bunt may even have distant claim to an English title. Now what's yours, for instance? I'll see what I can make of it."

Fräulein Bunt broke in sharply. "No surnames here, Sair Hilary. It is a rule of the house. We use only first names for the girls. It is part of the Count's treatment. It is bound up with a change, a transference of identity, to help the cure. You understand?"

"No, I'm afraid that's way out of my depth," said Bond cheerfully.

"No doubt the Count will explain some of these matters to you tomorrow. He has special theories. One day the world will be startled when he reveals his methods."

"I'm sure," said Bond politely. "Well now"—he searched for a subject that would leave his mind free to roam on its own. "Tell me about your skiing. How are you getting on? Don't do it myself, I'm afraid. Perhaps I shall pick up some tips watching your classes."

It was an adequate ball which went bouncing on between Ruby and Violet, and Bond kept it in play while their food came and proved delicious. Poulet Gloria was spatchcocked, with a mustard-and-cream sauce. The girls fell silent over their dishes, consuming them with polite but concentrated greed. There was a similar pause in the chatter at the other tables. Bond made conversation about the décor of the room and this gave him a chance to have a good look at the waiters. There were twelve of them in sight. It was not difficult to sum them up as three Corsicans, three Germans, three vaguely Balkan faces, Turks, Bulgars or Yugoslavs, and three obvious Slavs. There would probably be three Frenchmen in the kitchen. Was this the old pattern of SPECTRE? The well-tried communist-cell pattern of three men from each of the great gangster and secret-service organizations in Europe? Were the three Slavs ex-Smersh men? The whole lot of them looked tough enough, had that quiet smell of the pro. The man at the airport was one of them. Bond recognized others as the reception steward and the man who had come to his room about the table. He heard the girls calling them Fritz, Joseph, Ivan, Achmed. And some of them were ski-guides during the day. Well, it was a nice little set-up if Bond was right.

Bond excused himself after dinner on the grounds of work. He went to his room and laid out his books and papers on the desk and on the extra table that had been provided. He bent over them studiously while his mind reviewed the day.

At ten o'clock he heard the good nights of the girls down the corridor and the click of the doors shutting. He undressed, turned the thermostat on the wall down from eighty-five to sixty, switched off the light and lay on his back for a while staring up into the darkness. Then he gave an authentic sigh of exhaustion for the microphones, if any, and turned over on his side and went to sleep.

Later, much later, he was awakened by a very soft murmuring that seemed to come from somewhere under the floor, but very, very far away. He identified it as a minute, spidery whispering that went on and on. But he could not make out any words and he finally put it down to the central-heating pipes, turned over and went to sleep again.

11 DEATH FOR BREAKFAST

James Bond awoke to a scream. It was a terrible, masculine scream out of hell. It fractionally held its first high, piercing note and then rapidly diminished as if the man had jumped off a cliff. It came from the right, from somewhere near the cable station perhaps. Even in Bond's room, muffled by the double windows, it was terrifying enough. Outside it must have been shattering.

Bond jumped up and pulled back the curtains, not knowing what scene of panic, of running men, would meet his eyes. But the only man in sight was one of the guides, walking slowly, stolidly up the beaten snow-path from the cable station to the club. The spacious wooden veranda that stretched from the wall of the club out over the slope of the mountain was empty, but tables had been laid for breakfast and the upholstered chaises-longue for the sunbathers had already been drawn up in their meticulous, colourful rows. The sun was blazing down out of a crystal sky. Bond looked at his watch. It was eight o'clock. Work began early in this place! People died early. For that had undoubtedly been the death-scream. He turned back into his room and rang the bell.

It was one of the three men Bond had suspected of being Russians. Bond became the officer and gentleman. "What is your name?"

"Peter, sir."

"Piotr?" Bond longed to say. "And how are all my old friends from SMERSH?" He didn't. He said, "What was that scream?"

"Pliss?" The granite-grey eyes were careful.

"A man screamed just now. From over by the cable station. What was it?"

"It seems there has been an accident, sir. You wish for breakfast?" He produced a large menu from under his arm and held it out clumsily.

"What sort of an accident?"

"It seems that one of the guides has fallen."

How could this man have know that, only minutes after the scream? "Is he badly hurt?"

"Is possible, sir." The eyes, surely trained in investigation, held Bond's blandly. "You wish for breakfast?" The menu was once again nudged forward.

Bond said, with sufficient concern, "Well, I hope the poor chap's all right." He took the menu and ordered. "Let me know if you hear what happened."

"There will no doubt be an announcement if the matter is serious. Thank you, sir." The man withdrew.

It was the scream that triggered Bond into deciding that, above all things, he must keep fit. He suddenly felt that, despite all the mystery and its demand for solution, there would come a moment when he would need all his muscle. Reluctantly he proceeded to a quarter of an hour of knee-bends and press-ups and deep-breathing chest-expansions—exercises of the skiing muscles. He guessed that he might have to get away from this place. But quick!

He took a shower and shaved. Breakfast was brought by Peter. "Any more news about this poor guide?"

"I have heard no more, sir. It concerns the outdoor staff. I work inside the club."

Bond decided to play it down. "He must have slipped

and broken an ankle. Poor chap! Thank you, Peter."

"Thank you, sir." Did the granite eyes contain a sneer?

James Bond put his breakfast on the desk and, with some difficulty, managed to prise open the double window. He removed the small bolster that lay along the sill between the panes to keep out draughts, and blew away the accumulated dust and small fly-corpses. The cold, savourless air of high altitudes rushed into the room and Bond went to the thermostat and put it up to 90 as a counter-attack. While, his head below the level of the sill, he ate a spare continental breakfast, he heard the chatter of the girls assembling outside on the terrace. The voices were high with excitement and debate. Bond could hear every word.

"I really don't think Sarah should have told on him."

"But he came in in the dark and started mucking her about."

"You mean actually *interfering* with her?"

"So she says. If I'd been her, I'd have done the same. And he's such a beast of a man."

"*Was*, you mean. Which one was it, anyway?"

"One of the Yugos. Bertil."

"Oh, I know. Yes, he was pretty horrible. He had such dreadful teeth."

"You oughtn't to say such things of the dead."

"How do you know he's dead? What happened to him, anyway?"

"He was one of the two you see spraying the start of the bob-run. You see them with hoses every morning. It's to get it good and icy so they'll go faster. Fritz told me he somehow slipped, lost his balance or something. And that was that. He just went off down the run like a sort of human bob-sleigh."

"Elizabeth! How can you be so heartless about it!"

"Well, that's what happened. You asked."

"But couldn't he save himself?"

"Don't be idiotic. It's sheet ice, a mile of it. And the bobs get up to sixty miles an hour. He hadn't got a prayer."

"But didn't he fly off at one of the bends?"

"Fritz said he went all the way to the bottom. Crashed into the timing hut. But Fritz says he must have been dead in the first hundred yards or so."

"Oh, here's Franz. Franz, can I have scrambled eggs and coffee? And tell them to make the scrambled eggs runny like I always have them."

"Yes, miss. And you, miss?" The waiter took the orders and Bond heard his boots creak off across the boards.

The sentantious girl was being sententious again. "Well,

all I can say is it must have been some kind of punishment for what he tried to do to Sarah. You always get paid off for doing wrong."

"Don't be ridiculous. God would never punish you as severely as that." The conversation followed this new hare off into a maze of infantile morality and the Scriptures.

Bond lit a cigarette and sat back, gazing thoughtfully at the sky. No, the girl was right. God wouldn't mete out such a punishment. But Blofeld would. Had there been one of those Blofeld meetings at which before the full body of men, the crime and the verdict had been announced? Had this Bertil been taken out and dropped on to the bob-run? Or had his companion been quietly dealt the card of death, told to give the sinner the trip or the light push that was probably all that had been needed? More likely. The quality of the scream had been of sudden, fully realized terror as the man fell, scrabbled at the ice with his finger-nails and boots, and then, as he gathered speed down the polished blue gully, the blinding horror of the truth. And what a death! Bond had once gone down the Cresta, from "Top," to prove to himself that he dared. Helmeted, masked against the blast of air, padded with leather and foam rubber, that had still been sixty seconds of naked fear. Even now he could remember how his limbs had shaken when he rose stiffly from the flimsy little skeleton bob at the end of the run-out. And that had been a bare three-quarters of a mile. This man, or the flayed remains of him, had done over a mile. Had he gone down head or feet first? Had his body started tumbling? Had he tried, while consciousness remained, to brake himself over the edge of one of the early, scientifically banked bends with the unspiked toe of his boot or . . . No. After the first few yards, he would already have been going too fast for any rational thought or action. God, what a death! A typical Blofeld death, a typical SPECTRE revenge for the supreme crime of disobedience. That was the way to keep discipline in the ranks! So, concluded Bond as he cleared the tray away and got down to his books, SPECTRE walks again! But down what road this time?

At ten minutes to eleven, Irma Bunt came for him. After an exchange of affabilities, Bond gathered up an armful of books and papers and followed her round the back of the club building and along a narrow, well-trodden path past a sign that said PRIVAT. EINTRITT VERBOTEN.

The rest of the building, whose outlines Bond had seen the night before, came into view. It was an undistinguished but powerfully built one-storey affair made of local granite blocks, with a flat cement roof from which, at the far end, protruded a small, professional-looking radio mast which, Bond assumed, had given the pilot his landing instructions on the previous night and which would also serve as the ears and mouth of Blofeld. The building was on the very edge of the plateau and below the final peak of Piz Gloria, but out of avalanche danger. Beneath it the mountain sloped sharply away until it disappeared over a cliff. Far below again was the tree line and the Bernina valley leading up to Pontresina, the glint of a railway track and the tiny caterpillar of a long goods train of the Rhätische Bahn, on its way, presumably, over the Bernina Pass into Italy.

The door to the building gave the usual pneumatic hiss, and the central corridor was more or less a duplicate of the one at the club, but here there were doors on both sides and no pictures. It was dead quiet and there was no hint of what went on behind the doors. Bond put the question.

"Laboratories," said Irma Bunt vaguely. "All laboratories. And of course the lecture-room. Then the Count's private quarters. He lives with his work, Sair Hilary."

"Good show."

They came to the end of the corridor. Irma Bunt knocked on the facing door.

"Herein!"

James Bond was tremendously excited as he stepped over the threshold and heard the door sigh shut behind him. He knew what not to expect, the original Blofeld, last year's model—about twenty stone, tall, pale, bland face with black crew-cut, black eyes with the whites showing all round, like Mussolini's, ugly thin mouth, long pointed hands and feet—but he had no idea what alterations had been contrived on the envelope that contained the man.

But Monsieur le Comte de Bleuville, who now rose from the chaise-longue on the small private veranda and came in out of the sun into the penumbra of the study, his hands outstretched in welcome, was surely not even a distant relative of the man on the files!

Bond's heart sank. This man was tallish, yes, and, all right, his hands and naked feet were long and thin. But there the resemblance ended. The Count had longish, carefully tended, almost dandified hair that was a fine silvery white. His ears, that should have been close to his head, stuck out slightly and, where they should have had heavy lobes, had none. The body that should have weighed twenty stone, now naked save for a black woollen slip, was not more than twelve stone, and there were no signs of the sagging flesh that comes from middle-aged weight-reduction. The mouth was full and friendly, with a pleasant, up-turned but perhaps rather unwavering smile. The forehead was serrated with wrinkles above a nose that, while the files said it should be short and squat, was aquiline and, round the right nostril, eaten away, poor chap, by what looked like the badge of tertiary syphilis. The eyes? Well, there might be something there if one could see them, but they were only rather frightening dark-green pools. The Count wore, presumably against the truly dangerous sun at these altitudes, dark-green tinted contact lenses.

Bond unloaded his books on to a conveniently empty table and took the warm, dry hand.

"My dear Sir Hilary. This is indeed a pleasure." Blofeld's voice had been said to be sombre and even. This voice was light and full of animation.

Bond said to himself, furiously, by God this has *got* to be Blofeld! He said, "I'm so sorry I couldn't come on the 21st. There's a lot going on at the moment."

"Ah, yes. So Fräulein Bunt told me. These new African states. They must indeed present a problem. Now, shall we settle down here"—he waved towards his desk—"or shall we go outside? You see"—he gestured at his brown body—"I am a heliotrope, a sun-worshipper. So much so that I have had to have these lenses devised for me. Otherwise, the ultra-violet rays, at this altitude . . ." He left the phrase unfinished.

"I haven't seen that kind of lens before. After all, I can leave the books here and fetch them if we need them for reference. I have the case pretty clear in my mind. And"—Bond smiled chummily—"it would be nice to go back to the fogs with something of a sunburn."

Bond had equipped himself at Lillywhites with clothing he thought would be both appropriate and sensible. He had avoided the modern elasticized vorlage trousers and had chosen the more comfortable but old-fashioned type of ski-trouser in a smooth cloth. Above these he wore an aged black wind-cheater that he used for golf, over his usual white sea-island cotton shirt. He had wisely reinforced this outfit with long and ugly cotton and wool pants and vests. He had conspicuously brand-new ski-boots with powerful ankle-straps. He said, "Then I'd better take off my sweater." He did so and followed the Count out on to the veranda.

The Count lay back again in his upholstered aluminium chaise-longue. Bond drew up a light chair made of similar materials. He placed it also facing the sun, but at an angle so that he could watch the Count's face.

"And now," said the Comte de Bleuville, "what have you got to tell me that necessitated this personal visit?" He turned his fixed smile on Bond. The dark-green glass eyes were unfathomable. "Not of course that the visit is not most welcome, most welcome. Now then, Sir Hilary."

Bond had been well trained in two responses to this obvious first question. The first was for the event that the Count had lobes to his ears. The second, if he had not. He now, in measured, serious tones, launched himself into Number Two.

"My dear Count"—the form of address seemed dictated by the silvery hair, by the charm of the Count's manners—"there are occasions in the work of the College when research and paper-work are simply not enough. We have, as you know, come to a difficult passage in our work on your case. I refer of course to the hiatus between the disappearance of the de Bleuville line around the time of the French Revolution and the emergence of the Blofeld family, or families, in the neighbourhood of Augsburg. And"—Bond paused impressively—"in the latter context I may later have a proposal that I hope will find favour with you. But what I am coming to is this. You have already expended serious funds on our work, and it would not have been fair to suggest that the researches should go forward unless there was a substantial ray of hope in the sky. The possibility of such a ray existed, but it was of such a nature that it definitely demanded a physical confrontation."

"Is that so? And for what purpose, may I inquire?"

James Bond recited Sable Basilisk's examples of the Habsburg lip, the royal tail and the others. He then leaned forward in his chair for emphasis. "And such a physical peculiarity exists in connection with the de Bleuvilles. You did not know this?"

"I was not aware of it. No. What is it?"

"I have good news for you, Count." Bond smiled his congratulations. "All the de Bleuville effigies or portraits that we have been able to trace have been distinctive in one vital respect, in one inherited characteristic. It appears that the family had no lobes to their ears!"

The Count's hands went up to his ears and felt them. Was he acting?

"I see," he said slowly. "Yes, I see." He reflected. "And you had to see this for yourself? My word, or a photograph, would not have been sufficient?"

Bond looked embarrassed. "I am sorry, Count. But

that was the ruling of Garter King of Arms. I am only a junior free-lance research worker for one of the Pursuivants. He in turn takes his orders in these matters from above. I hope you will appreciate that the College has to be extremely strict in cases concerned with a most ancient and honourable title such as the one in question."

The dark pools aimed themselves at Bond like the muzzles of guns. "Now that you have seen what you came to see, you regard the title as still in question?"

This was the worst hurdle. "What I have seen certainly allows me to recommend that the work should continue, Count. And I would say that our chances of success have greatly multiplied. I have brought out the materials for a first sketch of the Line of Descent, and that, in a matter of days, I could lay before you. But alas, as I have said, there are still many gaps, and it is most important for me to satisfy Sable Basilisk particularly about the stages of your family's migration from Augsburg to Gdynia. It would be of the greatest help if I might question you closely about your parentage in the male line. Even details about your father and grandfather would be of the greatest assistance. And then, of course, it would be of the utmost importance if you could spare a day to accompany me to Augsburg to see if the handwriting of these Blofeld families in the Archives, their Christian names and other family details, awaken any memories or connections in your mind. The rest would then remain with us at the College. I could spare no more than a week on this work. But I am at your disposal if you wish it."

The Count got to his feet. Bond followed suit. He walked casually over to the railing and admired the view. Would this bedraggled fly be taken? Bond now desperately hoped so. During the interview he had come to one certain conclusion. There was not a single one of the peculiarities in the Count's appearance that could not have been achieved by good acting and by the most refined facial and stomach surgery applied to the original Blofeld. Only the eyes could not have been tampered with. And the eyes were obscured.

"You think that with patient work, even with the inclusion of a few question marks where the connecting links are obscure, I would achieve an Acte de Notoriété that would satisfy the Minister of Justice in Paris?"

"Most certainly," lied Bond. "With the authority of the College in support."

The fixed smile widened minutely. "That would give me much satisfaction, Sir Hilary. I *am* the Comte de Bleuville. I am certain of it in my heart, in my veins." There was real fervour in the voice. "But I am determined that my title shall be officially recognized. You will be most welcome to remain as my guest and I shall be constantly at your disposal to help with your researches."

Bond said politely, but with a hint of weariness, of resignation, "All right, Count. And thank you. I will go and make a start straightaway."

12 TWO NEAR MISSES

Bond was shown out of the building by a man in a white coat with the conventional white gauze of the laboratory worker over the lower half of his face. Bond attempted no conversation. He was now well inside the fortress, but he would have to continue to walk on tiptoe and be damned careful where he put his feet!

He returned to his room and got out one of the giant sheets of squared paper with which he had been furnished. He sat down at his table and wrote firmly at the top centre of the paper "Guillaume de Bleuville, 1207-1243." Now there were five hundred years of de Bleuvilles, with their wives and children, to be copied down from his books and notes. That would fill up an impressive number of pages with impeccable fact. He could certainly spread that chore over three days, interspersed with more tricky work—gassing with Blofeld about the Blofeld end of the story. Fortunately there were some English Blofelds he could throw in as make-weight. And some Bluefields and Blumfields. He could start some pretty hares running in those directions! And, in between these idiotic activities, he would ferret and ferret away at the mystery of what in hell the new Blofeld, the new SPECTRE, were up to!

One thing was certain, they had already been through his belongings. Before going for his interview, Bond had gone into the bathroom, away from that seemingly watchful hole in the ceiling, and had painfully pulled out half a dozen of his hairs. These, while he had selected the books he needed to take with him, he had dispersed inconspicuously among his other papers and in his passport. The hairs were all gone. Someone had been through all his books. He got up and went to the chest of drawers, ostensibly for a handkerchief. Yes, the careful patterns in which he had laid out his things had all been minutely disturbed.

Unemotionally he went back to his work, thanking heaven he had travelled as "clean" as a whistle! But by God he'd have to keep his cover solid! He didn't at all like the thought of that one-way trip down the bob-run!

Bond got as far as 1350 and then the noise from the veranda became too distracting. Anyway, he had done a respectable stint, almost to the bottom of the giant page. He would go out and do a little very discreet exploring. He wanted to get his bearings, or rather confirm them, and this would be a perfectly reasonable activity for a newcomer. He had left his door into the passage ajar. He went out and along to the reception lounge, where the man in the plum coat was busy entering the names of the morning's visitors in a book. Bond's greeting was politely answered. There was a ski-room and workshop to the left of the exit. Bond wandered in. One of the Balkan types was at the workbench, screwing a new binding on to a ski. He looked up and went on with his work while Bond gazed with seeming curiosity at the ranks of skis standing along the wall. Things had changed since his day. The bindings were quite different and designed, it seemed, to keep the heel dead flat on the ski. And there were new safety releases. Many of the skis were of metal and the ski-sticks were fibre-glass lances that looked to Bond extremely dangerous in the event of a bad fall. Bond wandered over to the workbench and feigned interest in what the man was doing. In fact he had seen something that excited him very much—an untidy pile of lengths of thin plastic strip for the boot to rest on in the binding, so that, on the shiny surface, snow would not ball under the sole. Bond leaned over the workbench, resting on his right elbow, and commented on the precision of the man's work. The man grunted and concentrated all the more closely to avoid further conversation. Bond's left hand slid under his leaning arm, secured one of the strips and slid it up his sleeve. He made a further inane comment, which was not answered, and strolled out of the ski-room.

(When the man in the workshop heard the front door hiss shut, he turned to the pile of plastic strips and counted them carefully twice. Then he went out to the man in the plum-coloured coat and spoke to him in German. The man nodded and picked up the telephone receiver and dialled O. The workman went stolidly back to his ski-room.)

As Bond strolled along the path that led to the cable station, he transferred the plastic strip from his sleeve to his trouser pocket, feeling pleased with himself. He had at least provided himself with one tool—the traditional burglar's tool for opening the Yale-type locks that secured the doors.

Away from the club-house, to which only a thin trickle of smart-looking people were making their way, he got into the usual mountain-top crowd—people swarming out of the cable-head, skiers wobbling or schussing down the easy nursery slopes on the plateau, little groups marshalled under individual teachers and guides from the valley. The terrace of the public restaurant was already crowded with the under-privileged who hadn't got the money or the connections to join the club. He walked below it on the well-trampled snow and stood amongst the skiers at the top of the first plunging schuss of the Gloria run. A large notice-board, crowned with the G and the coronet, announced GLORIA ABFAHFT! Then below, ROT—FREIE FAHRT. GELB—FREIE FAHRT. SCHWARZ—GESPERRT, meaning that the red and yellow runs were open but the black closed, presumably because of avalanche danger. Below this again was a painted metal map of the three runs. Bond had a good look at it, reflecting that it might be wise to commit to memory the red, which was presumably the easiest and most popular. There were red, yellow and black marker flags on the map, and Bond could see the actual flags fluttering way down the mountain until the runs, studded with tiny moving figures, disappeared to the left, round the shoulder of the mountain and under the cable railway. The red seemed to continue to zigzag under the cable and between the few high pylons until it met the tree line. Then there was a short stretch of wood-running until the final easy schuss across the undulating lower meadows to the bottom cable-head, beyond which lay the main railway line and then the Pontresina-Samaden road. Bond tried to get it all fixed in his mind. Then he watched some of the starts. These varied between the arrow-like dive of the Kannonen, the stars, who took the terrific schuss dead straight in a low crouch with their sticks jauntily tucked under their armpits, the average amateur who braked perhaps three or four times on his way down, and the terrified novice who, with stuck-out behind, stemmed his way down, his skis angled and edged like a snow-plough, with occasional straight runs diagonally across the polished slope—dashing little sprints that usually ended in a mild crash as he ran off the flattened surface into the thick powder snow that edged the wide, beaten piste.

The scene was the same as a thousand others Bond had

witnessed when, as a teen-ager, he learned his skiing in the old Hannes Schneider School at St Anton in the Arlberg. He had got pretty good and had won his golden K, but the style in those days was rudimentary compared with what he was now witnessing from the occasional expert who zoomed down and away from beside him. Today the metal skis seemed to run faster and truer than the old steel-edged hickory. There was less shoulder-work and the art of Wedeln, a gentle waggling of the hips, was a revelation. Would it be as effective in deep new snow as it was on the well-beaten piste? Bond was doubtful, but he was envious of it. It was so much more graceful than the old Arlberg crouch. Bond wondered how he would fare on this terrific run. He would certainly not dare to take the first schuss straight. He would brake at least twice, perhaps there and there. And his legs would be trembling before he had been going for five minutes. His knees and ankles and wrists would be giving out. He *must* get on with his exercises!

Bond, excited, left the scene and followed arrows that pointed to the GLORIA EXPRESS BOB-RUN. It lay on the other side of the cable station. There was a small wooden hut, the starter's hut, with telephone-wires connected to the station, and, beneath the cable station, a little "garage" that housed the bob-sleighs and one-man skeleton-bobs. A chain, with a notice on it saying ABFAHRTEN TAGLICH 0900-1100, was stretched across the wide mouth of the gulch of blue ice that curved away to the left and then disappeared over the shoulder. Here again was a metal map showing the zigzag course of the run down into the valley. In deference to the English traditions at the sport, outstanding curves and hazards were marked with names such as "Dead Man's Leap," "Whizz-Bang Straight," "Battling S," "Hell's Delight," "The Bone-shaker," and the finishing straight down "Paradise Alley." Bond visualized the scene that morning, heard again that heart-rending scream. Yes, that death certainly had the old Blofeld touch!

"Sair Hilary! Sair Hilary!"

Startled out of his thoughts, Bond turned. Fräulein Irma Bunt, her short arms akimbo, was standing on the path to the club.

"Lunchtime! Lunch!"

"Coming," Bond called back, and strolled up the slope towards her. He noted that, even in that hundred yards, his breathing was shallow and his limbs were heavy. This blasted height! He really must get into training!

He came up with her. She looked surly. He said that

he was sorry, he had not noticed the time. She said nothing. The yellow eyes surveyed him with active dislike before she turned her back and led the way along the path.

Bond looked back over the morning. What had he done? Had he made a mistake? Well, he just might have. Better re-insure! As they came through the entrance into the reception lounge, Bond said casually, "Oh, by the way, Fräulein Bunt, I was in the ski-room just now."

She halted. Bond noticed that the head of the receptionist bent a fraction lower over his visitors' book.

"Yes?"

Bond took the length of plastic out of his pocket. "I found just what I wanted." He stitched a smile of innocent pleasure on his face. "Like an idiot I forgot to bring a ruler with me. And there were these things on the workbench. Just right. So I borrowed one. I hope that was all right. Of course I'll leave it behind when I go. But for these family trees, you know"—Bond sketched a series of descending straight lines in the air—"one has to get them on the right levels. I hope you don't mind." He smiled charmingly. "I was going to confess the next time I saw you."

Irma Bunt veiled her eyes. "It is of no consequence. In future, anything you need you will perhaps ring for, isn't it? The Count wishes you to have every facility. Now" —she gestured—"if you will perhaps go out on the terrace. You will be shown to our table. I will be with you in a moment."

Bond went through the restaurant door. Several of the interior tables were occupied by those who had had enough sun. He went across the room and out through the now open french windows. The man Fritz, who appeared to be the maître d'hôtel, came towards him through the crowded tables. His eyes too were cold with hostility. He held up a menu. "Please to follow me."

Bond followed him to the table up against the railing. Ruby and Violet were already there. Bond felt almost light-hearted with relief at having clean hands again. By God, he must pay attention, take care! This time he had got away with it. And he still had the strip of plastic! Had he sounded innocent enough, stupid enough? He sat down and ordered a double medium-dry vodka martini, on the rocks, with lemon peel, and edged his foot up against Ruby's.

She didn't withdraw hers. She smiled. Violet smiled. They all started talking at once. It was suddenly a beautiful day.

Fräulein Bunt appeared and took her place. She was

gracious again. "I am so pleased to hear that you will be staying with us for a whole week, Sair Hilary. You enjoyed your interview with the Count? Is he not an interesting man?"

"Very interesting. Unfortunately our talk was too short and we discussed only my own subject. I was longing to ask him about his research work. I hope he didn't think me very rude."

Irma Bunt's face closed perceptibly. "I am sure not. The Count does not often like to discuss his work. In these specialized scientific fields, you understand, there is much jealousy and, I am sorry to say, much intellectual thieving." The box-like smile. "I do not of course refer to yourself, my dear Sair Hilary, but to scientists less scrupulous than the Count, to spies from the chemical companies. That is why we keep ourselves very much to ourselves in our little Eagle's Nest up here. We have total privacy. Even the police in the valley are most co-operative in safeguarding us from intruders. They appreciate what the Count is doing."

"The study of allergies?"

"Just so." The maître d'hôtel was standing by her side. His feet came together with a perceptible click. Menus were handed round and Bond's drink came. He took a long pull at it and ordered Oeufs Gloria and a green salad. Chicken again for Ruby, cold cuts "with stacks of potatoes" for Violet. Irma Bunt ordered her usual cottage cheese and salad.

"Don't you girls eat anything but chicken and potatoes? Is this something to do with your allergies?"

Ruby began, "Well, yes, in a way. Somehow I've come to simply love. . . . "

Irma Bunt broke in sharply. "Now then, Ruby. No discussion of treatments, you remember? Not even with our good friend Sair Hilary." She waved a hand towards the crowded tables around them. "A most interesting crowd, do you not find, Sair Hilary? Everybody who is anybody. We have quite taken the international set away from Gstaad and St Moritz. That is your Duke of Marlborough over there with such a gay party of young things. Nearby that is Mistair Whitney and Lady Daphne Straight. Is she not chic? They are both wonderful skiers. And that beautiful girl with the long fair hair at the big table, that is Ursula Andress, the film star. What a wonderful tan she has! And Sir George Dunbar, he always has the most enchanting companions." The box-like smile. "Why, we only need the Aga Khan and perhaps your Duke of Kent and we would have everybody, but everybody. Is it not sensational for the first season?"

Bond said it was. The lunch came. Bond's eggs were delicious—chopped hard-boiled eggs, with a cream and cheese sauce laced with English mustard (English mustard seemed to be the clue to the Gloria specialities) gratinés in a copper dish. Bond commented on the excellence of the cooking.

"Thank you," said Irma Bunt. "We have three expert Frenchmen in the kitchen. Men are very good at cooking, is it not?"

Bond felt rather than saw a man approaching their table. He came up to Bond. He was a military-looking man, of about Bond's age, and he had a puzzled expression on his face. He bowed slightly to the ladies and said to Bond, "Excuse me, but I saw your name in the visitors' book. It is Hilary Bray, isn't it?

Bond's heart sank. This situation had always been a possibility and he had prepared a fumbling counter to it. But this was the worst possible moment with that damned woman watching and listening!

Bond said, "Yes, it is," with heartiness.

"*Sir* Hilary Bray?" The pleasant face was even more puzzled.

Bond got to his feet and stood with his back to his table, to Irma Bunt. "That's right." He took out his handkerchief and blew his nose to obscure the next question, which might be fatal.

"In the Lovat Scouts during the war?"

"Ah," said Bond. He looked worried, lowered his voice appropriately. "You're thinking of my first cousin. From Ben Trilleachan. Died six months ago, poor chap. I inherited the title."

"Oh, lord!" The man's puzzlement cleared. Grief took its place. "Sorry to hear that. Great pal of mine in the war. Funny! I didn't see anything about it in *The Times*. Always read the 'Births, Marriages and Deaths.' What was it?"

Bond felt the sweat running down under his arms. "Fell off one of those bloody mountains of his. Broke his neck."

"My God! Poor chap! But he was always fooling around the tops by himself. I must write to Jenny at once." He held out his hand. "Well, sorry to have butted in. Thought this was a funny place to find old Hilary. Well, so long, and sorry again." He moved off between the tables. Out of the corner of his eye, Bond saw him rejoin a very English-looking table of men and, obviously, wives, to whom he began talking animatedly.

Bond sat down, reached for his drink and drained it and went back to his eggs. The woman's eyes were on him. He felt the sweat running down his face. He took out his handkerchief and mopped at it. "Gosh, it's hot out here in the sun! That was some pal of my first cousin's. My cousin had the same name. Collateral branch. Died not long ago, poor chap." He frowned sadly. "Didn't know this man from Adam. Nice-looking fellow." Bond looked bravely across the table. "Do you know any of his party, Fräulein Bunt?"

Without looking at the party, Fräulein Bunt said shortly, "No, I do not know everyone who comes here." The yellow eyes were still inquisitive, holding his. "But it was a curious coincidence. Were you very alike, you and your cousin?"

"Oh, absolutely," said Bond, gushing. "Spit image. Often used to get taken for each other." He looked across at the English group. Thank God they were picking up their things and going. They didn't look particularly smart or prosperous. Probably staying at Pontresina or under the ex-officers' scheme at St Moritz. Typical English skiing party. With any luck they were just doing the big runs in the neighbourhood one by one. Bond reviewed the way the conversation had gone while coffee came and he made cheerful small talk with Ruby, whose foot was again clamped against his, about her skiing progress that morning.

Well, he decided, the woman couldn't have heard much of it with all the clatter and chatter from the surrounding tables. But it had been a narrow squeak, a damned narrow squeak. The second of the day!

So much for walking on tiptoe inside the enemy lines!

Not good enough! Definitely not good enough!

13 PRINCESS RUBY?

My dear Sable Basilisk,

I arrived safely—by helicopter, if you please!—at this beautiful place called Piz Gloria, 10,000 feet up somewhere in the Engadine. Most comfortable with an excellent male staff of several nationalities and a most efficient secretary to the Count named Fräulein Irma Bunt who tells me that she comes from Munich.

I had a most profitable interview with the Count this morning as a result of which he wishes me to stay on for a week to complete the first draft of his genealogical tree. I do hope you can spare me for so long. I warned the Count that we had much work to do on the new Commonwealth states. He himself, though busily engaged on what sounds like very public-spirited research work on allergies and their cause (he has ten English girls here as his patients), has agreed to see me daily in the hope that together we may be able to bridge the gap between the migration of the de Bleuvilles from France and their subsequent transference, as Blofelds, from Augsburg to Gdynia. I have suggested to him that we conclude the work with a quick visit to Augsburg for the purposes you and I discussed, but he has not yet given me his decision.

Please tell my cousin Jenny Bray that she may be hearing from a friend of her late husband who apparently served with him in the Lovat Scouts. He came up to me at lunch today and took me for the other Hilary! Quite a coincidence!

Working conditions are excellent. We have complete privacy here, secure from the madding world of skiers, and very sensibly the girls are confined to their rooms after ten at night to put them out of the temptation of roaming and gossiping. They seem a very nice lot, from all over the United Kingdom, but rather on the dumb side!

Now for my most interesting item. The Count has *not* got lobes to his ears! Isn't that good news! He also is of a most distinguished appearance and bearing with a fine head of silvery hair and a charming smile. His slim figure also indicates noble extraction. Unfortunately he has to wear dark-green contact lenses because of weak eyes and the strength of the sunshine at this height, and his aquiline nose is blemished by a deformed nostril which I would have thought could easily have been put right by facial surgery. He speaks impeccable English with a gay lilt to his voice and I am sure that we will get on very well.

Now to get down to business. It would be most helpful if you would get in touch with the old printers of the Almanach de Gotha and see if they can help us over our gaps in the lineage. They may have some traces. Cable anything helpful. With the new evidence of the ear lobes I am quite confident that the connection exists.

That's all for now.

Yours ever,
HILARY BRAY

P.S. Don't tell my mother, or she will be worried for my safety among the eternal snows! But we had a nasty accident here this morning. One of the staff, a Yugoslav it seems, slipped on the bob-run and went the whole way to the bottom! Terrible business. He's apparently being buried in Pontresina tomorrow. Do you think we ought to send some kind of a wreath? H.B.

Bond read the letter several times. Yes, that would give the officers in charge of Operation "Corona" plenty to bite on. Particularly the hint that they should get the dead man's name from the registrar in Pontresina. And he had covered up a bit on the Bray mix-up when the letter, as Bond was sure it would be, was steamed open and photostated before dispatch. They might of course just destroy it. To prevent this, the bit of bogosity about the Almanach de Gotha would be a clincher. This source of heraldic knowledge hadn't been mentioned before. It would surely excite the interest of Blofeld.

Bond rang the bell, handed out the letter for dispatch and got back to his work, which consisted initially of going into the bathroom with the strip of plastic and his scissors in his pocket and snipping two-inch-wide strips off the end. These would be enough for the purposes he and, he hoped, Ruby would put them to. Then, using the first joint of his thumb as a rough guide, he marked off the remaining eighteen inches into inch measures, to support his lie about the ruler, and went back to his desk and to the next hundred years of the de Bleuvilles.

At about five o'clock the light got so bad that Bond got up from his table and stretched, preparatory to going over to the light-switch near the door. He took a last look out of the window before he closed it. The veranda was completely deserted and the foam rubber cushions for the reclining-chairs had already been taken in. From the direction of the cable-head there still came the whine of machinery that had been part of the background noises to the day. Yesterday the railway had closed at about five, and it must be time for the last pair of gondolas to complete their two-way journey and settle in their respective stations for the night. Bond closed the double windows, walked across to the thermostat and put it down to seventy. He was just about to reach for the light-switch when there came a very soft tapping at the door.

Bond kept his voice low. "Come in!"

The door opened and quickly closed to within an inch

of the lock. It was Ruby. She put her fingers to her lips and gestured towards the bathroom. Bond, highly intrigued, followed her in and shut the door. Then he turned on the light. She was blushing. She whispered imploringly, "Oh, please forgive me, Sir Hilary. But I did so want to talk to you for a second."

"That's fine, Ruby. But why the bathroom?"

"Oh, didn't you know? No, I suppose you wouldn't. It's supposed to be a secret, but of course I can tell you. You won't let on, will you?"

"No, of course not."

"Well, all the rooms have microphones in them. I don't know where. But sometimes we girls have got together in each other's rooms, just for a gossip, you know, and Miss Bunt has always known. We think they've got some sort of television too." She giggled. "We always undress in the bathroom. It's just a sort of feeling. As if one was being watched the whole time. I suppose it's something to do with the treatment."

"Yes, I expect so."

"The point is, Sir Hilary, I was tremendously excited by what you were saying at lunch today, about Miss Bunt perhaps being a duchess. I mean, is that really possible?"

"Oh, yes," said Bond airily.

"I was so disappointed at not being able to tell you my surname. You see, you see"—her eyes were wide with excitement—"it's Windsor!"

"Gosh," said Bond, "that's interesting!"

"I knew you'd say that. You see, there's always been talk in my family that we're distantly connected with the Royal Family!"

"I can quite understand that." Bond's voice was thoughtful, judicious. "I'd like to be able to do some work on that. What were your parents' names? I must have them first."

"George Albert Windsor and Mary Potts. Does that mean anything?"

"Well, of course, the Albert's significant." Bond felt a cur. "You see, there was the Prince Consort to Queen Victoria. He was Albert."

"Oh, golly!" Ruby's knuckles went up to her mouth.

"But of course all this needs a lot of working on. Where do you come from in England? Where were you born?"

"In Lancashire. Morecambe Bay, where the shrimps come from. But a lot of poultry too. You know."

"So that's why you love chicken so much."

"Oh, no." She seemed surprised by the remark. "That's just the point. You see, I was allergic to chickens. I simply couldn't bear them—all those feathers, the stupid pecking, the mess and the smell. I loathed them. Even eating chicken brought me out in a sort of rash. It was awful, and of course my parents were mad at me, they being poultry farmers in quite a big way and me being supposed to help clean out the batteries—you know, those modern mass-produced chicken places. And then one day I saw this advertisement in the paper, in the *Poultry Farmer's Gazette.* It said that anyone suffering from chicken allergy—then followed a long Latin name—could apply for a course of re . . . of re . . . for a cure in a Swiss institute doing research work on the thing. All found and ten pounds a week pocket-money. Rather like those people who go and act as rabbits in that place that's trying to find a cure for colds."

"I know," said Bond encouragingly.

"So I applied and my fare was paid down to London and I met Miss Bunt and she put me through some sort of exam." She giggled. "Heaven only knows how I passed it, as I failed my G.C.E. twice. But she said I was just what the Institute wanted and I came out here about two months ago. It's not bad. They're terribly strict. But the Count has absolutely cured my trouble. I simply love chickens now." Her eyes became suddenly rapt. "I think they're just the most beautiful, wonderful birds in the world."

"Well, that's a jolly good show," said Bond, totally mystified. "Now about your name. I'll get to work on it right away. But how are we going to talk? You all seem to be pretty carefully organized. How can I see you by yourself? The only place is my room or yours."

"You mean *at night?*" The big blue eyes were wide with fright, excitement, maidenly appraisal.

"Yes, it's the only way." Bond took a bold step towards her and kissed her full on the mouth. He put his arms round her clumsily. "And you know I think you're terribly attractive."

"Oh, Sir Hilary!"

But she didn't recoil. She just stood there like a great lovely doll, passive, slightly calculating, wanting to be a princess. "But how would you get out of here? They're terribly strict. A guard goes up and down the passage every so often. Of course"—the eyes were calculating—"it's true that I'm next door to you, in Number Three actually. If only we had some way of getting out."

Bond took one of the inch strips of plastic out of his pocket and showed it to her. "I knew you were somewhere close to me. Instinct, I suppose. [Cad!] I learned a thing or two in the Army. You can get out of these sort of doors by slipping this in the door crack in front of the lock and pushing. It slips the latch. Here, take this, I've got another. But hide it away. And promise not to tell anyone."

"Ooh! You are a one! But of course I promise. But do you think there's any hope—about the Windsors, I mean?" Now she put her arms round his neck, round the witch-doctor's neck, and the big blue orbs gazed appealingly into his.

"You definitely mustn't rely on it," said Bond firmly, trying to get back an ounce of his self-respect. "But I'll have a quick look now in my books. Not much time before drinks. Anyway, we'll see." He gave her another long and, he admitted to himself, extremely splendid kiss, to which she responded with an animalism that slightly salved his conscience. "Now then, baby." His right hand ran down her back to the curve of her behind, to which he gave an encouraging and hastening pat. "We've got to get you out of here."

His bedroom was dark. They listened at the door like two children playing hide-and-seek. The building was in silence. He inched open the door. He gave the behind an extra pat and she was gone.

Bond paused for a moment. Then he switched on the light. The innocent room smiled at him. Bond went to his table and reached for the *Dictionary of British Surnames*. Windsor, Windsor, Windsor. Here we are! Now then! As he bent over the small print, an important reflection seared his spy's mind like a shooting star. All right. So sexual perversions, and sex itself, were a main security risk. So was greed for money. But what about status? What about that most insidious of vices, snobbery?

Six o'clock came. Bond had a nagging headache, brought on by hours of poring over small-print reference books and aggravated by the lack of oxygen at the high altitude. He needed a drink, three drinks. He had a quick shower and smartened himself up, rang his bell for the "warder" and went along to the bar. Only a few of the girls were already there. Violet sat alone at the bar and Bond joined her. She seemed pleased to see him. She was drinking a daiquiri. Bond ordered another and, for himself, a double bourbon on the rocks. He took a deep pull at it and put the squat glass down. "By God, I needed that! I've been working like a slave all day while you've been waltzing about the ski-slopes in the sun!"

"Have I indeed!" A slight Irish brogue came out with

the indignation. "Two lectures this morning, frightfully boring, and I had to catch up with my reading most of this afternoon. I'm way behind with it."

"What sort of reading?"

"Oh, sort of agricultural stuff." The dark eyes watched him carefully. "We're not supposed to talk about our cures, you know."

"Oh, well," said Bond cheerfully, "then let's talk about something else. Where do you come from?"

"Ireland. The South. Near Shannon."

Bond had a shot in the dark. "All that potato country."

"Yes, that's right. I used to hate them. Nothing but potatoes to eat and potato crops to talk about. Now I'm longing to get back. Funny, isn't it?"

"Your family'll be pleased."

"You can say that again! And my boy friend! He's on the wholesale side. I said I wouldn't marry anyone who had anything to do with the damned, dirty, ugly things. He's going to get a shock all right . . ."

"How's that?"

"All I've learned about how to improve the crop. The latest scientific ways, chemicals and so on." She put her hand up to her mouth. She glanced swiftly round the room, at the bartender. To see if anyone had heard this innocent stuff? She put on a hostess smile. "Now you tell me what you've been working on, Sir Hilary."

"Oh, just some heraldic stuff for the Count. Like I was talking about at lunch. I'm afraid you'd find it frightfully dry stuff."

"Oh, no, I wouldn't. I was terribly interested in what you were saying to Miss Bunt. You see"—she lowered her voice and spoke into her raised glass—"I'm an O'Neill. They used to be almost kings of Ireland. Do you think . . ." She had seen something over his shoulder. She went on smoothly, "And I simply can't get my shoulders round enough. And when I try to I simply over-balance."

" 'Fraid I don't know anything about skiing," said Bond loudly.

Irma Bunt appeared in the mirror over the bar. "Ah, Sair Hilary." She inspected his face. "But yes, you are already getting a little of the sunburn, isn't it? Come! Let us go and sit down. I see poor Miss Ruby over there all by herself."

They followed her meekly. Bond was amused by the little undercurrent of rule-breaking that went on among the girls—the typical resistance pattern to strict discipline and the governessy ways of this hideous matron. He must be careful how he handled it, useful though it was proving. It wouldn't do to get these girls too much "on his side." But, if only because the Count didn't want him to know them, he must somehow ferret away at their surnames and addresses. Ferret! That was the word! Ruby would be his ferret. Bond sat down beside her, the back of his hand casually brushing against her shoulder.

More drinks were ordered. The bourbon was beginning to uncoil Bond's tensions. His headache, instead of occupying his whole head, had localized itself behind the right temple. He said gaily, "shall we play the game again?"

There was a chorus of approval. The glass and paper napkins were brought from the bar and now more of the girls joined in. Bond handed round cigarettes and the girls puffed vigorously, occasionally choking over the smoke. Even Irma Bunt seemed infected by the laughter and squeals of excitement as the cobweb of paper became more and more tenuous. "Careful! Gently, Elizabeth! Ayee! But now you have done it! And there was still this little corner that was safe!"

Bond was next to her. Now he sat back and suggested that the girls should have a game among themselves. He turned to Fräulein Bunt. "By the way, if I can find the time, it crossed my mind that it might be fun to go down in the cable car and pay a visit to the valley. I gathered from talk among the crowds today that St Moritz is the other side of the valley. I've never been there. I'd love to see it."

"Alas, my dear Sair Hilary, but that is against the rules of the house. Guests here, and the staff too, have no access to the Seilbahn. That is only for the tourists. Here we keep ourselves to ourselves. We are—how shall I say?—a little dedicated community. We observe the rules almost of a monastery. It is better so, isn't it? Thus we can pursue our researches in peace."

"Oh, I quite see that." Bond's smile was understanding, friendly. "But I hardly count myself as a patient here, really. Couldn't an exception be made in my case?"

"I think that would be a mistake, Sair Hilary. And surely you will need all the time you have to complete your duties for the Count. No"—it was an order—"I am afraid, with many apologies, that what you ask is out of the question." She glanced at her watch and clapped her hands. "And now, girls," she called, "it is time for the supper. Come along! Come along!"

It had only been a try-on, to see what form the negative answer would take. But, as Bond followed her into the dining-room, it was quite an effort to restrain his right shoe from giving Irma Bunt a really tremendous kick in her tight, bulging behind.

14 SWEET DREAMS—SWEET NIGHTMARE!

It was eleven o'clock and the place was as quiet as the grave. Bond, with due respect for the eye in the ceiling, went through the motions of going to the bathroom and then climbing into bed and switching off his light. He gave it ten minutes, then got quietly out of bed and pulled on his trousers and shirt. Working by touch, he slipped the end of the inch of plastic into the door crack, found the lock and pressed gently. The edge of the plastic caught the curve of the lock and slid it back. Bond now only had to push gently and the door was open. He listened, his ears pricked like an animal's. Then he carefully put his head out. The empty corridor yawned at him. Bond slipped out of the door, closed it softly, took the few steps along to Number Three and gently turned the handle. It was dark inside but there was a stirring in the bed. Now to avoid the click of the shutting door! Bond took his bit of plastic and got it against the lock, holding it in the mortice. Then he inched the door shut, at the same time gently withdrawing the plastic. The lock slid noiselessly into place.

There came a whisper from the bed. "Is that you?"

"Yes, darling." Bond slid out of his clothes and, assuming the same geography as in his own room, walked gingerly over to the bed and sat down on its edge.

A hand came out of the darkness and touched him. "Ooh, you've got nothing on!"

Bond caught the hand and reached along it. "Nor have you," he whispered. "That's how it should be."

Gingerly he lay down on the bed and put his head beside hers on the pillow. He noticed with a pang of pleasure that she had left room for him. He kissed her, at first softly and then with fierceness. Her body stirred. Her mouth yielded to his and when his left hand began its exploration she put her arms round him. "I'm catching cold." Bond followed the lie by pulling the single sheet away from under him and then covering them both with it. The warmth and softness of her splendid body were now all his. Bond lay against her. He drew the fingernails of his left hand softly down her flat stomach. The velvety skin fluttered. She gave a small groan and reached down for his hand and held it. "You do love me a little bit?"

That awful question! Bond whispered, "I think you're the most adorable, beautiful girl. I wish I'd met you before."

The stale, insincere words seemed to be enough. She removed her restraining hand.

Her hair smelt of new-mown summer grass, her mouth of Pepsodent and her body of Mennen's Baby Powder. A small night wind rose up outside and moaned round the building, giving an extra sweetness, an extra warmth, even a certain friendship to what was no more than an act of physical passion. There was real pleasure in what they did to each other, and in the end, when it was over and they lay quietly in each other's arms, Bond knew, and knew that the girl knew, that they had done nothing wrong, done no harm to each other.

After a while Bond whispered into her hair, "Ruby!"

"Mmmm."

"About your name. About the Windsors. I'm afraid there's not much hope."

"Oh, well, I never really believed. You know these old family stories."

"Anyway, I haven't got enough books here. When I get back I'll dig into it properly. Promise. It'll be a question of starting with your family and going back—church and town records and so forth. I'll have it done properly and send it to you. Great slab of parchment with a lot of snazzy print. Heavy black italics with coloured letters to start each line. Although it mayn't get you anywhere, it might be nice to have."

"You mean like old documents in museums?"

"That's right."

"That'd be nice."

There was silence in the little room. Her breathing became regular. Bond thought: how extraordinary! Here on top of this mountain, a death's run away from the nearest hamlet in the valley, in this little room were peace, silence, warmth, happiness—many of the ingredients of love. It was like making love in a balloon. Which nineteenth-century rake had it been who had recorded a bet in a London club that he would make love to a woman in a balloon?

Bond was on the edge of sleep. He let himself slide down the soft, easy slope. Here it was wonderful. It would be just as easy for him to get back to his room in the early hours. He softly eased his right arm from under the sleeping girl, took a lazy glance at his left wrist. The big luminous numerals said midnight.

Bond had hardly turned over on his right side, up against the soft flanks of the sleeping girl, when, from underneath the pillow, under the floor, deep in the bowels of the building, there came the peremptory ringing of a deep-toned, melodious electric bell. The girl stirred. She said sleepily, "Oh damn!"

"What is it?"

"Oh, it's only the treatment. I suppose it's midnight?"

"Yes."

"Don't pay any attention. It's only for me. Just go to sleep."

Bond kissed her between the shoulder-blades but said nothing.

Now the bell had stopped. In its place there started up a droning whine, rather like the noise of a very fast electric fan, with, behind it, the steady, unvarying tick-pause-tock, tick-pause-tock of some kind of metronome. The combination of the two sounds was wonderfully soothing. It compelled attention, but only just on the fringe of consciousness—like the night-noises of childhood, the slow tick of the nursery clock combined with the sound of the sea or the wind outside. And now a voice, the Count's voice, came over the distant wire or tape that Bond assumed was the mechanical source of all this. The voice was pitched in a low, singsong murmur, caressing yet authoritative, and every word was distinct. "You are going to sleep." The voice fell on the word "sleep." "You are tired and your limbs feel like lead." Again the falling cadence on the last word. "Your arms feel as heavy as lead. Your breathing is quite even. Your breathing is as regular as a child's. Your eyes are closed and the eyelids are heavy as lead. You are becoming tireder and tireder. Your whole body is becoming tired and heavy as lead. You are warm and comfortable. You are slipping, slipping, slipping down into sleep. Your bed is as soft and downy as a nest. You are as soft and sleepy as a chicken in a nest. A dear little chicken, fluffy and cuddly." There came the sound of a sweet cooing and clucking, the gentle brushing together of wings, the dozy murmuring of mother hens with their chicks. It went on for perhaps a full minute. Then the voice came back. "The little darlings are going to sleep. They are like you, comfortable and sleepy in their nests. You love them dearly, dearly, dearly. You love all chickens. You would like to make pets of them all. You would like them to grow up beautiful and strong. You would like no harm to come to them. Soon you will be going back to your darling chickens. Soon you will be able to look after them again. Soon you will be able to help all the chickens of England. You will be able to improve the breed of chickens all over England. This will make you very, very happy. You will be doing so much good that it will make you very, very happy. But you will keep quiet about it. You will say nothing of your methods. They will be your own secret, your very own secret. People will try and find out your secret. But you will say nothing because they might try and take your secret away from you. And then you would not be able to make your darling chickens happy and healthy and strong. Thousands, millions of chickens made happier because of you. So you will say nothing and keep your secret. You will say nothing, nothing at all. You will remember what I say. You will remember what I say." The murmuring voice was getting farther and farther away. The sweet cooing and clucking of chickens softly obscured the vanishing voice, then that too died away and there was only the electric whine and the tick-pause-tock of the metronome.

Ruby was deeply asleep. Bond reached out for her wrist and felt the pulse. It was plumb on beat with the metronome. And now that, and the whine of the machine, receded softly until all was dead silence again save for the soft moan of the night wind outside.

Bond let out a deep sigh. So now he had heard it all! He suddenly wanted to get back to his room and think. He slipped out from under the sheet, got to his clothes and put them on. He manipulated the lock without trouble. There was no movement, no sound, in the passage. He slipped back into Number Two and eased the door shut. Then he went into his bathroom, closed the door, switched on the light and sat down on the lavatory and put his head in his hands.

Deep hypnosis! That was what he had heard. The Hidden Persuader! The repetitive, singsong message injected into the brain while it was on the twilight edge of consciousness. Now, in Ruby's subconscious, the message would work on all by itself through the night, leaving her, after weeks of repetition, with an in-built mechanism of obedience to the voice that would be as deep, as compelling, as hunger.

But what in hell was the message all about? Surely it was a most harmless, even a praiseworthy message to instil in the simple mind of this country girl. She had been cured of her allergy and she would return home fully capable of helping with the family poultry business—more than that, enthusiastic, dedicated. Had the leopard changed his spots? Had the old lag become, in the corny, hackneyed tradition, a do-gooder? Bond simply couldn't believe it. What about all those high-powered security arrangements?

What about the multi racial staff that positively stank of SPECTRE? And what about the bob-run murder? Accident? So soon after the man's attempted rape of this Sarah girl? An impossible coincidence? Malignity must somewhere lie behind the benign, clinical front of this maddeningly innocent research outfit! But where? How in hell could he find out?

Bond, exhausted, got up and turned off the light in the bathroom and quietly got himself into bed. The mind whirred on for a sterile half-hour in the overheated brain and then, mercifully, he went to sleep.

When, at nine o'clock, he awoke and threw open his windows, the sky was overcast with the heavy blank grey that meant snow. Over by the Berghaus, the Schneefinken and Schneevögel, the snow-finches and Alpine choughs, which lived on the crumbs and leftovers of the picnickers, were fluttering and swooping close round the building—a sure storm-warning. The wind had got up and was blowing in sharp, threatening gusts, and no whine of machinery came from the cable railway. The light aluminium gondolas would have too bad a time in winds of this strength, particularly over the last great swoop of cable that brought them a good quarter of a mile over the exposed shoulder beneath the plateau.

Bond shut the windows and rang for his breakfast. When it came there was a note from Fräulein Bunt on the tray. "The Count will be pleased to receive you at eleven o'clock. I.B."

Bond ate his breakfast and got down to his third page of de Bleuvilles. He had quite a chunk of work to show up, but this was easy stuff. The prospect of successfully bamboozling his way along the Blofeld part of the trail was not so encouraging. He would start boldly at the Gdynia end and work back—get the old rascal to talk about his youth and his parents. Old rascal? Well, dammit, whatever he had become since Operation "Thunderball," there weren't two Ernst Stavro Blofelds in the world!

They met in the Count's study. "Good morning, Sir Hilary. I hope you slept well? We are going to have snow." The Count waved towards the window. "It will be a good day for work. No distractions."

Bond smiled a man-to-man smile. "I certainly find those girls pretty distracting. But most charming. What's the matter with them, by the way? They all look healthy enough."

The Count was off-hand. "They suffer from allergies, Sir Hilary. Crippling allergies. In the agricultural field. They are country girls and their disabilities affect the possibility of their employment. I have devised a cure for such symptoms. I am glad to say that the signs are propitious. We are making much progress together." The telephone by his side buzzed. "Excuse me." The Count picked up the receiver and listened. "Ja. Machen Sie die Verbindung." He paused. Bond politely studied the papers he had brought along. "Zdies de Bleuville . . . Da . . . Da . . . Kharascho!" He put the receiver back. "Forgive me. That was one of my research workers. He has been purchasing some materials for the laboratories. The cable railway is closed, but they are making a special trip up for him. Brave man. He will probably be very sick, poor fellow." The green contact lenses hid any sympathy he may have felt. The fixed smile showed none. "And now, my dear Sir Hilary, let us get on with our work."

Bond laid out his big sheets on the desk and proudly ran his finger down through the generations. There was excitement and satisfaction in the Count's comments and questions. "But this is tremendous, really tremendous, my dear fellow. And you say there is mention of a broken spear or a broken sword in the arms? Now when was that granted?"

Bond rattled off a lot of stuff about the Norman Conquest. The broken sword had probably been awarded as a result of some battle. More research in London would be needed to pin the occasion down. Finally Bond rolled up the sheets and got out his notebook. "And now we must start working back from the other end, Count." Bond became inquisitorial, authoritative. "We have your birth date in Gdynia, May 28th, 1908. Yes?"

"Correct."

"Your parents' names?"

"Ernst George Blofeld and Maria Stavro Michelopoulos."

"Also born in Gdynia?"

"Yes."

"Now your grandparents?"

"Ernst Stefan Blofeld and Elizabeth Lubomirskaya."

"Hm, so the Ernst is something of a family Christian name?"

"It would seem so. My great-grandfather, he was also Ernst."

"That is most important. You see, Count, among the Blofelds of Augsburg there are no less than two Ernsts!"

The Count's hands had been lying on the green blotting-pad on his desk, relaxed. Now, impulsively, they joined together and briefly writhed, showing white knuckles.

My God, you've got it bad! thought Bond.

"And that is important?"

"Very. Christian names run through families. We regard them as most significant clues. Now, can you remember any farther back? You have done well. We have covered three generations. With the dates I shall later ask you for, we have already got back to around 1850. Only another fifty years to go and we shall have arrived at Augsburg."

"No." It was almost a cry of pain. "My great-great-grandfather. Of him I know nothing." The hands writhed on the blotting-paper. "Perhaps, perhaps. If it is a question of money. People, witnesses could be found." The hands parted, held themselves out expansively. "My dear Sir Hilary, you and I are men of the world. We understand each other. Extracts from archives, registry offices, the churches—these things, do they have to be completely authentic?"

Got you, you old fox! Bond said affably, with a hint of conspiracy, "I don't quite understand what you mean, Count."

The hands were now flat on the desk again, happy hands. Blofeld had recognized one of his kind. "You are a hard-working man, Sir Hilary. You live modestly in this remote region of Scotland. Life could perhaps be made easier for you. There are perhaps material benefits you desire—motor-cars, a yacht, a pension. You have only to say the word, name a figure." The dark-green orbs bored into Bond's modestly evasive eyes, holding them. "Just a little co-operation. A visit here and there in Poland and Germany and France. Of course your expenses would be heavy. Let us say five hundred pounds a week. The technical matters, the documents and so forth. Those I can arrange. It would only require your supporting evidence. Yes? The Ministry of Justice in Paris, for them the word of the College of Arms is the word of God. Is that not so?"

It was too good to be true! But how to play it? Diffidently, Bond said, "What you are suggesting, Count, is—er—not without interest. Of course"—Bond's smile was sufficiently expansive, sufficiently bland—"if the documents were convincing, so to speak solid, very solid, then it would be quite reasonable for me to authenticate them." Bond put spaniel into his eyes, asking to be patted, to be told that everything would be all right, that he would be completely protected. "You see what I mean?"

The Count began, with force, sincerity, "You need have absolutely no . . ." when there was the noise of an approaching hubbub down the passage. The door burst open. A man, propelled from behind, lurched into the room and fell, writhing, to the floor.

Two of the guards came stiffly to attention behind him. They looked first at the Count and then, sideways, towards Bond, surprised to see him there.

The Count said sharply, "Was ist denn los?"

Bond knew the answer and, momentarily, he died. Behind the snow and the blood on the face of the man on the floor, Bond recognized the face of a man he knew.

The blond hair, the nose broken boxing for the Navy, belonged to a friend of his in the Service. It was, unmistakably, Number 2 from Station Z in Zürich!

15 THE HEAT INCREASES

Yes, it was Shaun Campbell all right! Christ Almighty, what a mess! Station Z had especially been told nothing about Bond's mission. Campbell must have been following a lead of his own, probably trailing this Russian who had been "buying supplies." Typical of the sort of balls-up that over-security can produce!

The leading guard was talking in rapid, faulty German with a Slav accent. "He was found in the open ski compartment at the back of the gondola. Much frozen, but he put up strong resistance. He had to be subdued. He was no doubt following Captain Boris." The man caught himself up. "I mean, your guest from the valley, Herr Graf. He says he is an English tourist from Zürich. That he had not got the money for the fare. He wanted to pay a visit up here. He was searched. He carried five hundred Swiss francs. No identity papers." The man shrugged. "He says his name is Campbell."

At the sound of his name, the man on the ground stirred. He lifted his head and looked wildly round the room. He had been badly battered about the face and head with a pistol or a cosh. His control was shot to pieces. When his eyes lit on the familiar face of Bond, he looked astonished, then, as if a lifebuoy had been thrown to him, he said hoarsely, "Thank God, James. Tell 'em it's me! Tell 'em I'm from Universal Export. In Zürich. You know! For God's sake, James! Tell 'em I'm O.K." His head fell forward on the carpet.

The Count's head slowly turned towards Bond. The opaque green eyes caught the pale light from the window and glinted whitely. The tight, face-lifted smile was grotesquely horrible. "You know this man, Sir Hilary?"

Bond shook his head sorrowfully. He knew he was pronouncing the death sentence on Campbell. "Never seen him before in my life. Poor chap. He sounds a bit daft to me. Concussed, probably. Why not ship him down to a hospital in the valley? He looks in a pretty bad way."

"And Universal Export?" The voice was silky. "I seem to have heard that name before."

"Well, *I* haven't," said Bond indifferently. "Never heard of it." He reached in his pocket for his cigarettes, lit one with a dead steady hand.

The Count turned back to the guards. He said softly, "Zur Befragungszelle." He nodded his dismissal. The two guards bent down and hauled Campbell up by his arm-pits. The hanging head raised itself, gave one last terrible look of appeal at Bond. Then the man who was Bond's colleague was hustled out of the room and the door was closed softly behind his dragging feet.

To the interrogation cell! That could mean only one thing, under modern methods, total confession! How long would Campbell hold out for? How many hours had Bond got left?

"I have told them to take him to the sick-room. He will be well looked after." The Count looked from the papers on his desk to Bond. "I am afraid this unhappy intrusion has interfered with my train of thought, Sir Hilary. So perhaps you will forgive me for this morning?"

"Of course, of course. And, regarding your proposition, that we should work a little more closely together on your interests, I can assure you, Count, that I find it most interesting." Bond smiled conspiratorially. "I'm sure we could come to some satisfactory arrangement."

"Yes? That is good." The Count linked his hands behind his head and gazed for a moment at the ceiling and then, reflectively, back at Bond. He said casually, "I suppose you would not be connected in any way with the British Secret Service, Sir Hilary?"

Bond laughed out loud. The laugh was a reflex, forced out of him by tension. "Good God, no! Didn't even know we had one. Didn't all that sort of thing go out with the end of the war?" Bond chuckled to himself, fatuously amused. "Can't quite see myself running about behind a false moustache. Not my line of country at all. Can't bear moustaches."

The Count's unwavering smile did not seem to share Bond's amusement. He said coldly, "Then please forget my question, Sir Hilary. The intrusion by this man has made me over-suspicious. I value my privacy up here, Sir Hilary. Scientific research can only be pursued in an atmosphere of peace."

"I couldn't agree more." Bond was effusive. He got to his feet and gathered up his papers from the desk. "And now I must get on with my own research work. Just getting into the fourteenth century. I think I shall have some interesting data to show you tomorrow, Count."

The Count got politely to his feet and Bond went out of the door and along the passage.

He loitered, listening for any sound. There was none, but half-way down the corridor one of the doors was ajar. A crack of blood-red light showed. Bond thought, I've probably had it anyway. In for a penny, in for a pound! He pushed the door open and stuck his head into the room. It was a long, low laboratory with a plastic-covered workbench extending its whole length beneath the windows, which were shuttered. Dark red light, as in a film-developing chamber, came from neon strips above the cornice. The bench was littered with retorts and test-tubes, and there were line upon line of test-tubes and phials containing a cloudy liquid in racks against the far wall. Three men in white, with gauze pads over the bottoms of their faces and white surgical caps over their hair, were at work, absorbed. Bond took in the scene, a scene from a theatrical hell, withdrew his head and walked on down the corridor and out into what was now a driving snow-storm. He pulled the top of his sweater over his head and forced his way along the path to the blessed warmth of the club-house. Then he walked quickly to his room, closed the door and went into the bathroom and sat down on his usual throne of reflection and wondered what in God's name to do.

Could he have saved Campbell? Well, he could have had a desperate shot at it. "Oh, yes. I know this man. Perfectly respectable chap. We used to work for the same export firm, Universal, in London. You look in pretty bad shape, old boy. What the devil happened?" But it was just as well he hadn't tried. As cover, solid cover, Universal was "brulé" with the pros. It had been in use too long. All the secret services in the world had penetrated it by now. Obviously Blofeld knew all about it. Any effort to save Campbell would simply have tied Bond in with him. There had been no alternative except to throw him to the wolves. If Campbell had a chance to get his wits back before they really started on him, he would know that Bond was there for some purpose, that his disavowal by Bond was desperately important to Bond, to the Service. How long would he have the strength to cover for Bond, retrieve his recognition of Bond? At most a few hours. But how many hours? That was the vital question. That and how long the storm would last. Bond couldn't possibly get away in this stuff. If it stopped, there might be a chance, a damned slim one, but better than the alternatives, of which, if and when Campbell talked, there was only one—death, probably a screaming death.

Bond surveyed his weapons. They were only his hands and feet, his Gillette razor and his wrist-watch, a heavy Rolex Oyster Perpetual on an expanding metal bracelet. Used properly, these could be turned into most effective knuckledusters. Bond got up, took the blade out of his Gillette and dropped the razor into his trouser pocket. He slipped the shaft between the first and second fingers of his left hand so that the blade-carrier rested flat along his knuckles. Yes, that was the way! Now was there anything, any evidence he should try and take with him? Yes, he must try and get more, if not all, of the girls' names and, if possible, addresses. For some reason he knew they were vital. For that he would have to use Ruby. His head full of plans for getting the information out of her, Bond went out of the bathroom and sat down at his desk and got on with a fresh page of de Bleuvilles. At least he must continue to show willing, if only to the recording eye in the ceiling.

It was about twelve-thirty when Bond heard his doorknob being softly turned. Ruby slipped in and, her finger to her lips, disappeared into his bathroom. Bond casually threw down his pen, got up and stretched and strolled over and went in after her.

Ruby's blue eyes were wide and frightened. "You're in trouble," she whispered urgently. "What *have* you been doing?"

"Nothing," said Bond innocently. "What's up?"

"We've all been told that we mustn't talk to you unless Miss Bunt is there." Her knuckles went distractedly up to her teeth. "Do you think they know about *us?*"

"Couldn't possibly," said Bond, radiating confidence."I think I know what it is." (With so much obfuscation in the air, what did an extra, a reassuring, lie matter?) "This morning the Count told me I was an upsetting influence here, that I was what he called 'disruptive,' interfering with your treatments. He asked me to keep myself more to myself. Honestly"—how often that word came into a lie!—"I'm sure that's all it is. Rather a pity really. Apart from you—I mean you're sort of special—I think all you girls are terribly sweet. I'd like to have helped you all."

"How do you mean? Helped us?"

"Well, this business of surnames. I talked to Violet last night. She seemed awfully interested. I'm sure it would have amused all the others to have theirs done. Everyone's interested in where they came from. Rather like palmistry in a way." Bond wondered how the College of Arms would have liked *that* one! He shrugged. "Anyway, I've decided to get the hell away from here. I can't bear being shepherded and ordered about like this. Who the hell do they think I am? But I'll tell you what I'll do. If you can give me the names of the girls, as many as you know, I'll do a piece on each of them and post them when you all get back to England. How much longer have you got, by the way?"

"We're not told exactly, but the rumour is about another week. There's another batch of girls due about then. When we're slow at our work or get behind-hand with our reading, Miss Bunt says she hopes the next lot won't be so stupid. The old bitch! But Sir Hilary"—the blue eyes filled with concern—"how *are* you going to get away? You know we're practically prisoners up here."

Bond was off-hand. "Oh, I'll manage somehow. They can't hold *me* here against my will. But what about the names, Ruby? Don't you think it would give the girls a treat?"

"Oh, they'd love it. Of course I know all of them. We've found plenty of ways of exchanging secrets. But you won't be able to remember. Have you got anything to write down on?"

Bond tore off some strips of lavatory paper and took out a pencil. "Fire away!"

She laughed. "Well, you know me and Violet, then there's Elizabeth Mackinnon. She's from Aberdeen. Beryl Morgan from somewhere in Herefordshire. Pearl Tampion, Devonshire—by the way, all those simply loathed every kind of cattle. Now they live on steaks! Would you believe it? I must say the Count's a wonderful man."

"Yes, indeed."

"Then there's Anne Charter from Canterbury and Caresse Ventnor from the National Stud, wherever that is—fancy her working there and she came up in a rash all over whenever she went near a horse! Now all she does is dream of pony clubs and read every word she can get hold of about Pat Smythe! And Denise Robertson . . ."

The list went on until Bond had got the whole ten.

He said, "What about that Polly somebody who left in November?"

"Polly Tasker. She was from East Anglia. Don't remember where, but I can find out the address when I get back to England. Sir Hilary"—she put her arm round his neck—"I *am* going to see you again, aren't I?"

Bond held her tight and kissed her. "Of course, Ruby. You can always get me at the College of Arms in Queen Victoria Street. Just send me a postcard when you get back. But for God's sake cut out the 'Sir.' You're my girl friend. Remember?"

"Oh, yes, I will—er—Hilary," she said fervently. "And you will be careful, getting away I mean. You're sure it's all right? Is there anything I can do to help?"

"No, darling. Just don't breathe a word of all this. It's a secret between us. Right?"

"Of course, darling." She glanced at her watch. "Oh lord! I must simply fly. Only ten minutes to lunchtime. Now, can you do your trick with the door? There shouldn't be anyone about. It's their lunchtime from twelve till one."

Bond, out of any possible line of vision from the eye in the ceiling, did his trick with the door and she was gone with a last whispered goodbye.

Bond eased the door shut. He let out a deep sigh and went over to the window and peered out through the snow-heaped panes. It was thick as Hades outside and the fine powder snow on the veranda was whirling up in little ghosts as the wind tore at the building. Pray God it would let up by night-time! Now, what did he need in the way of equipment? Goggles and gloves were two items he might harvest over lunch. Bond went into the bathroom again and rubbed soap into his eyes. It stung like hell, but the blue-grey eyes emerged from the treatment realistically bloodshot. Satisfied, Bond rang for the "warden" and went thoughtfully off to the restaurant.

Silence fell as he went through the swing doors, followed by a polite, brittle chatter. Eyes followed him discreetly as he crossed the room and the replies to his good mornings were muted. Bond took his usual seat between Ruby and Fräulein Bunt. Apparently oblivious to her frosty greeting, he snapped his fingers for a waiter and ordered his double vodka dry martini. He turned to Fräulein Bunt and smiled into the suspicious yellow eyes. "Would you be very kind?"

"Yes, Sair Hilary. What is it?"

Bond gestured at his still watering eyes. "I've got the Count's trouble. Sort of conjunctivitis, I suppose. The tremendous glare up here. Better today of course, but there still a lot of reflection from the snow. And all this paper-worl Could you get me a pair of snow-goggles? I'll only nee to borrow them for a day or two. Just till my eyes get use to the light. Don't usually have this sort of trouble."

"Yes. That can be done. I will see that they are pu in your room." She summoned the head waiter and gav the order in German. The man, looking at Bond wit overt dislike, said, "Sofort, gnädiges Fräulein" and clicke his heels.

"And one more thing, if you will," said Bond politely "A small flask of schnapps." He turned to Fräulein Bun "I find I am not sleeping well up here. Perhaps a nightca would help. I always have one at home—generally whisky But here I would prefer schnapps. When in Gloria, d as the Glorians do. Ha ha!"

Fräulein Bunt looked at him stonily. She said to th waiter curtly, "In Ordnung!" The man took Bond's orde of Paté Maison followed by Oeufs Gloria and the chees tray (Bond thought he had better get some stuffing int him!), clicked his heels and went away. Was he one o those who had been at work in the interrogation room Bond silently ground his teeth. By God, if it came to hittin any of these guards tonight, he was going to hit them damne hard, with everything he'd got! He felt Fräulein Bunt's eye inquisitively on him. He untensed himself and began t make amiable conversation about the storm. How lon would it last? What was the barometer doing?

Violet, guardedly but helpfully, said the guides though it would clear up during the afternoon. The baromete was rising. She looked nervously at Fräulein Bunt to se if she had said too much to the pariah, and then, not re assured, went back to her two vast baked potatoes with poached eggs in them.

Bond's drink came. He swallowed it in two gulps and ordered another. He felt like making any gesture that would startle and outrage. He said, combatively, to Fräulein Bunt, "And how is that poor chap who came up in the cable car this morning? He looked in terrible shape. I do hope he's up and about again."

"He makes progress."

"Oh! Who was that?" asked Ruby eagerly.

"It was an intruder." Fräulein Bunt's eyes were hard with warning. "It is not a subject for conversation."

"Oh, but why not?" asked Bond innocently. "After all, you can't get much excitement up here. Anything out of the ordinary should be a bit of a relief."

She said nothing. Bond raised his eyebrows politely and then accepted the snub with a good grace. He asked if any newspapers came up. Or was there a radio bulletin like on board ship? Did they get any news from the outside world?

"No."

Bond gave up the struggle and got on with his lunch. Ruby's foot crept up against his in sympathy with the man sent to Coventry. Bond gave it a gentle kick of warning and withdrew his. The girls at the other tables began to leave. Bond toyed with his cheese and coffee until Fräulein Bunt got to her feet and said, "Come, girls." Bond rose and sat down again. Now, except for the waiters clearing up, he was alone in the restaurant. That was what he wanted. He got up and strolled to the door. Outside, on pegs against the wall, the girls' outdoor coats and skiing gloves hung in an orderly row. The corridor was empty. Bond swept the largest pair of leather gauntlets he could see off the peg where they hung by their joining cord and stuffed them inside his sweater. Then he sauntered along to the reception room. It was empty. The door to the ski-room was open and the surly man was at his workbench. Bond went in and made one-sided conversation about the weather. Then, under cover of desultory talk about whether the metal skis were not more dangerous than the old wooden ones, he wandered, his hands innocently in his pockets, round the numbered racks in which the skis stood against the wall. They were mostly the girls' skis. No good! The bindings would be too small for his boots. But, by the door, in unnumbered slots, stood the guides' skis. Bond's eyes narrowed to slits as he scanned them, measuring, estimating. Yes, the pair of metal Heads with the red V's painted on the black curved tips was the best bet. They were of the stiffer, Master's, category, designed for racing. Bond remembered reading somewhere that the Standard model was inclined to "float" at speed. His choice had the Attenhofer Flex forward release with the Marker lateral release. Two transverse leather thongs wound round the ankle and buckled over the instep would, if he fell, which he was certain to do, ensure against losing a ski.

Bond made a quick guess at how much the bindings would need adjustment to fit his boots and went off down the corridor to his room.

16 DOWNHILL ONLY

Now it was just a question of sitting out the hours. When would they have finished with Campbell? Quick, rough torture is rarely effective against a professional, apart from the likelihood of the man rapidly losing consciousness, becoming so punch-drunk that he is incoherent. The pro, if he is a tough man spiritually, can keep the "game" alive for hours by minor admissions, by telling long, rambling tales and sticking to them. Such tales need verification. Blofeld would undoubtedly have his man in Zürich, would be able to contact him on his radio, get him to check this or that date or address, but that also would require time. Then, if it was proved that Campbell had told lies, they would have to begin again. So far as Bond and his identity were concerned, it all depended on Campbell's reading of why Bond was up at the Gloria Club. He must guess, because of Bond's curt disavowal of him, that it was something clandestine, something important. Would he have the wits to cover up Bond, the guts, against the electrical and mechanical devices they would surely use against him? He could say that, when he came to and saw Bond, in his semi-conscious state he had for a moment thought Bond was his brother, James Campbell. Some story like that. If he had the wits! If he had the guts! Had Campbell got a death pill, perhaps one of the buttons on his ski-jacket or trousers? Bond sharply put the thought away. He had been on the edge of wishing that Campbell had!

Well, he would be wise to assume that it was only a matter of hours and then they would come for him. They wouldn't do it until after lights-out. To do it before would cause too much talk among the girls. No, they would fetch him at night and the next day it would be put about that he had left by the first cable car down to the valley. Meanwhile he would be buried deep in a snow overcoat, or more likely deposited in a high crevasse in the near-by Piz Languard glacier, to come out at the bottom, fifty years later, out of his deep freeze, with multiple contusions but no identification marks—a nameless victim of "les neiges éternelles"!

Yes, he must plan for that. Bond got up from the desk where he had been automatically scribbling down lists of fifteenth-century de Bleuvilles and opened the window.

The snow had stopped and there was broken blue in the sky. It would be perfect powder snow, perhaps a foot of it, on the Gloria Run. Now to make everything ready!

There are hundreds of secret inks, but there was only one available to Bond, the oldest one in the world, his own urine. He went into the bathroom (what must the televising eye think of his digestive tracts?) with his pen, a clean nib, and his passport. Then he sat down and proceeded to transcribe, from the flimsy pieces of paper in his pocket on to a blank page of his passport, the names and approximate locations by county of the girls. The page showed nothing. Held in front of a flame, the writing would come up brown. He slipped the passport into his hip-pocket. Next he took the gloves from under his sweater, tried them on and found them an adequate but tight fit, took the top off the lavatory cistern and laid the gloves along the arm of the stop-cock.

What else? It was going to be fiendishly cold at the start, but his body would soon be drenched in sweat. He would just have to make do with the ski-clothes he possessed, the gloves, the goggles that had been placed on his table and the flat glass flask of schnapps that he would carry in one of his side pockets and not, in case of a fall, in his hip-pocket. Extra covering for his face? Bond thought of using one of his warm vests and cutting eye-holes in it. But it would surely slip and perhaps blind him. He had some dark-red silk bandana handkerchiefs. He would tie one tight over his face below the goggles and discard it if it interfered with his breathing. So! That was the lot! There was nothing else he could do or insure against. The rest was up to the Fates. Bond relaxed his thoughts and went out and back to his desk. He sat down and bent to his paper-work and tried not to listen to the hastening tick of the Rolex on his wrist, tried to fix in his mind the rough geography of the Gloria Run he had inadequately learned from the metal map. It was too late now to go and have another look at it. He must stay put and continue to play the toothless tiger!

Dinner was as ghastly as lunch. Bond concentrated on getting plenty of whisky and food under his belt. He made urbane conversation and pretended he didn't notice the chill in the air. Then he gave Ruby's foot one warm press under the table, excused himself on the grounds of work and strode with dignity out of the room.

He had changed for dinner and he was relieved to find his ski-clothes in the half-tidy heap in which he had left them. He went, with utter normalcy, about his work—sharpened pencils, laid out his books, bent to the squared paper: "Simon de Bleuville, 1510-1507. Alphonse de Bleuville, 1546-1580, married 1571 Mariette d'Escourt, and had issue, Jean, Françoise, Pierre." Thank God he would soon be released from all this blether!

9.15, 9.30, 9.45, 10! Bond felt the excitement ball up inside him like cat's fur. He found that his hands were wet. He wiped them down the sides of his trousers. He got up and stretched. He went into the bathroom and made appropriate noises, retrieved the gloves and laid them on the bathroom floor just inside the door. Then, naked, he came back into the room and got into bed and switched off the light. He regularized his breathing and, in ten minutes, began to snore softly. He gave it another ten, then slid out of bed and, with infinite precaution, dressed himself in his ski-clothes. He softly retrieved his gloves from the bathroom, put on the goggles so that they rested in his hair above the forehead, tied the dark-red handkerchief tightly across his nose, schnapps into pocket, passport into hip-pocket and, finally, Gillette through the fingers of the left hand and the Rolex transferred to his right, the bracelet clasped in the palm of his hand and round the fingers so that the face of the watch lay across his middle knuckles.

James Bond paused and ran over his equipment. The ski-gloves, their cord drawn through his sweater and down the sleeves, hung from his wrists. They would be a hindrance until he was outside. Nothing to be done about that. The rest was all right. He was set! He bent to the door, manipulated the lock with the plastic and, praying that the television eye had been closed down and would not see the light shining in from the passage, listened briefly and slipped out.

There was, as usual, light from the reception room to his left. Bond crept along, inched round the door jamb. Yes! The guard was there, bent over something that looked like a time sheet. The neck was offered. Bond dropped the Gillette in his pocket and stiffened the fingers of his left hand into the old Commando cutting edge. He took the two steps into the room and crashed the hand down on the back of the offered neck. The man's face hit the table top with a thud, bounced up and half turned towards Bond. Bond's right flashed out and the face of the Rolex disintegrated against the man's jaw. The body slid sluggishly off its chair on to the carpet and lay still, its legs untidy as if in sleep. The eyes fluttered and stared, unseeing, upwards. Bond went round the desk and bent down. There was no heartbeat. Bond straightened himself. It was the man he had seen coming back alone from the bob-run on his first morning, when Bertil had met with his accident. So! Rough justice!

The telephone on the desk buzzed like a trapped wasp. Bond looked at it. He picked up the receiver and spoke through the handkerchief across his mouth. "Ja?"

"Alles in Ordnung?"

"Ja."

"Also hör zu! Wir kommen für den Engländer in zehn Minuten. Verstanden?"

"Is' recht."

"Also, aufpassen. Ja?"

"Zu Befehl!"

At the other end the receiver went down. The sweat was beading on Bond's face. Thank God he had answered! So they were coming for him in ten minutes! There was a bunch of keys on the desk. Bond snatched them up and ran to the front door. After three misfits, he had the right one. He tried the door. It was now only held by its air-pressure device. Bond leaped for the ski-room. Unlocked! He went in and, by the light from the reception room, found his skis. There were sticks beside them. Carefully he lifted everything out of its wooden slot and strode to the main door and opened it. He laid the skis and sticks softly down in the snow, turned back to the door, locked it from the outside and threw the keys far away into the snow.

The three-quarter moon burned down with an almost dazzling fire and the snow crystals scintillated back at it like a carpet of diamond dust. Now minutes would have to be wasted getting the bindings absolutely right. James Bond kicked one boot into the groove of the Marker toe-hold and knelt down, feeling for the steel cable that went behind his heel. It was too short. Coolly, unhurriedly, he adjusted the regulating screw on the forward latch and tried again. This time it was all right. He pressed down on the safety latch and felt it lock his boot into the toe-hold. Next, the safety throng round the top of his boot that would keep the ski prisoner if the latch sprung, which it would do with a fall. His fingers were beginning to freeze. The tip of the thong refused to find its buckle! A full minute wasted! Got it! And now the same job on the other ski. At last Bond stood up, slipped the gloves over his aching fingers, picked up the lance-like sticks and pushed himself off along the faint ridge that showed the outlines of yesterday's well trodden path. It felt all right! He pulled the goggles down over his eyes and now the vast snow-scape was a silvery green as if he was swimming under sunny water. The skis hissed smoothly through the powder snow. Bond tried to get up more speed down the gentle slope by langlaufing, the sliding, forward stride of the first Norwegian skiers. But it didn't work. The heels of his boots felt nailed to the skis. He punted himself forward as fast as he could with his sticks. God, what a trail he must be leaving—like a tram-line! As soon as they got the front door open, they would be after him. Their fastest guide would certainly catch him easily unless he got a good start! Every minute, every second was a bonus. He passed between the black outlines of the cable-head and the Berghaus. There was the starting point of the Gloria Run, the metal notices beside it hatted with snow! Bond didn't pause. He went straight for it and over the edge.

The first vertical drop had a spine-chilling bliss to it. Bond got down into his old Arlberg crouch, his hands forward of his boots, and just let himself go. His skis were an ugly six inches apart. The Kannonen he had watched had gone down with their boots locked together, as if on a single ski. But this was no time for style, even if he had been capable of it! Above all he must stay upright!

Bond's speed was now frightening. But the deep cushion of cold, light powder snow gave him the confidence to try a paralled swing. Minimum of shoulder turn needed at this speed—weight on to the left ski—and he came round and held it as the right-hand edges of his skis bit against the slope, throwing up a shower of moonlit snow crystals. Danger was momentarily forgotten in the joy of speed, technique and mastery of the snow. Bond straightened up and almost dived into his next turn, this time to the left, leaving a broad S on the virgin mountain behind him. Now he could afford to schuss the rest down to the hard left-hand turn round the shoulder. He pointed his skis down and felt real rapture as, like a black bullet on the giant slope, he zoomed down the forty-five-degree drop. Now for the left-hand corner. There was the group of three flags, black, red and yellow, hanging limply, their colours confused by the moonlight! He would have to stop there and take a recce over the next lap. There was a slight upward slope short of the big turn. Bond took it at speed, felt his skis leave the ground at the crest of it, jabbed into the snow with his left stick as an extra lever and threw his skis and his right shoulder and hips round to the left. He landed in a spray of snow, at a dead halt. He was delighted with himself! A Sprung-Christiana is a showy and not an easy turn at speed. He wished his old teacher, Fuchs, had been there to see that one!

He was now on the shoulder of the mountain. High overhead the silver strands of the cable railway plunged downwards in one great swoop towards the distant black line of the trees, where the moonlight glinted on a spidery pylon. Bond remembered that there now followed a series of great zigs and zags more or less beneath the cables. With the piste unobscured, it would have been easy, but the new snow made every descent look desirable. Bond jerked up his goggles to see if he could spot a flag. Yes, there was one away down to the left. He would do some S turns down the next slope and then make for it.

As he pulled down his goggles and gripped his sticks, two things happened. First there came a deep boom from high up the mountain; and a speck of flame, that wobbled in its flight, soared into the sky above him. There was a pause at the top of its parabola, a sharp crack and a blazing magnesium flare on a parachute began its wandering descent, wiping out the black shadows in the hollows, turning everything into a hideous daylight. Another and another sprayed out across the sky, lighting every cranny over the mountain side.

And, at the same time, the cables high above Bond's head began to sing! They were sending the cable car down after him!

Bond cursed into the sodden folds of his silk handkerchief and got going. The next thing would be a man after him—probably a man with a gun!

He took the second lap more carefully than the first, got across to the second flag, turned at it and made back across the plunging slope for the series of linked S's under the cables. How fast did these bloody gondolas go? Ten, fifteen, twenty miles an hour? This was the latest type. It would be the fastest. Hadn't he read somewhere that the one between Arosa and the Weisshorn did twenty-five? Even as he got into his first S, the tune of the singing cable above him momentarily changed and then went back to its usual whine. That was the gondola passing the first pylon! Bond's knees, the Achilles heel of all skiers, were beginning to ache. He cut his S's narrower, snaking down faster, but now feeling the rutted tracks of the piste under his skis at every turn. Was that a flag away over to the left? The magnesium flares were swaying lower, almost directly over him. Yes. It looked all right. Two more S-turns and he would do a traverse schuss to it!

Something landed with a tremendous crack amidst a fountain of snow to his right! Another to his left! They had a grenade-thrower up front in the cable car! A bracket! Would the next one be dead on? Almost before the thought flashed through his mind, there came a tremendous explosion just ahead of him and he was hurled forward and sideways in a catherine wheel of sticks and skis.

Bond got gingerly to his feet, gasping and spitting snow. One of his bindings had opened. His trembling fingers found the forward latch and banged it tight again. Another sharp crack, but wide by twenty yards. He must get away from the line of fire from the blasted railway! Feverishly he thought, the left-hand flag! I must do the traverse now. He took a vague bearing across the precipitous slope and flung himself down it.

17 BLOODY SNOW

It was tricky, undulating ground. The magnesium flares had sailed lower and there were ugly patches of black shadow, any of which might have been a small ravine. Bond had to check at all of them and each time the sharp Christie reminded him of his legs and ankles. But he got across without a fall and pulled up at the flag, panting. He looked back. The gondola had stopped. They had telephone communication with the top and bottom stations, but why had it stopped? As if in answer, blue flames fluttered gaily from the forward cabin. But Bond heard no bullets. The gondola would be swaying on its cable. But then, high up above him, from somewhere near the first flags on the shoulder, came more rapid fire, from two points, and the snow kicked up daintily around him. So the guides had finally got after him! His fall would have cost him minutes. How much lead had he got? Certainly less than ten minutes. A bullet whanged into one of his skis and sang off down the mountain. Bond took a last gulp of breath and got going again, still left-handed, away from the cable railway, towards the next flag, a distant dot on the edge of the shadow thrown by the great Matterhorn-shaped peak of Piz Gloria, which knifed up into the spangled sky in dreadful majesty.

It looked as if the run was going to take him dangerously close to the skirts of the peak. Something was nagging at his mind, a tiny memory. What was it? It was something unpleasant. Yes, by God! The last flag! It had been black. He was on the Black Run, the one closed because of avalanche danger! God! Well, he'd had it now. No time to try and get back on the Red Run. And anyway the Red had a long stretch close to the cables. He'd just have to chance it. And what a time to chance it, just after a heavy fall of new snow, and with all these detonations to loosen up the stuff! When there was danger of an avalanche, guides forbade even speech! Well, to hell with it! Bond zoomed on across the great unmarked slope, got to the next flag, spotted the next, away down the mountain side towards the tree line. Too steep to schuss! He would just have to do it in S's.

And then the bastards chose to fire off three more flares followed by a stream of miscellaneous rockets that burst prettily among the stars. Of course! Bright idea! This was for the sake of watchers in the valley who might be inquisitive about the mysterious explosions high up the mountain. They were having a party up there, celebrating something. What fun these rich folk had, to be sure! And then Bond remembered. But of course! It was Christmas Eve! God rest ye merry gentlemen, let nothing ye dismay! Bond's skis hissed an accompaniment as he zigzagged fast down the beautiful snow slope. White Christmas! Well, he'd certainly got himself that!

But then, from high up above him, he heard that most dreaded of all sounds in the high Alps, that rending, booming crack! The Last Trump! Avalanche!

The ground shook violently under Bond's skis and the swelling rumble came down to him like the noise of express trains roaring through a hundred tunnels. God Almighty, now he really had had it! What was the rule? Point the skis straight downhill! Try and race it! Bond pointed his skis down towards the tree line, got down in his ugly crouch and shot, his skis screaming, into white space.

Keep forward, you bastard! Get your hands way in front of you! The wind of his speed was building up into a great wall in front of him, trying to knock him off balance. Behind him the giant roar of the mountain seemed to be gaining. Other, smaller cracks sounded high up among the crags. The whole bloody mountain was on the move! If he beat the gigantic mass of hurtling snow to the tree line, what comfort would he find there? Certainly no protection until he was deep in the wood. The avalanche would snap perhaps the first hundred yards of firs down like match-sticks. Bond used his brain and veered slightly left-handed. The opening, the glade cut for the Black Run, would surely be somewhere below the last flag he had been aiming for. If it wasn't, he was a dead duck!

Now the wild schuss was coming to an end. The trees were rushing towards him. Was there a break in the bloody black line of them? Yes! But more to the left. Bond veered, dropping his speed, gratefully, but with his ears strained to gauge the range of the thunder behind and above him. It couldn't be far from him. The shudder in the ground had greatly increased and a lot of the stuff would also find the hole through the trees, funnel itself in and pursue him even down there! Yes! There was the flag! Bond hurtled into a right-hand Christie just as, to his left, he heard the first trees come crashing down with the noise of a hundred monster crackers being pulled—Christmas crackers! Bond flung himself straight down the wide white glade between the trees. But he could hear that he was losing! The crashing of the trees was coming closer. The first froth of the white tide couldn't be far behind his heels! What did one do when the avalanche hit? There was only one rule. Get your hands to your boots and grip your ankles. Then, if you were buried, there was some hope of undoing your skis, being able, perhaps, to burrow your way to the surface—if you knew in your tomb where the surface lay! If you couldn't go down like a ball, you would end up immovable, a buried tangle of sticks and skis at all angles. Thank God the opening at the end of the glade, the shimmer of the last, easily sloping fields before the finish, was showing up! The crackling roar behind him was getting louder! How high would the wall of snow be? Fifty feet? A hundred? Bond reached the end of the glade and hurled himself into a right-hand Christie. It was his last hope, to get below the wide belt of trees and pray that the avalanche wouldn't mow down the lot of them. To stay in the path of the roaring monster at his heels would be suicide!

The Christie came off, but Bond's right ski snarled a root or a sapling and he felt himself flying through space. He landed with a crash and lay gasping, all the wind knocked out of him. Now he was done for! Not even enough strength to get his hands to his ankles! A tremendous buffet of wind hit him and a small snowstorm covered him. The ground shook wildly and a deep crashing roar filled his ears. And then it had passed him and given way to a slow, heavy rumble. Bond brushed the snow out of his eyes and got unsteadily to his feet, both skis loose, his goggles gone. Only a cricket pitch away a great torrent of snow, perhaps twenty feet high, was majestically pouring out of the wood and down into the meadows. Its much higher, tumbling snout, tossing huge crags of broken snow around it, was already a hundred yards ahead and still going fast. But, where Bond stood, it was now silent and peaceful except for the machine-gun-fire crackling of the trees as they went down in the wood that had finally protected him. The crackling was getting nearer! No time to hang about! But Bond took off one sodden glove and dug into his trouser pocket. If ever he needed a drink it was now! He tilted the little flask down his throat, emptied it and threw the bottle away. Happy Christmas! he said to himself, and bent to his bindings.

He got to his feet and, rather light-headed but with the wonderful glow of the Enzian in his stomach, started on the last mile of finishing schuss across the meadows to the right, away from the still hurtling river of snow. Blast! There was a fence across the bottom of the meadows! He would have to take the normal outlet for the runs beside the cable station. It looked all right. There was no sign of the gondola, but he could now hear the song of the cables. Had the down-coming car reversed back up to Piz Gloria, assuming him to have been killed by the avalanche? There was a large black saloon car in the forecourt to the cable station, and lights on in the station, but otherwise no sign of life. Well, it was his only way to get off the run and on to the road that was his objective. Bond schussed easily downwards, resting his limbs, getting his breath back.

The sharp crack of a heavy-calibre pistol and the phut as the bullet hit the snow beside him pulled him together. He jinked sideways and glanced quickly up to the right, where the shot had come from. The gun blazed again. A man on skis was coming fast after him. One of the guides! Of course! He would have taken the Red Run. Had the other followed Bond on the Black? Bond hoped so, gave a deep sigh of anger and put on all the speed he could, crouching low and jinking occasionally to spoil the man's aim. The single shots kept on coming. It was going to be a narrow shave who got to the end of the run first!

Bond studied the finishing point that was now coming at him fast. There was a wide break in the fence to let the skiers through, a large parking place in front of the cable station and then the low embankment that protected the main line of the Rhätische Bahn up to Pontresina and the Bernina Pass. On the other side of the rails the railway embankment dropped into the road from Pontresina to Samaden, the junction for St Moritz, perhaps two miles down the valley.

Another shot kicked up the snow in front of him. That was six that had gone. With any luck the man's pistol was empty. But that wouldn't help much. There was no stuffing left in Bond for a fight.

Now a great blaze of light showed coming up the railway line, and, before it was hidden by the cable station, Bond identified an express and could just hear the thudding of its electro-diesels. By God, it would just about be passing the cable station as he wanted to get across the track! Could he make it—take a run at the low embankment and clear it and the lines before the train got there? It was his only hope! Bond dug in with his sticks to get on extra speed. Hell! A man had got out of the black car and was crouching, aiming at him. Bond jinked and jinked again as fire bloomed from the man's hand. But now Bond was on top of him. He thrust hard with the rapier point of a ski-stick and felt it go through clothing. The man gave a scream and went down. The guide, now only yards behind, yelled something. The great yellow eye of the diesel glared down the tracks, and Bond caught a sideways glimpse of a huge red snow-fan below the headlight that was fountaining the new snow to right and left of the engine in two white wings. Now! He flashed across the parking place, heading straight at the mound of the embankment and, as he hit, dug both his sticks in to get his skis off the ground and hurled himself forward into the air. There was a brief glimpse of steel rails below, a tremendous thudding in his ears and a ferocious blast, only yards away, from the train's siren. Then he crashed on to the icy road, tried to stop, failed and fetched up in an almighty skid against the hard snow wall on the other side. As he did so, there came a terrible scream from behind him, a loud splintering of wood and the screech of the train's brakes being applied.

At the same time, the spray from the snow-fan, that had now reached Bond, turned pink!

Bond wiped some of it off his face and looked at it. His stomach turned. God! The man had tried to follow him, had been too late or had missed his jump, and had been caught by the murderous blades of the snow-fan! Mincemeat! Bond dug a handful of snow off the bank and wiped it over his face and hair. He rubbed more of it down his sweater. He suddenly realized that people were pulling down the windows in the brilliantly lit train above him. Others had got down on the line. Bond pulled himself together and punted off down the black ice of the road. Shouts followed him—the angry bawls of Swiss citizens. Bond edged his skis a little against the camber of the road and kept going. Ahead of him, down the black gulch of the road, in his mind's eye, the huge red propeller whirred, sucking him into its steel whirlpool. Bond, close to delirium, slithered on towards its bloody, beckoning vortex.

Bond, a grey-faced, lunging automaton, somehow stayed upright on the two miles of treacherous Langlauf down the gentle slope to Samaden. Once a passing car, its snow-chains clattering, forced him into the bank. He leaned against the comforting soft snow for a moment, the breath sobbing in his throat. Then he drove himself on again. He had got so far, done so well! Only a few more hundred yards to the lights of the darling, straggling little paradise of people and shelter! The slender campanile of the village church was floodlit and there was a great warm lake of light on the left of the twinkling group of houses. The strains of a waltz came over the still, frozen air. The skating-rink! A Christmas Eve skaters' ball. That was the place for him! Crowds! Gaiety! Confusion! Somewhere to lose himself from the double hunt that would now be on—by SPECTRE and the Swiss police, the cops and the robbers hand in hand!

Bond's skis hit a pile of horse's dung from some merry-maker's sleigh. He lurched drunkenly into the snow wall of the road and righted himself, cursing feebly. Come on! Pull yourself together! Look respectable! Well, you needn't look *too* respectable. After all, it's Christmas Eve. Here were the first houses. The noise of accordion music, deliciously nostalgic, came from a Gasthaus with a beautiful iron sign over its door. Now there was a twisty, uphill bit—the road to St Moritz. Bond shuffled up it, placing his sticks carefully. He ran a hand through his matted hair and pulled the sweat-soaked handkerchief down to his neck, tucking the ends into his shirt collar. The music lilted down towards him from the great pool of light over the skating-rink. Bond pulled himself a little more upright. There were a lot of cars drawn up, skis stuck in mounds of snow, luges and tobaggans, festoons of paper streamers, a big notice in three languages across the entrance: "Grand Christmas Eve Ball! Fancy Dress! Entrance two Francs! Bring your friends! Hooray!"

Bond dug in his sticks and bent down to unlatch his skis. He fell over sideways. If only he could just lie there, go to sleep on the hard, trodden snow that felt like swans down! He gave a small groan and heaved himself gingerly into a crouch. The bindings were frozen solid, caked, like his boots, with ice. He got one of his sticks and hacked feebly at the metal and tried again. At last the latches sprang and the thongs were off. Where to put the bloody things, hide their brilliant red markings? He lugged them down the trodden path towards the entrance, gay with fairy lights, shoved the skis and the sticks under a big saloon car and staggered on. The man at the ticket-table was as drunk as Bond seemed. He looked up blearily: "Zwo Franken. Two francs. Deux francs." The routine incantation was slurred into one portmanteau word. Bond held on to the table, put down the coins and got his ticket. The man's eyes focused. "The fancy dress, the travesti, it is obligatoire." He reached into a box by his side and threw a black and white domino-mask on the table. "One franc." He gave a lop-sided smile. "Now you are the gangster, the spy. Yes?"

"Yeah, that's right." Bond paid and put on the mask. He reluctantly let go of the table and wove through the entrance. There were raised tiers of wooden benches round the big square rink. Thank God for a chance to sit down! There was an empty seat on the aisle in the bottom row at rink level. Bond stumbled down the wooden steps and fell into it. He righted himself, said "Sorry" and put his head in the hands. The girl beside him, part of a group of harlequins, Wild Westerners and pirates, drew her spangled skirt away, whispered something to her neighbour. Bond didn't care. They wouldn't throw him out on a night like this. Through the loud speakers the violins sobbed into "The Skaters' Waltz." Above them the voice of the M.C. called, "Last dance, ladies and gentlemen. And then all out on to the rink and join hands for the grand finale. Only ten minutes to go to midnight! Last dance, ladies and gentlemen. Last dance!" There was a rattle of applause. People laughed excitedly.

God in Heaven! thought Bond feebly. Now this! Won't anybody leave me alone? He fell asleep.

Hours later he felt his shoulder being shaken. "On to the rink, sir. Please. All on to the rink for the grand finale. Only a minute to go." A man in purple and gold uniform was standing beside him, looking down impatiently.

"Go away," said Bond dully. Then some inner voice told him not to make a scene, not to be conspicuous. He struggled to his feet, made the few steps to the rink, somehow stood upright. His head lowered, like a wounded bull, he looked to left and right, saw a gap in the human chain round the rink and slid gingerly towards it. A hand was held out to him and he grasped it thankfully. On the other side someone else was trying to get hold of his free hand.

And then there came a diversion. From right across the rink a girl in a short black skating-skirt topped by a shocking pink fur-lined parka, sped like an arrow across the ice and came to a crash-stop in front of Bond. Bond felt the ice particles hit his legs. He looked up. It was a face he recognized—those brilliant blue eyes, the look of authority now subdued beneath golden sunburn and a brilliant smile of excitement. Who in hell?

The girl slipped in beside him, seized his right hand in her left, joined up on her right. "James"—it was a thrilling whisper—"oh, James. It's me! Tracy! What's the matter with you? Where have you come from?"

"Tracy," said Bond dully. "Tracy. Hold on to me. I'm in bad shape. Tell you later."

Then Auld Lang Syne began and everybody swung linked hands in unison to the music.

18 FORK LEFT FOR HELL

Bond had no idea how he managed to stay upright, but at last it was over and everyone cheered and broke up into pairs and groups.

Tracy got her arm under his. Bond pulled himself together. He said hoarsely, "Mix with the crowd, Tracy. Got to get away from here. People after me." A sudden hope came to him. "Got your car?"

"Yes, darling. Everything'll be all right. Just hang on to me. Are people waiting for you outside?"

"Could be. Watch out for a big black Mercedes. There may be shooting. Better stay away from me. I can make it. Where's the car?"

"Down the road to the right. But don't be silly. Here, I've got an idea. You get into this parka." She ran the zip down and stripped it off. "It'll be a tight fit. Here, put your arm into this sleeve."

"But you'll get cold."

"Do as I tell you. I've got a sweater and plenty on underneath. Now the other arm. That's right." She pulled up the zip. "Darling James, you look sweet."

The fur of the parka smelt of Guerlain's "Ode." It took Bond back to Royale. What a girl! The thought of her, of having an ally, of not being on his own, of being away from that bloody mountain, revived Bond. He held her hand and followed her through the crowd that was now streaming towards the exit. This was going to be a bad moment! Whether or not that cable car had come on down the mountain, by now Blofeld would have had time to get one down full of SPECTRE men. Bond had been seen from the train, would be known to have made for Samaden. By now they would have covered the railway station. They would expect him to try and hide in a crowd. Perhaps the drunken man at the entrance had remembered him. If that saloon moved off and revealed the red-arrowed skis, it would be a cert. Bond let go the girl's hand and slipped the shattered Rolex back over the knuckles of his right hand. He had gathered enough strength, mostly from the girl, to have one more bash at them!

She looked at him. "What are you doing?"

He took her hand again. "Nothing."

They were getting near the exit. Bond peered through the slits in his mask. Yes, by God! Two of the thugs were standing beside the ticket man watching the throng with deadly concentration. On the far side of the road stood the black Mercedes, petrol vapour curling up from its exhaust. No escape. There was only bluff. Bond put his arm round Tracy's neck and whispered, "Kiss me all the way past the ticket-table. They're there, but I think we can make it."

She flung an arm over his shoulder and drew him to her. "How did you know that that's what I've been waiting for?" Her lips crushed down sideways on his and, in a tide of laughing, singing people, they were through and on the street.

They turned, still linked, down the road. Yes! There was the darling little white car!

And then the horn on the Mercedes began sounding urgently. Bond's gait, or perhaps his old-fashioned ski-trousers, had given him away to the man in the car!

"Quick, darling!" Bond said urgently.

The girl threw herself in under the wheel, pressed the starter and the car was moving as Bond scrambled in through the opposite door. Bond looked back. Through the rear window he could see the two men standing in the road. They would not shoot with so many witnesses about. Now they ran to the Mercedes. Thank God it was pointing up the hill towards St Moritz! And then Tracy had done a controlled skid round the S bend in the village and they were on the main road that Bond had staggered down half an hour before.

It would be five minutes at least before the Mercedes could turn and get after them. The girl was going like hell, but there was traffic on the road—tinkling sleighs full of fur-wrapped merry-makers on their way back to Pontresina, an occasional car, its snow-chains rattling. She drove on her brakes and her horn, the same triple wind-horn that sounded the high discord Bond remembered so well. Bond said, "You're an angel, Tracy. But take it easy. We don't want to end up in the ditch."

The girl glanced sideways at him and laughed with pleasure. "That sounds as if you were feeling better. But I cannot see you. Now you can take off that silly mask and my parka. In a minute the heat will come on and you will be roasted. And I would like to see you as I remember you. But you are pleased with me?"

Life was beginning to come back into Bond. It was so wonderful to be in this little car with this marvellous girl. The memory of the dreadful mountain, of all that he had been through, was receding. Now there was hope again, after so much dread and despair. He could feel the tensions uncoiling in his stomach. He said, "I'll tell you if I'm pleased when we get to Zürich. Can you make it? It's a hell of a way to spend Christmas." He wound down the window and threw the domino-mask out, stripped off the parka and draped it over her shoulders. The big sign for the main road down into the valley came up. He said, "Left here, Tracy. Filisur and then Coire."

She took the turning, in Bond's estimation, dangerously fast. She went into a skid that Bond swore was going to be uncontrolled. But, even on the black ice of the road, she got out of it and motored blithely on. Bond said, "For God's sake, Tracy! How in hell did you manage that? You haven't even got chains on."

She laughed, pleased at the awe in his voice. "Dunlop Rally studs on all the tyres. They're only supposed to be for Rally drivers, but I managed to wangle a set out of them. Don't worry. Just sit back and enjoy the drive."

There was something entirely new in the girl's voice, a lilt and happiness that had certainly not been there at Royale. Bond turned and looked at her carefully for the first time. Yes, she was somehow a new woman, radiating health and a kind of inner glow. The tumbled fair hair glittered with vitality and the half-open, beautiful lips seemed always to be on the verge of a smile.

"Satisfied?"

"You look absolutely wonderful. But now for God's sake tell me how you happened to be at Samaden. It was a bloody miracle. It saved my life."

"All right. But then you tell. I've never seen a man look so dead on his feet. I couldn't believe my eyes. I thought you must be plastered." She gave him a quick glance. "You still look pretty bad. Here"—she leant forward to the dashboard—"I'll switch on the blower. Get you properly warmed up." She paused. "Well, my bit of the story's quite simple really. Papa rang me up one day from Marseilles to find out how I was. He asked if I had seen you and seemed very annoyed when he heard I hadn't. He practically ordered me to go and find you." She glanced at him. "He's quite taken to you, you know. Anyway he said he had found out the address of a certain man you were looking for. He said he was sure that by now you would have found out that address too. He said that, knowing you, I would find you somewhere close to this address. It was the Piz Gloria Club. He told me if I found you to tell you to watch your step, to look after yourself." She laughed. "How right he was! Well, so I left Davos, which had really put me on my feet again, as you said it would, and I came up to Samaden the day before yesterday. The Seilbahn wasn't running yesterday, so I was going to come up today to look for you. It was all as simple as that. Now you tell."

They had been keeping up a good speed down the sloping, winding road into the valley. Bond turned to look through the rear window. He swore under his breath. Perhaps a mile behind, twin lights were coming after them. The girl said, "I know. I've been watching in the mirror. I'm afraid they're gaining a little. Must be a good driver who knows the road. Probably got snow-chains. But I think I can hold them. Now go on. What have you been up to?"

Bond gave her a garbled version. There was a big gangster up the mountain, living under a false name. He was wanted by the police in England. Bond was vaguely connected with the police, with the Ministry of Defence. (She snorted, "Don't try and fool me. I know you're in the Secret Service. Papa told me so." Bond said curtly, "Well, Papa's talking through his hat." She laughed knowingly). Anyway, Bond continued, he had been sent out to make sure this was the man they wanted. He had found out that he was. But the man had become suspicious of Bond and Bond had had to get out quickly. He gave her a graphic account of the moonlit nightmare of the mountain, of the avalanche, of the man who had been killed by the train, of how he had got to Samaden, dead beat, and had tried to hide in the crowd on the skating-rink. "And then," he ended lamely, "you turned up like a beautiful angel on skates, and here we are."

She thought the story over for a minute. Then she said

calmly, "And now, my darling James, just tell me how many of them you killed. And tell me the truth."

"Why?"

"I'm just curious."

"You promise to keep this between you and me?"

She said enigmatically, "Of course. Everything's between you and me from now on."

"Well, there was the main guard at the so-called Club. That had to be done or I'd be dead myself by now. Then I suppose one got caught by the avalanche. Then, at the bottom, one of them shot at me and I had to spear him with my ski-stick—self-defence. I don't know how badly he's hurt. And then there was the man killed by the train. He'd fired six shots at me. And anyway it was his own fault. Let's say three and a half got themselves killed one way or another."

"How many are left?"

"What are you getting at?"

"I just want to know. Trust me."

"Well, I think there were about fifteen up there all told. So that leaves eleven and a half—plus the big man."

"And there are three in the car behind? Would they kill us if they caught us?"

"I'm afraid so. I haven't got any weapons. I'm sorry, Tracy, but I'm afraid you wouldn't have much chance either, being a witness and a sort of accomplice of mine. These people think I'm pretty bad news for them."

"And you are?"

"Yes. From now on, I'm the worst."

"Well, I've got pretty bad news for you. They're gaining on us and I've only got a couple of gallons left in the tank. We'll have to stop in Filisur. There won't be a garage open and it'll mean waking someone up. Can't hope to do it under ten minutes and they'll have us. You'll have to think up something clever."

There was a ravine and an S-turn over a bridge. They were coming out of the first curve over the bridge. Lights blazed at them from across the ravine. There was half a mile between the two cars, but the range across the ravine was perhaps only three hundred yards. Bond wasn't surprised to see the familiar blue flames flutter from the front of the car. Chips of granite from the overhang splattered down on the bonnet of the car. Then they were into the second half of the S-bend and out of sight of their pursuers.

Now came a stretch of reconstruction work where there had been a landslide. There were big warning notices: "Achtung! Baustelle! Vorsichtig Fahren!" The broken road hugged the mountain side on the right. On the left was rickety fencing and then a precipice falling hundreds of feet down into a gorge with an ice-floed river. In the middle of the bad stretch, a huge red wooden arrow pointed right to a narrow track across a temporary bridge. Bond suddenly shouted "Stop!"

Tracy pulled up, her front wheels on the bridge. Bond tore open the door. "Get on! Wait for me round the next corner. It's the only chance."

Good girl! She got going without a word. Bond ran back the few yards to the big red arrow. It was held in the forks of two upright poles. Bond wrenched it off, swung it round so that it pointed to the left, towards the flimsy fence that closed off the yards of old road leading to the collapsed bridge. Bond tore at the fence, pulling the stakes out, flattening it. Glare showed round the corner behind him. He leaped across the temporary road into the shadow of the mountain, flattened himself against it, waited, holding his breath.

The Mercedes was coming faster than it should over the bumpy track, its chains clattering inside the mudguards. It made straight for the black opening to which the arrow now pointed. Bond caught a glimpse of white, strained faces and then the desperate scream of brakes as the driver saw the abyss in front of him. The car seemed almost to stop, but its front wheels must have been over the edge. It balanced for a moment on its iron belly and then slowly, slowly toppled and there was a first appalling crash as it hit the rubble beneath the old bridge. Then another crash and another. Bond ran forward past the lying arrow and looked down. Now the car was flying upside-down through the air. It hit again and a fountain of sparks flashed from a rock ledge. Then, somersaulting, and with its lights somehow still blazing, it smashed on down into the gorge. It hit a last outcrop that knocked it sideways and, spinning laterally, but now with its lights out and only the glint of the moon on metal, it took the last great plunge into the iced-up river. A deep rumble echoed up from the gorge and there was the patter of rocks and stones following the wreckage. And then all was peaceful, moonlit silence.

Bond let out his breath in a quiet hiss between his clenched teeth. Then, mechanically, he straightened things out again, put up the remains of the fence, lifted the arrow and put it back facing to the right. Then he wiped his sweating hands down the side of his trousers and walked unsteadily down the road and round the next corner.

The little white car was there, pulled in to the side,

with its lights out. Bond got in and slumped into his seat. Tracy said nothing but got the car going. The lights of Filisur appeared, warm and yellow in the valley below. She reached out a hand and held his tightly. "You've had enough for one day. Go to sleep. I'll get you to Zürich. Please do what I say."

Bond said nothing. He pressed her hand weakly, leaned his head aginst the door-jamb and was instantly asleep.

He was out for the count.

19 LOVE FOR BREAKFAST

In the grey dawn, Zürich airport was depressing and almost deserted, but, blessedly, there was a Swissair Caravelle, delayed by fog at London Airport, waiting to take off for London. Bond parked Tracy in the restaurant and, regretfully forsaking the smell of coffee and fried eggs, went and bought himself a ticket, had his passport stamped by a sleepy official (he had half-expected to be stopped, but wasn't), and went to a telephone booth and shut himself in. He looked up Universal Export in the telephone book, and read underneath, as he had hoped, "Hauptvertreter Alexander Muir. Privat Wohnung" and the number. Bond glanced through the glass window at the clock in the departure hall. Six o'clock. Well, Muir would just have to take it.

He rang the number and, after minutes, a sleepy voice said, "Ja! Hier Muir."

Bond said, "Sorry, 410, but this is 007. I'm calling from the airport. This is bloody urgent so I'll have to take a chance on your line being bugged. Got a paper and pencil?"

The voice at the other end had grown brisker. "Hang on, 007. Yes, got it. Go ahead."

"First of all I've got some bad news. Your Number Two has had it. Almost for sure. Can't give you any details over this line, but I'm off to London in about an hour—Swissair Flight 110—and I'll signal the dope back straight away. Could you put that on the teleprinter? Right. Now I'm guessing that in the next day or so a party of ten girls, British, will be coming in here by helicopter from the Engadine. Yellow Sud Aviation Alouette. I'll be teleprinting their names back from London some time today. My bet is they'll be flying to England, probably on different flights and perhaps to Prestwick and Gatwick as well as London Airport, if you've any planes using those airports. Anyway, I guess they'll be dispersed. Now I think it may be very important to tell London their flight numbers and E.T.A. Rather a big job, but I'll get you authority in a few hours to use men from Berne and Geneva to lend a hand. Got it? Right. Now I'm pretty certain you're blown. Remember the old Operation Bedlam that's just been cancelled? Well, it's him and he's got radio and he'll probably have guessed I'd be contacting you this morning. Just take a look out of the window and see if there's any sign of watchers. He's certainly got his men in Zürich."

"Christ, what a shambles!" The voice at the other end was tight with tension. "Hang on." There was a pause. Bond could visualize Muir, whom he didn't know except as a number, going over to the window, carefully drawing aside the curtain. Muir came back on the wire. "Looks damn like it. There's a black Porsche across the road. Two men in it. I'll get my friends in the Sécurité to chase them away."

Bond said, "Be careful how you go about it. My guess is that our man has got a pretty good fix in with the police. Anyway, put all this on the telex to M personally, would you? Ciphered of course. And tell him if I get back in one piece I must see him today, with 501 [the Chief Scientific Officer to the Service] and if possible with someone in the same line of business from the Ministry of Agriculture and Fisheries. Sounds daft, but there it is. It's going to upset their paper hats and Christmas pudding, but I can't help that. Can you manage all that? Good lad. Any questions?"

"Sure I oughtn't to come out to the airport and get some more about my Number Two? He was tailing one of Redland's men. Chap's been buying some pretty odd stuff from the local rep. of Badische Anilin. Number Two thought it seemed damned fishy. Didn't tell me what the stuff was. Just thought he'd better see where it was being delivered to."

"I thought it must be some kind of a spiel like that. No. You stay away from me. I'm hot as a pistol, going to be hotter later in the day when they find a certain Mercedes at the bottom of a precipice. I'll get off the line now. Sorry to have wrecked your Christmas. 'Bye."

Bond put down the receiver and went up to the restaurant. Tracy had been watching the door. Her face lit up when she saw him. He sat down very close to her and took her hand, a typical airport farewell couple. He ordered plenty of scrambled eggs and coffee. "It's all right, Tracy. I've fixed everything at my end. But now about you. That car of yours is going to be bad news. There'll be people who'll have seen you drive away with the Mercedes on your tail. There always are, even at midnight on Christmas Eve. And the big man on top of the mountain has got his men down here too. You'd better finish your breakfast and get the hell on over the frontier. Which is the nearest?"

"Schaffhausen or Konstanz, I suppose, but"—she pleaded—"James, do I have to leave you now? It's been so long waiting for you. And I *have* done well, haven't I? Why do you want to punish me?" Tears, that would never have been there in the Royale days, sparkled in her eyes. She wiped them angrily away with the back of her hand.

Bond suddenly thought, Hell! I'll never find another girl like this one. She's got everything I've ever looked for in a woman. She's beautiful, in bed and out. She's adventurous, brave, resourceful. She's exciting always. She seems to love me. She'd let me go on with my life. She's a lone girl, not cluttered up with friends, relations, belongings. Above all, she needs me. It'll be someone for me to look after. I'm fed up with all these untidy, casual affairs that leave me with a bad conscience. I wouldn't mind having children. I've got no social background into which she would or wouldn't fit. We're two of a pair, really. Why not make it for always?

Bond found his voice saying those words that he had never said in his life before, never expected to say.

"Tracy. I love you. Will you marry me?"

She turned very pale. She looked at him wonderingly. Her lips trembled. "You mean that?"

"Yes, I mean it. With all my heart."

She took her hand away from his and put her face in her hands. When she removed them she was smiling. "I'm sorry, James. It's so much what I've been dreaming of. It came as a shock. But yes. Yes, of course I'll marry you. And I won't be silly about it. I won't make a scene. Just kiss me once and I'll be going." She looked seriously at him, at every detail of his face. Then she leant forward and they kissed.

She got up briskly. "I suppose I've got to get used to doing what you say. I'll drive to Munich. To the Vier Jahreszeiten. It's my favourite hotel in the world. I'll wait for you there. They know me. They'll take me in without any luggage. Everything's at Samaden. I'll just have to send out for a tooth-brush and stay in bed for two days until I can go out and get some things. You'll telephone me? Talk to me? When can we get married? I must tell Papa. He'll be terribly excited."

"Let's get married in Munich. At the consulate. I've

got a kind of diplomatic immunity. I can get the papers through quickly. Then we can be married again in an English church, or Scottish rather. That's where I come from. I'll call you up tonight and tomorrow. I'll get to you just as soon as I can. I've got to finish this business first."

"You promise you won't get hurt?"

Bond smiled. "I wouldn't think of it. For once I'll run away if someone starts any shooting."

"All right then." She looked at him carefully again. "It's time you took off that red handkerchief. I suppose you realize it's bitten to ribbons. Give it to me. I'll mend it."

Bond undid the red bandanna from round his neck. It was a dark, sweat-soaked rag. And she was right. Two corners of it were in shreds. He must have got them between his teeth and chewed on them when the going was bad down the mountain. He couldn't remember having done so. He gave it to her.

She took it and, without looking back, walked straight out of the restaurant and down the stairs towards the exit.

Bond sat down. His breakfast came and he began eating mechanically. What had he done? What in hell had he done? But the only answer was a feeling of tremendous warmth and relief and excitement. James and Tracy Bond! Commander and Mrs Bond! How utterly, utterly extraordinary!

The voice of the Tannoy said, "Attention, please. Passengers on Swissair Flight Number 110 for London, please assemble at gate Number 2. Swissair Flight Number 110 for London. Passengers to gate Number 2, please."

Bond stubbed out his cigarette, gave a quick glance round their trysting-place to fix its banality in his mind, and walked to the door, leaving the fragments of his old life torn up amidst the debris of an airport breakfast.

20 'M EN PANTOUFLES

Bond slept in the plane and was visited by a terrible nightmare. It was the hallway of a very grand town-house, an embassy perhaps, and a wide staircase led up under a spangled chandelier to where the butler was standing at the door of the drawing-room, from which came the murmur of a large crowd of guests. Tracy, in oyster satin, was on his arm. She was loaded with jewels and her golden hair had been piled up grandly into one of those fancy arrangements you see in smart hairdressers' advertisements. On top of the pile was a diamond tiara that glittered gorgeously. Bond was dressed in tails (where in hell had he got *those* from?) and the wing collar stuck into his neck below the chin. He was wearing his medals, and his order as C.M.G., on its blue and scarlet ribbon, hung below his white tie. Tracy was chattering, gaily, excitedly, looking forward to the grand evening. Bond was cursing the prospect before him and wishing he was playing a tough game of bridge for high stakes at Blades. They got to the top of the stairs and Bond gave his name.

"Commander and Mrs James Bond!" It was the stentorian bellow of a toast-master. Bond got the impression that a sudden hush fell over the elegant crowd in the gilt and white drawing-room.

He followed Tracy through the double doors. There was a gush of French from Tracy as she exchanged those empty "Mayfair" kisses, that end up wide of the kissers' ears, with her hostess. Tracy drew Bond forward. "And this is James. Doesn't he look sweet with that beautiful medal round his neck? Just like the old De Reszke cigarette advertisements!"

"Fasten your seat belts, please, and extinguish your cigarettes."

Bond awoke, sweating. God Almighty! What had he done? But no! It wouldn't be like that! Definitely not. He would still have his tough, exciting life, but now there would be Tracy to come home to. Would there be room in his flat in Chelsea? Perhaps he could rent the floor above. And what about May, his Scottish treasure? That would be tricky. He must somehow persuade her to stay.

The Caravelle hit the runway and there came the roar of jet deflection, and then they were trundling over the tarmac in a light drizzle. Bond suddenly realized that he had no luggage, that he could go straight to Passport Control and then out and back to his flat to change out of these ridiculous ski-clothes that stank of sweat. Would there be a car from the pool for him? There was, with Miss Mary Goodnight sitting beside the driver.

"My God, Mary, this is the hell of a way to spend your Christmas! This is far beyond the line of duty. Anyway, get in the back and tell me why you're not stirring the plum-pudding or going to church or something."

She climbed in to the back seat and he followed. She said, "You don't seem to know much about Christmas. You make plum-puddings at least two months before and let them sort of settle and mature. And church isn't till eleven." She glanced at him. "Actually I came to see how you were. I gather you've been in trouble again. You certainly look pretty ghastly. Don't you own a comb? And you haven't shaved. You look like a pirate. And"—she wrinkled her nose—"when did you last have a bath? I wonder they let you out of the airport. You ought to be in quarantine."

Bond laughed. "Winter sports are very strenuous—all that snowballing and tobogganing. Matter of fact, I was at a Christmas Eve fancy-dress party last night. Kept me up till all hours."

"In those great clod-hopping boots? I don't believe you."

"Well, sucks to you! It was on a skating-rink. But seriously, Mary, tell me the score. Why this V.I.P. treatment?"

"M. You're to check with H.Q. first and then go down to lunch with him at Quarterdeck. Then, after lunch, he's having these men you wanted brought down for a conference. Everything top priority. So I thought I'd better stand by too. As you're wrecking so many other people's Christmases, I thought I might as well throw mine on the slag-heap with the others. Actually, if you want to know, I was only having lunch with an aunt. And I loathe turkey and plum-pudding. Anyway, I just didn't want to miss the fun and when the duty officer got on to me about an hour ago and told me there was a major flap, I asked him to tell the car to pick me up on the way to the airport."

Bond said seriously, "Well, you're a damned good girl. As a matter of fact it's going to be the hell of a rush getting down the bare bones of a report. And I've got something for the lab to do. Will there be someone there?"

"Of course there will. You know M insists on a skeleton staff in every Section, Christmas Day or not. But seriously, James. Have you been in trouble? You really do look awful."

"Oh, somewhat. You'll get the photo as I dictate." The car drew up outside Bond's flat. "Now be an angel and stir up May while I clean myself up and get out of these bloody clothes. Get her to brew me plenty of black coffee and to pour two jiggers of our best brandy into the pot. You ask May for what you like. She might even have some plum-pudding. Now then, it's nine-thirty. Be a good girl and call the Duty Officer and say O.K. to M's orders and that we'll be along by ten-thirty. And get him to ask the lab to stand by in half an hour." Bond took his passport out of his hip-pocket. "Then give this to the driver and ask him to get the hell over and give it to the Duty Officer personally. Tell the D.O."—Bond turned down the corner of a page—"to tell the lab that the ink used is—er—homemade. All it needs is exposure to heat. They'll understand. Got that? Good girl. Now come on and we'll get May going." Bond went up the steps and rang two shorts and a long on the bell.

When Bond got to his desk a few minutes after ten-thirty, feeling back to nine-tenths human, he found a folder on his desk with the red star in the top right corner that meant Top Secret. It contained his passport and a dozen copies of blown-up photostats of its page twenty-one. The list of girls' names was faint but legible. There was also a note marked "personal." Bond opened it. He laughed. It just said, "The ink showed traces of an excess of uric acid. This if often due to a super-abundance of alcohol in the blood-stream. You have been warned!" There was no signature. So the Christmas spirit had permeated even into the solemn crevices of one of the most secret Sections in the building! Bond crumpled the paper and then, thinking of Mary Goodnight's susceptibilities, more prudently burned it with his lighter.

She came in and sat down with her shorthand book. Bond said, "Now this is only a first draft, Mary, and it's got to be fast. So don't mind about mistakes. M'll understand. We've got about an hour and a half if I'm to get down to Windsor by lunch-time. Think you can manage it? All right then, here goes. 'Top Secret. Personal to M. As instructed, on December 22nd I arrived at Zürich Central Airport at 1330 by Swissair to make first contact in connection with Operation "Corona" . . .' "

Bond turned sideways to his secretary and, as he talked, looked out across the bare trees in Regent's Park, remembering every minute of the last three days—the sharp, empty smell of the air and the snow, the darkgreen pools of Blofeld's eyes, the crunch as the edge of his left hand, still bruised, thudded down across the offered neck of the guard. And then all the rest until Tracy, whom, without mention of romance, he left in his report on her way to the Vier Jahreszeiten in Munich. Then the report was finished and the muted clack of Mary's typewriter came from behind the closed door. He would ring Tracy up that night when he got back to his flat. He could already hear her laughing voice at the other end of the wire. The nightmare in the plane was forgotten. Now there was only the happy, secret looking-forward to the days to come. Bond lost himself in his plans—how to get the days off, how to get the necessary papers, where to have the service in Scotland. Then he pulled himself together, picked up the photostat containing the girls' names and went up to the Communications Centre to get on the teleprinter to Station Z.

M would have preferred to live by the sea, near Plymouth perhaps or Bristol—anywhere he could see the stuff whenever he wanted to and could listen to it at night. As it was, and since he had to be within easy call of London, he had chosen the next best thing to water, trees, and had found a small Regency manor-house on the edge of Windsor Forest. This was on Crown Lands, and Bond had always suspected that an ounce of "Grace and Favour" had found its way into M's lease. The head of the Secret Service earned £5,000 a year, with the use of an ancient Rolls-Royce and driver thrown in. M's naval pay (as a vice-admiral on the retired list) would add perhaps another £1,500. After taxes, he would have about £4,000 to spend. His London life would probably take at least half of that. Only if his rent and rates came to no more than £500 would he be able to keep a house in the country, and a beautiful small Regency house at that.

These thoughts ran again through Bond's mind as he swung the clapper of the brasship's-bell of some former H.M.S. *Repulse*, the last of whose line, a battle-cruiser, had been M's final sea-going appointment. Hammond, M's Chief Petty Officer in that ship who had followed M into retirement, greeted Bond as an old friend, and he was shown into M's study.

M had one of the stock bachelor's hobbies. He painted in water-colour. He painted only the wild orchids of England, in the meticulous but uninspired fashion of the naturalists of the nineteenth century. He was now at his painting-table up against the window, his broad back hunched over his drawing-board, with, in front of him, an extremely dim little flower in a tooth-glass full of water. When Bond came in and closed the door, M gave the flower one last piercingly inquisitive glance. He got to his feet with obvious reluctance. But he gave Bond one of his rare smiles and said, "Afternoon, James." (He had the sailor's meticulous observance of the exact midday.) "Happy Christmas and all that. Take a chair." M himself went behind his desk and sat down. He was about to come on duty. Bond automatically took his traditional place across the desk from his Chief.

M began to fill a pipe. "What the devil's the name of that fat American detective who's always fiddling about with orchids, those obscene hybrids from Venezuela and so forth? Then he comes sweating out of his orchid house, eats a gigantic meal of some foreign muck and solves the murder. What's he called?"

"Nero Wolfe, sir. They're written by a chap called Rex Stout. I like them."

"They're readable," condescended M. "But I was thinking of the orchid stuff in them. How in hell can a man like those disgusting flowers? Why, they're damned near animals, and their colours, all those pinks and mauves and the blotchy yellow tongues, are positively hideous! Now that"—M waved at the meagre little bloom in the tooth-glass—"that's the real thing. That's an Autumn Lady's Tresses—*spiranthes spiralis*, not that I care particularly. Flowers in England as late as October and should be under the ground by now. But I got this forced-late specimen from a man I know—assistant to a chap called Summerhayes who's the orchid king at Kew. My friend's experimenting with cultures of a fungus which oddly enough is a parasite on a lot of orchids, but, as the same time, gets eaten by the orchids and acts as its staple diet. Mycorhiza it's called." M gave another of his rare smiles. "But you needn't write it down. Just wanted to take a leaf out of this fellow Nero Wolfe's book. However"—M brushed the topic aside—"can't expect you to get excited about these things. Now then." He settled back. "What the devil have you been up to?" The grey eyes regarded Bond keenly. "Looks as if you haven't been getting much sleep. Pretty gay these winter sports places, they tell me."

Bond smiled. He reached into his inside pocket and took out the pinned sheets of paper. "This one provided plenty of miscellaneous entertainment, sir. Perhaps you'd like to have a look at my report first. 'Fraid it's only a draft. There wasn't much time. But I can fill in anything that isn't clear."

M reached across for the papers, adjusted his spectacles and began reading.

Soft rain scratched at the windows. A big log fell in the grate. The silence was soft and comfortable. Bond looked round the walls at M's treasured collection of naval prints. Everywhere there were mountainous seas, crashing cannon, bellying sails, tattered battle pennants—the fury of ancient engagements, the memories of ancient enemies, the French, the Dutch, the Spaniards, even the Americans. All gone, all friends now with one another. Not a sign of the enemies of today. Who was backing Blofeld, for instance, in the inscrutable conspiracy in which he was now certainly engaged? The Russians? The Chinese? Or was it an independent job, as Thunderball had been? And what was the conspiracy? What was the job for the protection of which six or seven of Blofeld's men had died within less than a week? Would M read anything into the evidence? Would the experts who were coming that afternoon? Bond lifted his left wrist. Remembered that he no longer had a watch. *That* he would certainly be allowed on expenses. He would get another one as soon as the shops opened after Boxing Day. Another Rolex? Probably. They were on the heavy side, but they worked. And at least you could see the time in the dark with those big phosphorus numerals. Somewhere in the hall, a clock struck the half-hour. 1.30. Twelve hours before, he must have just set up the trap that killed the three men in the Mercedes. Self-defence, but the hell of a way to celebrate Christmas!

M threw the papers down on his desk. His pipe had gone out and he now slowly lit it again. He tossed the spent match accurately over his shoulder into the fire. He put his hands flat on the desk and said—and there was an unusual kindness in his voice—"Well, you were pretty lucky to get out of that one, James. Didn't know you could ski."

"I only just managed to stay upright, sir. Wouldn't like to try it again."

"No. And I see you say you can't come to any conclusions about what Blofeld is up to?"

"That's right, sir. Haven't got a clue."

"Well, nor have I. I just don't understand any part of it. Perhaps the professors'll help us out this afternoon. But you're obviously right that it's SPECTRE all over again. By the way, your tip about Pontresina was a good one. He was a Bulgar. Can't remember his name, but Interpol turned him up for us. Plastic-explosives expert. Worked for KGB in Turkey. If it's true that the U.2 that fellow Powers was piloting was brought down by delayed charges and not by rockets, it may be this man was implicated. He was on the list of suspects. Then he turned free-lance. Went into business on his own. That's probably when SPECTRE picked him up. We were doubtful about your identification of Blofeld. The Pontresina lead helped a lot. You're absolutely sure of him, are you? He certainly seems to have done a good job on his face and stomach. Better set him up on the Identicast when you get back this evening. We'll have a look at him and get the views of the medical gentry."

"I think it must be him, sir. I was really getting the

uthentic smell of him on the last day—yesterday, that ;. It seems a long time ago already."

"You were lucky to run into this girl. Who is she? Some ld flame of yours?" M's mouth turned down at the orners.

"More or less, sir. She came into my report on the first ıews we got that Blofeld was in Switzerland. Daughter of his man Draco, head of the Union Corse. Her mother vas an English governess."

"Hm. Interesting breeding. Now then. Time for lunch. told Hammond we weren't to be disturbed." M got up ınd pressed the bell by the fire-place. " 'Fraid we've got o go through the turkey and plum-pudding routine. Mrs. Iammond's been brooding over her pots and pans for veeks. Damned sentimental rubbish."

Hammond appeared at the door, and Bond followed M hrough and into the small dining-room beyond the hall vhose walls glittered with M's other hobby, the evolution of the naval cutlass. They sat down. M said, with mock erocity, to Hammond, "All right, Chief Petty Officer Hammond. Do your worst." And then, with real vehemence, 'What in hell are those things doing here?" He pointed ıt the centre of the table.

"Crackers, sir," said Hammond stolidly. "Mrs. Hammond hought that seeing as you have company . . ."

"Throw them out. Give 'em to the school-children. I'll go so far with Mrs. Hammond, but I'm damned if I'm going to have my dining-room turned into a nursery."

Hammond smiled. He said, "Aye, aye, sir," gathered up the shimmering crackers and departed.

Bond was aching for a drink. He got a small glass of very old Marsala and most of a bottle of very bad Algerian wine.

M treated his two glasses as if they had been Château Lafitte. "Good old 'Infuriator.' Staple drink for the fleet in the Mediterranean. Got real guts to it. I remember an old shipmate of mine, McLachlan, my Chief Gunnery Officer at the time, betting he could get down six bottles of the stuff. Damn fool. Measured his length on the wardroom floor after only three. Drink up, James! Drink up!"

At last the plum-pudding arrived, flaming traditionally. Mrs. Hammond had implanted several cheap silver gewgaws in it and M nearly broke a tooth on the miniature horseshoe. Bond got the bachelor's button. He thought of Tracy. It should have been the ring!

21 THE MAN FROM AG. AND FISH.

They had coffee in M's study and smoked the thin black cheroots of which M allowed himself two a day. Bond burnt his tongue on his. M continued with his stories about the Navy which Bond could listen to all day—stories of battles, tornadoes, bizarre happenings, narrow shaves, courts martial, eccentric officers, neatly worded signals, as when Admiral Somerville, commanding the battleship *Queen Elizabeth*, had passed the liner *Queen Elizabeth* in mid-Atlantic and had signalled the one word "SNAP"! Perhaps it was all just the stuff of boys' adventure books, but it was all true and it was about a great navy that was no more and a great breed of officers and seamen that would never be seen again.

It was three o'clock. A car's wheels scrunched on the gravel outside. Dusk was already creeping into the room. M got up and switched on the lights and Bond arranged two more chairs up against the desk. M said, "That'll be 501. You'll have come across him. Head of the Scientific Research Section. And a man called Franklin from the Ministry of Agriculture. 501 says he's the top on his subject—Pest Control. Don't know why Ag. and Fish. chose to send him in particular, but the Minister told me they've got a bit of trouble on their hands, wouldn't tell even me what it is, and they think you may have run into something pretty big. We'll let them have a look at your report and see what they make of it. All right?"

"Yes, sir."

The door opened and the two men came in.

Number 501 of the Secret Service, whose name Bond remembered was Leathers, was a big-boned, rangy man with the stoop and thick spectacles of the stage scientist. He had a pleasant, vague smile and no deference, but only politeness, towards M. He was appropriately dressed in shaggy tweeds and his knitted woollen tie didn't cover his collar stud. The other man was small and brisk and keen-looking, with darting, amused eyes. As became a senior representative of a Ministry who had received his orders from his Minister in person and who knew nothing of Secret Services, he had put on a neat dark-blue pinstripe and a stiff white collar. His black shoes gleamed efficiently. So did the leather of his fat brief-case. His greeting was reserved, neutral. He wasn't quite sure where he was or what this was all about. He was going to smell his way carefully in this business, be wary of what he said and how far he committed his Ministry. Of such, Bond reflected, is "Government."

When the appropriate greetings and apologies for disturbed Christmases had been made, and they were in their chairs, M said, "Mr. Franklin, if you'll forgive my saying so, everything you are going to see and hear in this room is subject to the Official Secrets Act. You will no doubt be in possession of many secret matters affecting your own Ministry. I would be grateful if you would respect those of the Ministry of Defence. May I ask you to discuss what you are about to hear only with your Minister personally?"

Mr. Franklin made a little bow of acquiescence. "My Minister has already instructed me accordingly. My particular duties in the Ministry have accustomed me to handling Top Secret matters. You need have no reservations in what you tell me. Now then"—the amused eyes rested on each of the other three in turn—"perhaps you can tell me what this is all about. I know practically nothing except that a man on top of an alp is making efforts to improve our agriculture and livestock. Very decent of him. So why are we treating him as if he had stolen atomic secrets?"

"He did once, as a matter of fact," said M drily. "I think the best course would be for you and Mr Leathers to read the report of my representative here. It contains code numbers and other obscure references which need not concern you. The story tells itself without them." M handed Bond's report to 501. "Most of this will be new to you also. Perhaps you would like to read a page at a time and then pass them on to Mr. Franklin."

A long silence fell in the room. Bond looked at his fingernails and listened to the rain on the window-panes and the soft noises of the fire. M sat hunched up, apparently in a doze. Across the table the sheets of paper rustled slowly. Bond lit a cigarette. The rasp of his Ronson caused M's eyes to open lazily and then close again. 501 passed across the last page and sat back. Franklin finished his reading, shuffled the pages together and stacked them neatly in front of him. He looked at Bond and smiled. "You're lucky to be here."

Bond smiled back but said nothing.

M turned to 501. "Well?"

501 took off his thick spectacles and polished them on a none too clean handkerchief. "I don't get the object of the exercise, sir. It seems perfectly above-board—praise-

worthy, in fact, if we didn't know what we do know about Blofeld. Technically, what he has done is this. He has obtained ten, or rather eleven, counting the one that's left the place, suitable subjects for deep hypnosis. These are all simple girls from the country. It is significant that the one called Ruby had failed her G.C.E. twice. They seem to suffer, and there's no reason to believe that they don't, from certain fairly common forms of allergy. We don't know the origins of their allergies and these are immaterial. They are probably psychosomatic—the adverse reaction to birds is a very common one, as is the one brought on by cattle. The reactions to crops and plants are less common. Blofeld appears to be attempting cures of these allergies by hypnosis, and not only cures, but a pronounced affinity with the cause of the allergy in place of the previous repulsion. In the case of Ruby, for instance, she is told, in the words of the report, to 'love' chickens, to wish to 'improve their breed' and so forth. The mechanical means of the cure are, in practice, simple. In the twilight stage, on the edge of sleep—the sharp ringing of the bell would waken those who were already asleep—the use of the metronome exactly on the pulsebeat, and the distant whirring noise, are both common hypnotic aids. The singsong, authoritative murmur is the usual voice of the hypnotist. We have no knowledge of what lectures these girls attended or what reading they did, but we can assume that these were merely additional means to influence the mind in the path desired by Blofeld. Now, there is plenty of medical evidence for the efficacy of hypnosis. There are well-authenticated cases of the successful treatment by these means of such stubborn disabilities as warts, certain types of asthma, bed-wetting, stammering and even alcoholism, drug-taking and homosexual tendencies. Although the British Medical Association frowns officially on the practitioners of hypnosis, you would be surprised, sir, to know how many doctors themselves, as a last resort, particularly in cases of alcoholism, have private treatment from qualified hypnotists. But this is by the way. All I can contribute to this discussion is that Blofeld's ideas are not new and that they can be completely efficacious."

M nodded. "Thank you, Mr Leathers. Now would you like to be unscientific and hazard any wild guesses that would contribute in any way to what you have told us?" M smiled briefly. "You will not be quoted, I can assure you."

501 ran a worried hand through his hair. "Well, sir, it may be nonsense, but a train of thought came to me

as I read the report. This is a very expensive set-up of Blofeld's. Whether his intentions are benign or malignant, and I must say that I think we can accept them as being malignant, who is paying for all this? How did he fall upon this particular field of research and find the finance for it? Well, sir, this may sound fanciful, looking for burglars under the bed, so to speak, but the leaders in this field, ever since Pavlov and his salivating dogs, have been the Russians. If you recall, sir, at the time of the first human orbiting of the earth by the Russians, I put in a report on the physiology of the astronaut Yuri Gagarin. I drew attention to the simple nature of this man, his equable temperament when faced with his hysterical welcome in London. This equability never failed him and, if you will remember, we kept him under discreet observation throughout his visit and on his subsequent tours abroad, at the request of the Atomic Energy authorities. That bland, smiling face, sir, those wide-apart, innocent eyes, the extreme psychological simplicity of the man, all added up, as I said in my report, to the perfect subject for hypnosis, and I hazarded the guess that, in the extremely complicated movements required of him in his space capsule, Gagarin was operating throughout in a state of deep hypnosis. All right, sir"—501 made a throw-away gesture of his hand—"my conclusions were officially regarded an fanciful. But, since you ask, I now repeat them, and I throw out the suggestion that the Power behind Blofeld in all this may well be the Russians." He turned to Bond. "Was there any sign of Russian inspiration or guidance at this Gloria place? Any Russians anywhere in the offing?"

"Well, there was this man, Captain Boris. I never saw him, but he was certainly a Russian. Otherwise nothing I can think of except the three SPECTRE men who I'd guess were ex-Smersh. But they seemed definitely staff men, what the Americans would call 'mechanics.' "

501 shrugged. He said to M, "Well, I'm afraid that's all I can contribute, sir. But, if you come to the conclusion that this is dirty business, for my money, this Captain Boris was either the paymaster or supervisor of the scheme and Blofeld the independent operator. It would fit in with the free-lance character of the old SPECTRE—an independent gang working for whoever was willing to pay them."

"Perhaps you've got something there, Mr Leathers," said M reflectively. "But what the devil's the object of the exercise?" He turned to Franklin. "Well, now, Mr. Franklin, what do *you* think of all this?"

The man from Ag. and Fish. had lit a small, highly polished

pipe. He kept it between his teeth and reached down for his brief-case and took out some papers. From among them he extracted a black and white outline map of Britain and Eire and smoothed it down across the desk. The map was dotted with symbols, forests of them here, blank spaces there. He said, "This is a map showing the total agricultural and livestock resources of Britain and Eire, leaving out grassland and timber. Now, at my first sight of the report, I admit I was completely confused. As Mr. Leathers said, these experiments seem perfectly harmless—more than that, to use his word, praiseworthy. But"—Franklin smiled—"you gentlemen are concerned with searching for the dark side of the moon. I adjusted my mind accordingly. The result was that I am filled with a very deep and terrible suspicion. Perhaps these black thoughts have entered my mind by a process of osmosis with the present company's way of looking at the world"—he looked deprecatingly at M—"but I also have one piece of evidence which may be decisive. Excuse me, but there was one sheet of paper missing from the report—the list of the girls and their addresses. Is that available?"

Bond took the photostat out of his inside pocket. "Sorry. I didn't want to clutter up the report too much." He slipped it across the table to Franklin.

Franklin ran his eyes down it. Then he said, and there was awe in his voice, "I've got it! I do believe I've got it!" He sat back heavily in his chair as if he couldn't believe what he had seen.

The three men watched him tensely, believing him, because of what was written on his face—waiting for it.

Franklin took a red pencil out of his breast pocket and leaned over the map. Glancing from time to time at the list, he made a series of red circles at seemingly unrelated points across Britain and Eire, but Bond noticed that they covered the areas where the forests of symbols were at their densest. As he made the circles he commented, "Aberdeen—Aberdeen Angus, Devon—Red Poll, Lancashire—poultry, Kent—fruit, Shannon—potatoes," until ten red circles stood out on the map. Finally he poised his pencil over East Anglia and made a big cross. He looked up, said "Turkeys" and threw his pencil down.

In the silence that followed, M said, rather testily, "Well, Mr Franklin, what have you in mind?"

The man from Ag. and Fish. had no intention of being pushed about by someone, however grand and hush-hush, from another Ministry. He bent and dug again into his brief-case. He came up with several papers. He selected one, a newspaper cutting. He said, "I don't expect you gentlemen have time to read much of the agricultural news in the paper, but this is from the *Daily Telegraph* of early December. I won't read it all. It's from their agricultural correspondent, good man by the name of Thomas. These are the headlines: 'CONCERN OVER TURKEYS. FLOCKS RAVAGED BY FOWL PEST.' Then it goes on: 'Supplies of turkeys to the Christmas market may be hit by recent fowl pest outbreaks which have resulted in large numbers of birds being slaughtered. . . .' and further down, 'Figures available show that 218,000 birds have been slaughtered . . . last year, total supplies for the Christmas market were estimated at between 3,700,000 and 4,000,000 birds, so much will depend now on the extent of further fowl pest outbreaks."

Mr. Franklin put the cutting down. He said seriously, "That news was only the tip of the iceberg. We managed to keep later details out of the press. But I can tell you this, gentlemen. Within the past four weeks or so we have slaughtered three million turkeys. And that's only the beginning of it. Fowl pest is running wild in East Anglia and there are signs of it in Suffolk and Hampshire, where a lot of turkey-raising goes on. What you ate at lunch today was almost certainly a foreign bird. We allowed the import of two million from America to cover up this position."

M said sourly, "Well, so far as I'm concerned, I don't care if I never eat another turkey again. However, I see you've had quite a problem on your hands. But to get back to our case. Where do we go from turkeys?"

Franklin was not amused. He said, "We have one clue. All the birds that died first were exhibited at the National Poultry Show at Olympia early this month. Olympia had been cleared and cleaned out for the next exhibition before we had reached that conclusion, and we could find no trace on the premises of the virus—Fowl Pest is a virus, by the way, highly infectious, with a mortality of one hundred per cent. Now then"—he held up a stout white pamphlet with the insignia of the United States on it—"how much do you gentlemen know about Biological Warfare?"

Leathers said, "We were indirectly concerned in the fringes of the subject during the war. But in the end neither side used it. Around 1944 the Americans had a plan for destroying the whole of the Japanese rice crop by the use of aerial sprays. But, as I recall, Roosevelt vetoed the idea."

"Right," said Franklin. "Dead right. But the subject is still very much alive. And very much so in my Ministry. We happen to be the most highly agriculturalized country in the world. We had to make ourselves so during the war to keep ourselves from starvation. So, in theory, we would be an ideal target for an attack of this kind." He slowly brought his hands down on the table for emphasis. "I don't think it would be too much to say, gentlemen, that if such an attack could be launched, and it can only be countered by slaughtering the poultry and animals and burning the crops, we would be a bankrupt country within a matter of months. We would literally be down on our knees, begging for bread!"

"Never thought of that," said M reflectively, "but it seems to make sense."

"Now this," continued Franklin, holding up the pamphlet, "is the latest thinking on the subject by our friends in America. It also covers Chemical and Radiological Warfare, but we're not concerned with those—CW, BW and RW they call them. It's a United States Senate paper, Number 58991, dated August 29th, 1960, prepared by 'The Subcommittee on Disarmament of the Committee on Foreign Relations.' My Ministry goes along with the general findings on BW, with the reservation that America is a vast country and we are a very small and tightly packed one. BW would hit us a thousand times harder than it would hit the States. May I read you a few extracts?"

M positively loathed the problems of other Ministries. In the end, on the Intelligence side, they all ended up on his plate. Bond, amused, watched him summon an expression of polite interest. "Go ahead, Mr Franklin."

22 SOMETHING CALLED "BW"

Franklin began reading in an even, expository tone of voice, frequently stopping to explain a point or when he skipped irrelevant passages.

"This section," he said, "is headed 'Biological Warfare Weapons and Defense.' This is how it goes on:

" 'Biological Warfare,' " he read, " 'is often referred to as bacteriological, bacterial or germ warfare but it is preferred over those terms because it includes all micro-organisms, insects and other pests, and toxic products of plant and animal life. The Army lists five groups of BW agents, including certain chemical compounds used to inhibit or destroy plant growth:

Microorganisms (bacteria, viruses, rickettsiae, fungi, protozoa).

Toxins (microbial, animal, plant).
Vectors of disease (arthropods [insects and acarids], birds and animals).
Pests (of animals and crops).
Chemical anticrop compounds (plant-growth inhibitors, herbicides, defoliants).

" 'Biological Warfare agents, like Chemical Warfare agents, vary in lethality, making it possible to select an agent best suited to accomplish the objective desired, whether it be temporary incapacity with little after-effects or serious illness and many deaths. There are some important differences between BW and CW other than their scientific classifications. BW agents have an incubation period of days, sometimes weeks' "—Franklin looked up. "See what I mean about Olympia?"—" 'which produces a lag in their action while CW weapons usually bring reactions within a few seconds to a few hours. CW agents are easier to detect than BW agents, and identification of the latter could often be too late to permit effective countermeasures.' "—Franklin again looked significantly at his audience—" '. . . BW agents theoretically are more dangerous, weight for weight, than CW agents, though this advantage may be canceled because of loss of virulence by BW agents under exposure.' "

Franklin paused. His finger went down the page. "Then it goes on to talk about antipersonnel BW agents like anthrax, typhus, smallpox, botulism and so on. Yes"—his finger stopped—"here we are." "Antianimal BW agents which might be used to incapacitate or destroy domestic animals are:

Bacteria: Anthrax, three closely related species of brucella, and glanders.
Viruses: Foot-and-mouth disease, rinderpest, Rift Valley fever, vesicular stomatitis, vesicular exanthema, hog cholera, African swine fever, fowl plague, Newcastle disease, and equine encephalomyelitis.' "

Franklin looked up apologetically. "Sorry about all this jaw-breaking stuff, but there's not much more of it. Then it goes on to 'Anticrop BW agents,' which they say would be used as economic weapons, as I personally think is the case with the Blofeld scheme, and they mention a whole list including potato blight, cereal stem disease, crown rust of oats, curly top disease of sugar beets, block rot of crucifers and potato ring rot, and insects such as the Colorado beetle and something called 'the Giant African

Land-snail,' which I somehow don't think we need worry about. Then they talk about 'chemical anticrop agents,' but I don't think we need worry about those either as they'd have to be sprayed from an aeroplane, though, for what it's worth, they're damned lethal. Now, this is more to the point." Franklin's finger halted on the page. " 'The nature of BW agents makes them very adaptable for covert or undercover operations. The fact that these agents are so concentrated, cannot be detected by physical senses, and have a delayed casualty effect would enable an operator quietly to introduce effective amounts into building-ventilation systems, food and water supplies, and other places where they would be spread rapidly through contact with a heavily concentrated population.' " Franklin paused. "And that means us. You see what I mean about livestock shows and so on? After the show, the virus gets carried off all over the country by the exhibits." He went back to his pamphlet. "And here it goes on, 'A significant factor is that the possible area of effective coverage is generally greater with BW than with CW agents. Tests have been made which show that coverage measured in the thousands of square miles is quite feasible with biological agents.' " Franklin tapped the paper in front of him. "How about that, gentlemen? We talk about the new poison gases, the nerve gases the Germans invented in the war. We march and counter-march about radiation and the atom bomb. 'Thousands of square miles' it says here. A Committee of the United States Senate says it. How many thousands of square miles are there in the United Kingdom and Eire, gentlemen?" The eyes, urgent and holding humour no longer, looked almost scornfully into the faces of these three top officers of the Secret Service. "I'll tell you. There are only something over one hundred thousand square miles of this little atoll of ours, including the little atoll of all Ireland." His eyes retained their fire. "And let me just give you a last quote and then perhaps"—the eyes regained some of their humour—"you'll realize why I'm getting so steamed up on this Day of Goodwill to all Men. Look here, what it says under 'Defensive Measures.' It says, 'Defense against BW warfare is greatly complicated by the difficulties involved in detection of BW agents, a situation which is almost unique as to these weapons.' " Franklin looked up and now he smiled. "Bad English. Perhaps we might improve on 'as to.' 'They cannot be detected by sight, smell or any other physical sense. So far no means have been devised for their quick detection and identification.' "

Franklin threw the pamphlet on to the desk. Suddenly

he gave a big, embracing smile. He reached for his little polished pipe and began filling it. "All right, gentlemen. The prosecution rests."

Franklin had had his day, a Christmas he would never forget.

M said, "Thank you, Mr Franklin. Am I right in thinking that you conclude that this man Blofeld is mounting Biological Warfare against this country?"

"Yes." Franklin was definite. "I am."

"And how do you work that out? It seems to me he's doing exactly the opposite—or rather it would if I didn't know something about the man. Anyway, what are your deductions?"

Franklin reached over and pointed to the red cross he had made over East Anglia. "That was my first clue. The girl, Polly Tasker, who left this Gloria place over a month ago, came from somewhere round here where you'll see from the symbols that there's the greatest concentration of turkey farmers. She suffered from an allergy against turkeys. She came back inspired to improve the breed. Within a week of her return, we have the biggest outbreak of Fowl Pest affecting turkeys in the history of England."

Leathers suddenly slapped his thigh. "By God, I think you've got it, Franklin! Go on!"

"Now"—Franklin turned to Bond—"When this officer took a look into the laboratory up there he saw rack upon rack of test-tubes containing what he describes as 'a cloudy liquid.' How would it be if those were viruses, Fowl Pest, anthrax, God knows what all? The report mentions that the laboratory was lit with a dim red light. That would be correct. Virus cultures suffer from exposure to bright light. And how would it be if before this Polly girl left she was given an aerosol spray of the right stuff and told that this was some kind of turkey elixir—a tonic to make them grow fatter and healthier. Remember that stuff about 'improving the breed' in the hypnosis talk? And suppose she was told to go to Olympia for the Show, perhaps even take a job for the meeting as a cleaner or something, and just casually spray this aerosol here and there among the prize birds. It wouldn't be bigger than one of those shaving-soap bombs. That'd be quite enough. She'd been told to keep it secret, that it was patent stuff. Perhaps even that she'd be given shares in the company if the tonic proved the success this man Blofeld claimed it would. It'd be quite easy to do. She'd just wander round the cages—perhaps she was even given a special purse to carry the thing in—lean up against the wire and psst! the job would be done. Easy as falling off a log. All right, if you'll go along with me so far, she was probably told to do the job on one of the last two days of the show, so that the effects wouldn't be seen too soon. Then, at the end of the show, all the prize birds are dispersed back to their owners all over England. And that's that! And"—he paused—"mark you, that *was* that. Three million birds dead and still dying all over the place, and a great chunk of foreign currency coughed up by the Treasury to replace them."

Leathers, his face red with excitement, butted in. He swept his hand over the map. "And the other girls! All from the danger spots. All from the areas of greatest concentration. Local shows taking place all the time—cattle, poultry, even potatoes—Colorado beetle for that crop, I suppose, swine fever for the pigs. Golly!" There was reverence in Leathers's voice. "And it's so damned simple! All you'd need would be to keep the viruses at the right temperature for a while. They'd be instructed in that, the little darlings. And all the time they'd be sure they were being saints! Marvellous. I really must hand it to the man."

M's face was thunderous with the fury of his indecision. He turned to Bond. He barked, "What do you think?"

"I'm afraid it fits, sir. The whole way along the line. We know the man. It fits him too. Right up his street. And it doesn't even matter who's paying him. He can pay himself, make a fortune. All he has to do is go a bear of sterling or Gilt-Edged. If Mr. Franklin's right, and that Senate paper's pretty solid backing for him, our currency'll literally go through the floor—and the country with it."

M got to his feet. He said, "All right, gentlemen. Mr. Franklin, will you tell your Minister what you've heard? It'll be up to him to tell the P.M. and the Cabinet as he thinks fit. I'll get on with the preventive measures, first of all through Sir Ronald Vallance of the C.I.D. We must pick up this Polly woman and get the others as they come into the country. They'll be gently treated. It's not their fault. Then we'll have to think what to do with Mister Blofeld." He turned to Bond. "Stay behind, would you?"

Goodbyes were said and M rang for Hammond to see the other two out. He then rang again. "Tea, please, Hammond." He turned to Bond. "Or rather have a whisky and soda?"

"Whisky, please, sir," said Bond with infinite relief.

"Rot-gut," commented M. He walked over to the window and looked out at the darkness and rain.

Bond drew Franklin's map towards him and studied it.

He reflected that he was learning quite a lot on this case—about other people's business, other people's secrets, from the innards of the College of Arms to the innards of Ag. and Fish. Odd how this gigantic, many-branched tree had grown from one tiny seed in September—a girl calling banco in a casino and not having the money to pay. And what about Bond's letter of resignation? That looked pretty silly now. He was up to his ears, as deeply as ever in his life before, in his old profession. And now a big mopping-up job would have to be done. And he would have to do it, or at any rate lead it, organize it. And Bond knew exactly what he was going to put to M when the tea and whisky came. Only *he* could do the cleaning up. It was written in his stars!

Hammond came in with the tray and withdrew. M came back to his desk, gruffly told Bond to pour himself a whisky, and himself took a vast cup, as big as a baby's chamber-pot, of black tea without sugar or milk, and put it in front of him.

At length he said moodily, "This is a dirty business, James. But I'm afraid it makes sense. Better do something about it, I suppose." He reached for the red telephone with scrambler attachment that stood beside the black one on his desk and picked up the receiver. It was a direct line to that very private switchboard in Whitehall to which perhaps fifty people in all Britain have access. "Put me on to Sir Ronald Vallance, would you? Home number, I suppose." He reached out and took a deep gulp at his cup of tea and put the cup back on its saucer. Then, "That you, Vallance? M here. Sorry to disturb your afternoon nap." There was an audible explosion at the other end of the line! M smiled. "Reading a report on teen-age prostitution? I'm ashamed of you. On Christmas Day too. Well, scramble, would you?" M pressed down the large black button on the side of the cradle. "Right? Now I'm afraid this is top priority. Remember Blofeld and the Thunderball case? Well, he's up to his tricks again. Too long to explain now. You'll get my side of the report in the morning. And Ag. and Fish. are mixed up in it. Yes, of all people. Man called Franklin is your contact. One of their top pest-control men. Only him and his Minister. So would your chaps report to him, copy to me? I'm only dealing with the foreign side. Your friend 007's got the ball. Yes, same chap. He can fill you in with any extra detail you may need on the foreign angles. Now, the point is this. Even though it's Christmas and all that, could your chaps try at once and lay their hands on a certain girl, Polly Tasker, aged about

25, who lives in East Anglia? Yes, I know it's a hell of a big area, but she'll probably come from a respectable lower-middle-class family connected with turkey farming. Certainly find the family in the telephone book. Can't give you any description, but she's just been spending several weeks in Switzerland. Got back the last week in November. Don't be ridiculous! Of course you can manage it. And when you find her, take her into custody for importing Fowl Pest into the country. Yes, that's right." M spelt it out. "The stuff that's been killing all our turkeys." M muttered "Thank God!" away from the receiver. "No, I didn't say anything. Now, be kind to the girl. She didn't know what she was doing. And tell the parents it'll be all right. If you need a formal charge, you'll have to get one out of Franklin. Then tell Franklin when you've got her and he'll come down and ask her one or two simple questions. When he's got the answers, you can let her go. Right? But we've *got* to find that girl. You'll see why all right when you've read the report. Now then, next assignment. There are ten girls of much the same type as this Polly Tasker who'll probably be flying from Zürich to England and Eire any day from tomorrow on. Each one has got to be held by the Customs at the port or airport of entry. 007 has a list of their names and fairly good descriptions. My people in Zürich may or may not be able to give us warning of their arrival. Is that all right? Yes, 007 will bring the list to Scotland Yard this evening. No, I can't tell you what it's all about. Too long a story. But have you ever heard of Biological Warfare? That's right. Anthrax and so on. Well, this is it. Yes. Blofeld again. I know. That's what I'm just going to talk to 007 about. Well now, Vallance, have you got all that? Fine." M listened. He smiled grimly. "And a Happy Christmas to *you*."

He put the receiver back and the scrambler button automatically clicked to OFF. He looked across at Bond. He said, with a hint of weariness, "Well, that's taken care of this end. Vallance said it was about time we had this fellow Blofeld in the bag. I agree. And that's *our* job. And I don't for a moment think we're going to get any help from the Swiss. Even if we were to, they'd trample all over the case with their big boots for weeks before we saw any action. By that time the man would be in Peking or somewhere, cooking up something else." M looked straight at Bond. "Any ideas?"

It had come, as Bond knew it would. He took a deep pull at his whisky and put the glass carefully down. He began talking, urgently, persuasively. As he expounded his plan, M's face sank deeper and deeper in gloom, and, when Bond concluded with "And that's the only way I can see, sir. All I need is two weeks' leave of absence. I could put in a letter of resignation if it would help." M turned in his chair and gazed deep into the dying flames of the log fire.

Bond sat quietly, waiting for the verdict. He hoped it would be yes, but he also hoped it would be no. That damned mountain! He never wanted to see the bloody thing again!

M turned back. The grey eyes were fierce. "All right, 007. Go ahead. I can't go to the P.M. about it. He'd refuse. But for God's sake bring it off. I don't mind being sacked, but we don't want to get the Government mixed up in another U.2 fiasco. Right?"

"I understand, sir. And I can have the two weeks' leave?"

"Yes."

23 GAULOISES AND GARLIC

With the Walther PPK in its leather holster warm against his stomach and his own name in his passport, James Bond looked out of the window at the English Channel sliding away beneath the belly of the Caravelle and felt more like his old, his pre-Sir-Hilary-Bray, self.

He glanced at the new Rolex on his wrist—the shops were still shut and he had had to blarney it out of Q Branch—and guessed they would be on time, 6 P.M. at Marseilles. It had been the hell of a rush to get off. He had worked until late in the night at H.Q. and all that morning, setting up the Identicast of Blofeld, checking details with Ronnie Vallance, fixing up the private, the Munich side of his life, chattering on the teleprinter to Station Z, even remembering to tell Mary Goodnight to get on to Sable Basilisk after the holiday and ask him to please do some kind of a job on the surnames of the ten girls and please to have the family tree of Ruby Windsor embellished with gold capitals.

At midnight he had called Tracy in Munich and heard her darling, excited voice. "I've got the toothbrush, James," she had said, "and a pile of books. Tomorrow I'm going to go up the Zugspitze and sit in the sun so as to look pretty for you. Guess what I had for dinner tonight in my room! Krebsschwänze mit Dilltunke. That's crayfish tails with rice and a cream and dill sauce. And Rehrücken mit Sahne. That's saddle of roebuck with a smitane sauce. I bet it was better than what you had."

"I had two ham sandwiches with stacks of mustard and half a pint of Harper's bourbon on the rocks. The bourbon was better than the ham. Now listen, Tracy, and stop blowing down the telephone."

"I was only sighing with love."

"Well, you must have got a Force Five sigh. Now listen. I'm posting my birth certificate to you tomorrow with a covering letter to the British Consul saying I want to get married to you as soon as possible. Look, you're going up to Force Ten! For God's sake pay attention. It'll take a few days, I'm afraid. They have to post the banns or something. He'll tell you all about it. Now, you must quickly get your birth certificate and give it to him too. Oh, you have, have you?" Bond laughed. "So much the better. Then we're all set. I've got three days or so of work to do and I'm going down to see your father tomorrow and ask for your hand, both of them, and the feet and all the rest, in marriage. No, you're to stay where you are. This is men's talk. Will he be awake? I'm going to ring him up now. Good. Well, now you go off to sleep or you'll be too tired to say 'Yes' when the time comes."

They had not wanted to let go of each other's voices, but finally the last good night, the last kiss, had been exchanged, and Bond called the Marseilles number of Appareils Électriques Draco, and Marc-Ange's voice, almost as excited as Tracy's, was on the line. Bond dampened down the raptures about the "fiançailles" and said, "Now listen, Marc-Ange. I want you to give me a wedding-present."

"Anything, my dear James. Anything I possess." He laughed. "And perhaps certain things of which I could take possession. What is it you would like?"

"I'll tell you tomorrow evening. I'm booked on the afternoon Air France to Marseilles. Will you have someone meet me? And it's business, I'm afraid. So could you have your other directors present for a little meeting? We shall need all our brains. It is about our sales organization in Switzerland. Something drastic needs to be done about it."

"Aha!" There was full understanding in the voice. "Yes, it is indeed a bad spot on our sales map. I will certainly have my colleagues available. And I assure you, my dear James, that anything that can be done will be done. And of course you will be met. I shall perhaps not be there in person—it is very cold out these winter evenings. But shall see that you are properly looked after. Good night, ny dear fellow. Good night."

The line had gone dead. The old fox! Had he thought Bond might commit an indiscretion, or had he got fitted o his telephone a "bug-meter," the delicate instrument hat measures the resonance on the line and warns of istening-in?

The winter sun spread a last orange glow over the thick vercast 10,000 feet below the softly whistling plane and witched itself off for the night.

Bond dozed, reflecting that he must somehow, and pretty oon, find a way of catching up on his sleep.

There was a stage-type Marseilles taxi-driver to meet Bond—the archetype of all Mariuses, with the face of . pirate and the razor-sharp badinage of the lower French nusic-halls. He was apparently known and enjoyed by veryone at the airport, and Bond was whisked through he formalities in a barrage of wise-cracks about "le nilord anglais," which made Marius, for his name turned ut in fact to be Marius, the centre of attraction and Bond nerely his butt, the dim-witted English tourist. But, once n the taxi, Marius made curt, friendly apologies over is shoulder. "I ask your pardon for my bad manners." His French had suddenly purified itself of all patois. It lso smelt like acetylene gas. "I was told to extract you rom the airport with the least possible lime-light directed pon you. I know all those 'flics' and douaniers. They ll know me. If I had not been myself, the cab-driver they now as Marius, if I had shown deference, eyes, inquisitive yes, would have been upon you, mon commandant. I lid what I thought best. You forgive me?"

"Of course I do, Marius. But you shouldn't have been o funny. You nearly made me laugh. That would have een fatal."

"You understand our talk here?"

"Enough of it."

"So!" There was a pause. Then Marius said, "Alas, ince Waterloo, one can never underestimate the English."

Bond said, seriously, "The same date applied to the French. t was a near thing." This was getting too gallant. Bond aid, "Now tell me, is the bouillabaisse chez Guido always s good?"

"It is passable," said Marius. "But this is a dish that s dead, gone. There is no more true bouillabaisse, because here is no more fish in the Mediterranean. For the bouil-abaisse, you must have the rascasse, the tender flesh of he scorpion fish. Today they just use hunks of morue.

The saffron and the garlic, they are always the same. But you could eat pieces of a woman soaked in those and it would be good. Go to any of the little places down by the harbour. Eat the plat du jour and drink the vin du Cassis that they give you. It will fill your stomach as well as it fills the fishermen's. The toilette will be filthy. What does that matter? You are a man. You can walk up the Canebière and do it at the Noailles for nothing after lunch."

They were now weaving expertly through the traffic down the famous Canebière and Marius needed all his breath to insult the other drivers. Bond could smell the sea. The accordions were playing in the cafés. He remembered old times in this most criminal and tough of all French towns. He reflected that it was rather fun, this time, being on the side of the devil.

At the bottom of the Canebière, where it crosses the Rue de Rome, Marius turned right and then left into the Rue St Ferréol, only a long stone's throw from the Quai des Belges and the Vieux Port. The lights from the harbour's entrance briefly winked at them and then the taxi drew up at a hideous, but very new apartment house with a broad vitrine on the ground floor, which announced in furious neon "Appareils Electriques Draco." The well-lit interior of the store contained what you would expect—television sets, radios, gramophones, electric irons, fans and so forth. Marius very quickly carried Bond's suitcase across the pavement and through the swing doors beside the vitrine. The close-carpeted hallway was more luxurious than Bond had expected. A man came out of the porter's lodge beside the lift and wordlessly took the suitcase. Marius turned to Bond, gave him a smile and a wink and a bone-crushing handshake, said curtly, "A la prochaine," and hurried out. The porter stood beside the open door of the lift. Bond noticed the bulge under his right arm and, out of curiosity, brushed against the man as he entered the lift. Yes, and something big, too, a real stopper. The man gave Bond a bored look, as much as to say, "Clever, Eh?" and pressed the top button. The porter's twin, or very nearly his twin—dark, chunky, brown-eyed, fit—was waiting at the top floor. He took Bond's suitcase and led the way down a corridor, close-carpeted and with wall brackets in good taste. He opened a door. It was an extremely comfortable bedroom with a bathroom leading off. Bond imagined that the big picture window, now curtained, would have a superb view of the harbour. The man put down his suitcase and said, "Monsieur Draco est immédiatement àvotre disposition."

Bond thought it time to make some show of independence. said firmly, "Un moment, je vous en prie," and went o the bathroom and cleaned himself up—amused to tice that the soap was that most English of soaps, Pears ansparent, and that there was a bottle of Mr Trumper's ucris" beside the very masculine brush and comb by nt. Marc-Ange was indeed making his English guest l at home!

Bond took his time, then went out and followed the n to the end door. The man opened it without knocking d closed it behind Bond. Marc-Ange, his creased walnut e split by his great golden-toothed smile, got up from desk (Bond was getting tired of desks!), trotted across broad room, threw his arms round Bond's neck and sed him squarely on both cheeks. Bond suppressed his oil and gave a reassuring pat to Marc-Ange's broad ck. Marc-Ange stood away and laughed. "All right! I ear never to do it again. It is once and for ever. Yes? t it had to come out—from the Latin temperament, isn't You forgive me? Good. Then come and take a drink"—he ved at a loaded sideboard—"and sit down and tell what I can do for you. I swear not to talk about Teresa til you have finished with your business. But tell me"—the own eyes pleaded—"it is all right between you? You ve not changed your mind?"

Bond smiled. "Of course not, Marc-Ange. And everything arranged. We will be married within the week. At consulate in Munich. I have two weeks' leave. I thought might spend the honeymoon in Kitzbühel. I love that ce. So does she. You will come to the wedding?"

"Come to the wedding!" Marc-Ange exploded. "You ll have a time keeping me away from Kitzbühel. Now n"—he waved at the sideboard—"take your drink while compose myself. I must stop being happy and be clever tead. My two best men, my organizers if you like, are iting. I wanted to have you for a moment to myself."

Bond poured himself a stiff Jack Daniel's sourmash bourbon the rocks and added some water. He walked over to desk and took the right-hand of the three chairs at had been arranged in a semicircle facing the "Capu." wanted that too, Marc-Ange. Because there are some ings I must tell you which affect my country. I have en granted leave to tell them to you, but they must remain, you put it, behind the Herkos Odonton—behind the dge of your teeth. Is that all right?"

Marc-Ange lifted his right hand and crossed his heart, wly, deliberately, with his forefinger. His face was now

deadly serious, almost cruelly implacable. He leaned forw
and rested his forearms on the desk. "Continue."

Bond told him the whole story, not even omitting
passage with Ruby. He had developed much love, and to
respect, for this man. He couldn't say why. It was pa
animal magnetism and partly that Marc-Ange had so ope
his heart to Bond, so completely trusted him with
own innermost secrets.

Marc-Ange's face remained impassive throughout. O
his quick, animal eyes flickered continually across Bon
face. When Bond had finished, Marc-Ange sat back.
reached for a blue packet of Gauloises, fixed one in
corner of his mouth and talked through the blue clo
of smoke that puffed continuously out through his li
as if somewhere inside him there was a small steam-engi
"Yes, it is indeed a dirty business. It must be finished wi
destroyed, and the man too. My dear James"—the vo
was sombre—"I am a criminal, a great criminal. I r
houses, chains of prostitutes, I smuggle, I sell protecti
whenever I can, I steal from the very rich. I break ma
laws and I have often had to kill in the process. Perha
one day, perhaps very soon, I shall reform. But it is diffic
to step down from being Capu of the Union. Without
protection of my men, my life would not be worth mu
However, we shall see. But this Blofeld, he is too ba
too disgusting. You have come to ask the Union to ma
war on him, to destroy him. You need not answer.
know it is so. This is something that cannot be done officia
Your Chief is correct. You would get nowhere with
Swiss. You wish me and my men to do the job."
smiled suddenly. "That is the wedding-present you talk
of. Yes?"

"That's right, Marc-Ange. But I'll do my bit. I'll
there too. I want this man for myself."

Marc-Ange looked at him thoughtfully. "That I
not like. And you know why I do not like it." He sa
mildly, "You are a bloody fool, James. You are alrea
lucky to be alive." He shrugged. "But I am wasting
breath. You started on a long road after this man. A
you want to come to the end of it. Is that right?"

"That's right. I don't want someone else to shoot
fox."

"O.K., O.K. We bring in the others, yes? They w
not need to know the reason why. My orders are my orde
But we all need to know *how* we are to bring this abo
I have some ideas. I think it can be done and swiftly do

t it must also be well done, cleanly done. There must no untidiness about this thing."

Marc-Ange picked up his telephone and spoke into A minute later the door opened and two men came and, with hardly a glance at Bond, took the other two ıirs.

Marc-Ange nodded at the one next to Bond, a great of a man with the splayed ears and broken nose of oxer or wrestler. "This is Ché-Ché—Ché-ché le Persuadeur. d"—Marc-Ange smiled grimly—"is he very adept at suading."

Bond got a glimpse of two hard yellow-brown eyes t looked at him quickly, reluctantly, and then went :k to the Capu. "Plaisir."

"And this is Toussaint, otherwise known as 'Le Pouff.' is our expert with le plastique. We shall need plenty plastique."

"We shall indeed," said Bond, "with pretty quick time-ıcils."

Toussaint leaned forward to show himself. He was thin l grey-skinned, with an almost fine Phoenician profile ted with smallpox. Bond guessed that he was on heroin, t not as a mainliner. He gave Bond a brief, conspiratorial ile. "Plaisir." He sat back.

"And this"—Marc-Ange gestured at Bond—"is my friend. absolute friend. He is simply 'Le Commandant.' And w to business." He had been speaking in French, but now broke into rapid Corsican which, apart from a Italian and French roots, was incomprehensible to nd. At one period he drew a largescale map of Switzerland t of a drawer of his desk, spread it out, searched with finger and pointed to a spot in the centre of the Engadine. e two men craned forward, examined the map carefully l then sat back. Ché-Ché said something which contained word Strasbourg and Marc-Ange nodded enthusiastically. turned to Bond and handed him a large sheet of paper l a pencil. "Be a good chap and get to work on this, uld you? A map of the Gloria buildings, with approximate es and distances from each other. Later we will do a nplete maquette in plasticine so that there is no confusion. ery man will have his job to do"—he smiled—"like the nmandos in the war. Yes?"

Bond bent to his task while the others talked. The telephone ıg. Marc-Ange picked it up. He jotted down a few words l rang off. He turned to Bond, his eyes momentarily picious. "It is a telegram for me from London signed

Universal. It says, 'The birds have assembled in the to and all fly tomorrow.' What is this, my friend?"

Bond kicked himself for his forgetfulness. "I'm sor Marc-Ange. I meant to tell you you might get a signal l that. It means that the girls are in Zürich and are fly to England tomorrow. It is very good news. It was import to have them out of the way."

"Ah, good! Very good indeed! That is fine news. A you were quite right not to have the telegram addres to you. You are not supposed to be here or to know at all. It is better so." He fired some more Corsican the two men. They nodded their understanding.

After that, the meeting soon broke up. Marc-Ange exami Bond's handiwork and passed it over to Toussaint. T man glanced at the sketch and folded it as if it were valuable share-certificate. With short bows in Bond's directi the two men left the room.

Marc-Ange sat back with a sigh of satisfaction. goes well," he said. "The whole team will receive g danger money. And they love a good rough fight. A they are pleased that I am coming to lead them." laughed slyly. "They are less certain of you, my dear Jam They say you will get in the way. I had to tell them t you could outshoot and outfight the lot of them. Wher say something like that, they have to believe me. have never let them down yet. I hope I am right?"

"Please don't try me," said Bond. "I've never taken a Corsican and I don't want to start now."

Marc-Ange was delighted. "You might win with gu But not in close combat. They are pigs, my men. Gr pigs. The greatest. I am taking five of the best. With y and me that is seven. How many did you say there on the mountain?"

"About eight. And the big one."

"Ah yes, the big one," said Marc-Ange reflectively. "T is one that must not get away." He got up. "And n my friend, I have ordered dinner, a good dinner, to served us up here. And then we will go to bed stinking garlic and, perhaps, just a little bit drunk. Yes?"

From his heart Bond said, "I can't think of anyth better."

24 BLOOD-LIFT

The next day, after lunch, Bond made his way by plane and train to the Hotel Maison Rouge at Strasbourg, his breath bearing him close company like some noisome, captive pet.

He was totally exhilarated by his hours with Marc-Ange in Marseilles and by the prospects before him—the job that was to be done and, at the end of it, Tracy.

The morning had been an endless series of conferences round the model of Piz Gloria and its buildings that had been put up in the night. New faces came, received their orders in a torrent of dialect and disappeared—rough, murderous faces, bandits' faces, but all bearing one common expression, devotion to their Capu. Bond was vastly impressed by the authority and incisiveness of Marc-Ange as he dealt with each problem, each contingency, from the obtaining of a helicopter down to the pensions that would be paid to the families of the dead. Marc-Ange hadn't liked the helicopter business. He had explained to Bond, "You see, my friend, there is only one source for this machine, the O.A.S., the French secret army of the right wing. It happens that they are under an obligation to me, a heavy one, and that is the way I would have it. I do not like being mixed up in politics. I like the country where I operate to be orderly, peaceful. I do not like revolutions. They make chaos everywhere. Today, I never know when an operation of my own is not going to be interfered with by some damned emergency concerning Algerian terrorists, the rounding up of some nest of these blasted O.A.S. And road blocks! House-to-house searches! They are the bane of my existence. My men can hardly move without falling over a nest of flics or S.D.T. spies—that, as I'm sure you know, is the latest of the French Secret Services. They are getting as bad as the Russians with their constant changes of initials. It is the Section Défense Territoire. It comes under the Ministry of the Interior and I am finding it most troublesome and difficult to penetrate. Not like the good old Deuxième. It makes life for the peace-loving very difficult. But I naturally have my men in the O.A.S. and I happen to know that the O.A.S. has a military helicopter, stolen from the French Army, hidden away at a château on the Rhine not far from Strasbourg. The château belongs to some crazy fascist count. He is one of those Frenchmen who cannot live without conspiring against something. So now he has put all his money and property behind this General Salan. His château is remote. He poses as an inventor. His farm people are not surprised that there is some kind of flying machine kept in an isolated barn with mechanics to tend it—O.A.S. mechanics, bien entendu. And now, early this morning, I have spoken on my radio to the right man and I have the machine on loan for twenty-four hours with the best pilot in their secret air force. He is already on his way to the place to make his preparations, fuel and so on. But it is unfortunate. Before, these people were in my debt. Now I am in theirs." He shrugged. "What matter? I will soon have them under my thumb again. Half the police and Customs officers in France are Corsicans. It is an important laissez-passer for the Union Corse. You understand?"

At the Maison Rouge, a fine room had been booked for Bond. He was greeted with exaggerated courtesy tinged with reserve. Where didn't the Freemasonry of the Union operate? Bond, obedient to the traditions of the town, made a simple dinner off the finest foie gras, pink and succulent and half a bottle of champagne, and retired gratefully to bed. He spent the next morning in his room, changed into his ski-clothes and sent out for a pair of snow-goggles and thin leather gloves, sufficient to give some protection to his hands but close-fitting enough for the handling of his gun. He took the magazine out of his gun, pumped out the single round in the chamber and practised shooting himself in the wardrobe mirror with the gloves on until he was satisfied. Then he reloaded and got the fitting of the stitched pigskin holster comfortable inside the waist-band of his trousers. He had his bill sent up and paid it, and ordered his suitcase to be forwarded on to Tracy at the Vier Jahreszeiten. Then he sent for the day's papers and sat in front of the window, watching the traffic in the street and forgetting what he read.

When, at exactly midday, the telephone rang, he went straight down and out to the grey Peugeot 403 he had been told to expect. The driver was Ché-Ché. He acknowledged Bond's greeting curtly and, in silence, they drove for an hour across the uninteresting countryside, finally turning left off a secondary road into a muddy lane that meandered through thick forest. In due course there was the ill-kept stone wall of a large property and then a vast broken-down iron gateway leading into a park. On the unweeded driveway were the recent tracks of vehicles. They followed them past the dilapidated façade of a once-imposing château, on through the forest to where the trees gave way to fields. On the edge of the trees was a large barn in good repair. They stopped outside and Ché-Ché sounded three shorts on his horn. A small door in the wide double doors of the barn opened and Marc-Ange came out. He greeted Bond cheerfully. "Come along in, my friend. You are just in time for some good Strasbourg sausage and a passable Riquewihr. Rather thin and bitter. I would have christened it 'Château Pis-de-Chat,' but it serves to quench the thirst."

Inside it was almost like a film set. Lights blazed down on the ungainly shape of the Army helicopter and from somewhere came the cough of a small generator. The place seemed to be full of people. Bond recognized the faces of the Union men. The others were, he assumed, the local mechanics. Two men on ladders were busily engaged painting red crosses on white backgrounds on the black-painted fuselage of the machine, and the paint of the recognition letters, FLBGS, presumably civilian and false, still glittered wetly. Bond was introduced to the pilot, a bright-eyed, fair-haired young man in overalls called Georges. "You will be sitting beside him," explained Marc-Ange. "He is a good navigator, but he doesn't know the last stretch up the valley and he has never heard of Piz Gloria. You had better go over the maps with him after some food. The general route is Basle-Zürich." He laughed cheerfully. He said in French, "We are going to have some interesting conversation with the Swiss Air Defences, isn't it, Georges?"

Georges didn't smile. He said briefly, "I think we can fool them," and went about his business.

Bond accepted a foot of garlic sausage, a hunk of bread and a bottle of the "Pis-de-Chat," and sat on an upturned packing-case while Marc-Ange went back to supervising the loading of the "stores"—Schmeisser sub-machine guns and six-inch square packets in red oilcloth.

In due course, Marc-Ange lined up his team, including Bond, and carried out a quick inspection of sidearms, which, in the case of the Union men, included well-used flick-knives. The men, as well as Marc-Ange, were clothed in brand-new ski-clothes of grey cloth. Marc-Ange handed to all of them armlets in black cloth bearing the neatly stitched words "Bundesalpenpolizei." When Marc-Ange gave Bond his, he commented, "There is no such force as the 'Federal Police of the Alps.' But I doubt if our SPECTRE friends will know that. At least the arm-bands will make an important first impression."

Marc-Ange looked at his watch. He turned and called

out in French, "Two forty-five. All ready? Then let us roll!"

The farm tractor attached to the wheel-base of the helicopter started up, the gates of the barn were thrown wide and the great metal insect moved slowly out on to the grassland under the pale winter sun. The tractor was uncoupled and the pilot, followed by Bond, climbed up the little aluminium ladder and then into the raised cockpit, where they strapped themselves in. The others followed into the ten-seat cabin, the ladder was pulled up and the door banged and locked. On the ground, the mechanics lifted their thumbs and the pilot bent to his controls. He pressed the starter and, after a first indecisive cough, the engine fired healthily and the great blades began to turn. The pilot glanced back at the whirring tail-rotor. He waited while the needle on the rotor speed-indicator crept up to 200, then he released the wheel-brakes and pulled up slowly on the pitch-lever. The helicopter trembled, unwilling to leave the earth, but then came a slight jerk and they were up and climbing rapidly above the trees. The pilot retracted his wheels above the inflated snow-floats, gave the machine left rudder, pushed forward the joystick and they were off.

Almost at once they were over the Rhine and Basle lay ahead under a thick canopy of chimney-smoke. They reached two thousand feet and the pilot held it, skirting the town to the north. Now there came a crackle of static over Bond's ear-phones and Swiss Air Control, in thick Schwyzerdütch, asked them politely to identify themselves. The pilot made no reply and the question was repeated with more urgency. The pilot said in French, "I don't understand you." There was a pause, then a French voice again queried them. The pilot said, "Repeat yourself more clearly." The voice did so. The pilot said, "Helicopter of the Red Cross flying blood plasma to Italy." The radio went dead. Bond could imagine the scene in the control room somewhere down below—the arguing voices, the doubtful faces. Another voice, with more authority to it, spoke in French. "What is your destination?" "Wait," said the pilot. "I have it here. A moment please." After minutes he said, "Swiss Air Control?" "Yes, yes." "FL-BGS reporting. My destination is Ospedale Santa Monica at Bellinzona." The radio again went dead, only to come to life five minutes later. "FL-BGS FL-BGS," "Yes," said the pilot. "We have no record of your identification symbol. Please explain." "Your registration manual must be out of date. The aircraft was commissioned only one month ago." Another long pause. Now Zürich lay ahead and the silver boomerang of the Zürichersee

Now Zürich Airport came on the air. They must have been listening to Swiss Air Control. "FL-BGS, FL-BGS." "Yes, yes. What is it now?" "You have infringed the Civil Airlines Channel. Land and report to Flying Control. I repeat. Land and report." The pilot became indignant. "What do you mean 'land and report'? Have you no comprehension of human suffering? This is a mercy flight carrying blood plasma of a rare category. It is to save the life of an illustrious Italian scientist at Bellinzona. Have you no hearts down there? You tell me to 'land and report' when a life is at stake? Do you wish to be responsible for murder?" This Gallic outburst gave them peace until they had passed the Zürichersee. Bond chuckled. He gave the thumbs-up sign to the pilot. But then Federal Air Control at Berne came on the air and a deep, resonant voice said, "FL-BGS, FL-BGS. Who gave you clearance? I repeat. Who gave you clearance for your flight?" "You did." Bond smiled into his mouthpiece. The Big Lie! There was nothing like it. Now the Alps were ahead of them—those blasted Alps, looking beautiful and dangerous in the evening sun. Soon they would be in the shelter of the valleys, off the radar screens. But records had been hastily checked in Berne and the sombre voice came over to them again. The voice must have realized that the long debate would have been heard at every airport and by most pilots flying over Switzerland that evening. It was extremely polite, but firm. "FL-BGS, we have no record at Federal Air Control of your proposed flight. I regret but you are transgressing Swiss air-space. Unless you can give further authority for your flight, kindly return to Zürich and report to Flying Control."

The helicopter rocked. There was a flash of silver and a Dassault Mirage with Swiss markings flashed by not a hundred yards away, turned, leaving a trail of black vapour from the slow-burning of its fuel at this low altitude, and headed straight back at them, swerving off to port only at the last moment. The helicopter gave another lurch. The pilot spoke angrily into his mouthpiece. "Federal Air Control. This is FL-BGS. For further information contact International Red Cross at Geneva. I am just a pilot. I am not a 'rond de cuir,' a chairborne flyer. If you have lost the papers, that is not my fault. I repeat, check with Geneva. And, in the meantime, kindly call off the whole of the Swiss Air Force which is at present trying to make my passengers air-sick." The voice came back, but now more faintly, because of the mountains. "Who are your passengers?" The pilot played his trump card. "Representatives of the world's press. They have been listening to all this nonsense coming from the home of the famous International Red Cross. I wish you happy reading of your newspapers at breakfasttime tomorrow, gentlemen. And now, a little peace, yes? And please record in your log-books that I am not, repeat, not, the Soviet Air Force invading Switzerland."

There was silence. The Dassault Mirage had disappeared. They were climbing up the valley and were already past Davos. The gold-tipped needles of the glittering mountains seemed to be closing in on them from right and left. Ahead were the great peaks. Bond looked at his watch. Barely another ten minutes to go.

He turned and glanced down the hatch. The faces of Marc-Ange and of the others looked up at him, tense and livid under the setting sun that poured in through the windows, their eyes glinting redly.

Bond held up this thumb encouragingly. He spread out his ten fingers in their thin leather gloves.

Marc-Ange nodded. There was a shifting of the bodies in their seats. Bond turned back and gazed ahead, looking for the soaring peak that he loathed and feared.

25 HELL'S DELIGHT. ETC.

Yes! There was the bloody place! Now only the peak was golden. The plateau and the buildings were in indigo shadow, soon to be lit by the full moon.

Bond pointed. The helicopter wasn't liking the altitude. At 10,000 feet its rotors were finding it hard to get a grip of the thin air and the pilot was struggling to keep it at maximum revs. As he turned to port, in towards the face of the mountain, his radio crackled sharply and a harsh voice said, in German and then in French, "Landing forbidden. This is private property. I repeat, landing forbidden!" The pilot reached up to the cockpit roof and switched off the radio. He had studied his landing-point on the plateau on the mock-up. He got to it, hovered and gently came down. The helicopter bounced once on its rubber floats and settled. Already there was a group of men waiting for them. Eight men. Bond recognized some of them. They all had their hands in their pockets or in their wind-jackets. The engine coughed to a stop and the rotors swung round briefly in neutral and halted. Bond heard the bang of the door being opened behind him and the rattle of the men piling down the ladder. The two groups lined up facing each other. Marc-Ange said, with authority, "This is the Federal Police Alpine Patrol. There was trouble up here on Christmas Eve. We have come to investigate."

Fritz, the "head waiter," said angrily, "The local police have already been here. They have made their report. All is in order. Please leave at once. What is the Federal Police Alpine Patrol? I have never heard of it."

The pilot nudged Bond and pointed over to the left, to the building that housed the Count and the laboratories. A man, clumsy in bob-sleigh helmet and padding, was running down the path towards the cable station. He would be out of sight of the men on the ground. Bond said "Blast!" and scrambled out of his seat and into the cabin. He leaned out of the door and shouted, "The Big One. He's getting away!"

As Bond jumped, one of the SPECTRE men shouted, "Der Engländer. Der Spion!" And then, as Bond started running away to the right, weaving and dodging, all hell broke loose. There came the boom of heavy automatics as the SPECTRE team got off their first rounds, and bullets, tracer, flashed past Bond with the noise of humming-birds' wings. Then came the answering roar of the Schmeissers and Bond was left alone.

Now he was round the corner of the club, and, a hundred yards down the slope, the man in the crash helmet had torn open the door of the "garage" for the bob-sleighs in the foundations of the cable station. He emerged carrying a one-man skeleton bob. Holding it in front of him as a shield, he fired a burst from a heavy automatic at Bond and again the humming-birds whirred past. Bond knelt and, steadying his gun with two hands, fired three rounds with his Walther, but the man was now running the few yards to the glistening ice-mouth of the Gloria Express bob-run. Bond got a glimpse of the profile under the moon. Yes, it was Bloefeld all right! Even as Bond ran on down the slope, the man had flung himself down on his skeleton and had disappeared as if swallowed up by the glistening landscape. Bond got to the "garage." Damn, they were all six-men or two-men models! No, there was one skeleton at the back! Bond hauled it out. No time to see if the runners were straight, the steering-arm shifting easily! He ran to the start and hurled himself under the protecting chain in a mad forward dive that landed him half on and half off his skeleton. He straightened himself and shifted his body well forward on the flimsy little aluminium platform and gripped the steering-arm, keeping his elbows well in to his sides. He was already going like hell down the dark-blue gutter! He tried braking with the toes of both his boots. Damned little difference! What came first on the blasted run? There was this lateral straight across the shoulder of the mountain, then a big banked curve. He was into it now! Bond kept his right shoulder down and inched right on the steering-arm. Even so, he went perilously near the top edge of the bank before he dived down into the dark gully again. What came next on that metal map? Why in hell hadn't he studied it more carefully? He got his answer! It looked like a straight, but the shadows camouflaged a sharp dip. Bond left the ground and flew. The crash of his landing almost knocked the wind out of his body. He frantically dug his toes into the ice, managed to get down from perhaps fifty m.p.h. to forty. Well, well! So that was "Dead Man's Leap." What in hell was the next bit of murder? "Whizz-Bang Straight!" And by God it was! —200 yards when he must have been doing around seventy. He remembered that on the finishing straight of the Cresta the stars got up to over eighty. No doubt something like that was still to come! But now, flashing towards him, in silver and black, came an S-bend—"Battling S." The toes of Bond's boots slid maddeningly on the black ice. Under his nose he could see the parallel tracks of Blofeld's runners and, between them, the grooves of his toe-spikes. The old fox! As soon as he heard the helicopter, he must have got himself fixed for his only escape route. But at this speed Bond must surely be catching up with him! For God's sake look out! Here comes the S! There was nothing he could do about it. He swayed his body as best he could, felt the searing crash of one elbow against one wall, was hurled across into the opposite one and was then spewed out into the straight again. God Almighty, but it hurt! He could feel the cold wind on both elbows. The cloth had gone! Then so had the skin! Bond clenched his teeth. And he was only half-way down, if that! But then, ahead, flashing through a patch of moonlight, was the other body, Blofeld! Bond took a chance, heaved himself up on one hand and reached down for his gun. The wind tried to tear him off the bob, but he had the gun. He opened his mouth wide and gripped the gun between his teeth, flexed the ice-caked leather on his right hand. Then he got the gun in his right hand, lifted his toes off the ice and went like hell. But now the man had disappeared into the shadows and a giant bank reared up ahead. This would be "Hell's Delight"! Oh well, if he could make this, there would be another straight and he could begin shooting. Bond dug his toes in, got a glimpse of an ice-wall ahead and to the left, and in a flash was climbing it, straight up! God, in a split second he would be over the edge! Bond hammered in his right boot and lurched his body to the right, tearing at the steering-arm. Reluctantly the sliver of aluminium answered and Bond, inches from the top of the wall, found himself swooping down into blackness and then out again on to a moonlit straight. Only fifty yards ahead was the flying figure, with chips of ice fountaining up from the braking spikes on his boots. Bond held his breath and got off two shots. He thought they were good ones, but now the man had gone into shadow again. But Bond was gaining, gaining. His lips drew back from his teeth in an almost animal snarl. You bastard! You're a dead duck! You can't stop or fire back. I'm coming after you like lightning! Soon I shall only be ten, five yards behind you. Then you'll have had it!

But the shadows concealed another hazard, long transverse waves in the ice—"The Bone-shaker"! Bond crashed from one to the next, felt his boots being almost torn from his feet as he tried to brake, nearly lost his gun, felt his stomach flatten against his spine with each shattering impact, felt his rib cage almost cracking. But then it was over and Bond sucked in air through his clenched teeth. Now for a length of straight! But what was that ahead on the track? It was something black, something the size of a big lemon that was bouncing along gaily like a child's rubber ball. Had Blofeld, now only about thirty yards ahead, dropped something, a bit of his equipment? *Had he?* The realization came to Bond in a surge of terror that almost made him vomit. He ground his toes into the ice. No effect! He was gaining on the gaily bouncing thing. Flashing down on it. On the grenade!

Bond, sick in the stomach, lifted his toes and let himself go. What setting had Blofeld put on it? How long had he held it with the pin out? The only hope was to pray to God and race it!

The next thing Bond knew was that the whole track had blown up in his face and that he and his skeleton bob were flying through the air. He landed in soft snow, with the skeleton on top of him and passed out like a light.

Later, Bond was to estimate that he lay there only a matter of minutes. It was a tremendous explosion from the mountain above him that brought him staggering to his feet, up to his belly in snow. He looked vaguely up to where it had come from. It must have been the club building going up, because now there was the glare of flames and a tower of smoke that rose towards the moon. There came the echoing crack of another explosion and Blofeld's block disintegrated, great chunks of it crashing down the mountain side, turning themselves into giant snowballs that bounded off down towards the tree line. By God, they'll start another avalanche! thought Bond vaguely. Then he realized that it didn't matter this time, he was away to the right, almost underneath the cable railway. And now the station went up and Bond stared fascinated as the great wires, their tension released, came hissing and snaking down the mountain towards him. There was nothing he could do about it but stand and watch. If they cut him down, they cut him down. But they lashed past in the snow, wrapped themselves briefly round the tall pylon above the tree line, tore it away in a metallic crackling and disappeared over the edge of the shoulder.

Bond laughed weakly with pleasure and began feeling himself for damage. His torn elbows he already knew about, but his forehead hurt like hell. He felt it gingerly, then scooped up a handful of snow and held it against the wound. The blood showed black in the moonlight. He ached all over, but there didn't seem to be anything broken. He bent dazedly to the twisted remains of the skeleton. The steering-arm had gone, had probably saved his head, and both runners were bent. There were a lot of rattles from the rivets, but perhaps the damned thing would run. It had bloody well got to! There was no other way for Bond to get down the mountain! His gun? Gone to hell, of course. Wearily Bond heaved himself over the wall of the track and slid carefully down, clutching the remains of his skeleton. As soon as he got to the bottom of the gutter, everything began to slip downwards, but he managed to haul himself on to the bob and get shakily going. In fact, the bent runners were a blessing and the bob scraped slowly down, leaving great furrows in the ice. There were more turns, more hazards, but, at a bare ten miles an hour, they were child's play and soon Bond was through the tree line and into "Paradise Alley," the finishing straight, where he slowly came to a halt. He left the skeleton where it stopped and scrambled over the low ice-wall. Here the snow was beaten hard by spectators' feet and he stumbled slowly along, nursing his aches and occasionally dabbing at his head with handfuls of snow. What would he find at the bottom, by the cable station? If it was Blofeld, Bond would be a dead duck! But there were no lights on in the station into which the cables now trailed limply along the ground. By God, that had been an expensive bang! But what of Marc-Ange and his merry men, and the helicopter?

As if to answer him, he heard the clatter of its engine high up in the mountains and in a moment the ungainly black shape crossed the moon and disappeared down the valley. Bond smiled to himself. They were going to have a tough time arguing themselves across Swiss air-space this time! But Marc-Ange had thought out an alternative route over Germany. That would also not be fun. They would have to argue the toss with N.A.T.O.! Well, if a Marseillais couldn't blarney his way across two hundred miles, nobody could!

And now, up the road from Samaden that Bond knew so well, came the iron hee-haw warning of the local fire-engine. The blinking red light on its cabin roof was perhaps a mile away. Bond, carefully approaching the corner of the darkened cable station, prepared his story. He crept up to the wall of the building and looked round. Nobody! No trace except fresh tyre-marks outside the entrance door. Blofeld must have telephoned his man down here before he started and used him and his car for the getaway. Which way had he gone? Bond walked out on to the road. The tracks turned left. Blofeld would be at the Bernina Pass or over it by now, on his way down into Italy and away. It might still have been possible to have him held at the frontier by alerting the fire-brigade, whose lights now held Bond in their beam. No! That would be idiotic. How had Bond got this knowledge unless he himself had been up at Piz Gloria that night? No, he must just play the part of the stupidest tourist in the Engadine!

The shining red vehicle pulled up in front of the cable station and the warning klaxons ran down with an iron groan. Men jumped to the ground. Some went into the station while others stood gazing up at the Piz Gloria, where a dull red glow still showed. A man in a peaked cap, presumably the captain of the team, came up to Bond and saluted. He fired off a torrent of Schwyzerdütch. Bond shook his head. The man tried French. Bond again showed incomprehension. Another man with fragmentary English was called over. "What is it that is happening?" he asked.

Bond shook his head dazedly. "I don't know. I was walking down from Pontresina to Samaden. I came on a day excursion from Zürich and missed my bus. I was going to take a train from Samaden. Then I saw these explosions up the mountain"—he waved vaguely—"and I walked up there past the station to see better, and the next thing I knew was a bang on the head and being dragged along the path." He indicated his bleeding head and the raw elbows that protruded from his torn sleeves. "It must have been the broken cable. It must have hit me and dragged me with it. Have you got a Red Cross outfit with you?"

"Yes, yes." The man called over to the group, and one of his colleagues wearing a Red Cross brassard on his arm fetched his black box from the vehicle and came over. He clucked his tongue over Bond's injuries and, while his interrogator told Bond's story to the Captain, bade Bond follow him into the toilette in the station. There, by the light of a torch, he washed Bond's wounds, applied quantities of iodine that stung like hell and then strapped wide strips of Elastoplast over the damage. Bond looked at his face in the mirror. He laughed. Hell of a bridegroom he was going to make! The Red Cross man cluck-clucked in sympathy, produced a flask of brandy out of his box and offered it to Bond. Bond gratefully took a long swig. The interpreter came in. "There is nothing we can do here. It will need a helicopter from the mountain rescue team. We must go back to Samaden and report. You wish to come?"

"I certainly do," said Bond enthusiastically, and, with many politenesses and no question of why he should attempt the icy walk to Samaden in the dark instead of taking a taxi, he was borne comfortably to Samaden and dropped off, with the warmest gestures of goodwill and sympathy at the railway station.

By a rattling Personenzug to Coire and then by express to Zürich, Bond got to the door of the flat of Head of Station Z in the Bahnhofstrasse at two in the morning. He had had some sleep in the train but he was almost out on his feet, and his whole body felt as if it had been beaten with wooden truncheons. He leaned wearily against the bell ticketed "Muir" until a tousled man in pyjamas came and opened the door and held it on the chain. "Um Gottes Willen! Was ist denn los?" he inquired angrily. The English accent came through. Bond said, "It's me that's 'los.' It's 007 again, I'm afraid."

"Good God, man, come in, come in!" Muir opened the door and looked quickly up and down the empty street. "Anyone after you?"

"Shouldn't think so," said Bond thickly, coming gratefully into the warmth of the entrance hall. Head of Z closed the door and locked it. He turned and looked at Bond. "Christ, old boy, what in hell's been happening to you? You look as if you'd been through a mangle. Here, come in and have a drink." He led the way into a comfortable sitting-room. He gestured at the sideboard. "Help yourself. I'll just tell hyllis not to worry—unless you'd like her to have a look t the damage. She's quite a hand at that sort of thing."

"No, it's all right, thanks. A drink'll fix me. Nice and 'arm in here. I never want to see a patch of snow again s long as I live."

Muir went out and Bond heard a quick comfabulation cross the passage. Muir came back. "Phyllis is fixing the pare room. She'll put some fresh dressings and stuff out 1 the bathroom. Now then"—he poured himself a thin 'hisky and soda to keep Bond company and sat down opposite im—"tell me what you can."

Bond said, "I'm terribly sorry, but I can't tell you much. 'he same business as the other day. Next chapter. I promise ou'd do better to know nothing about it. I wouldn't have ome here only I've got to get a signal off to M, personal, 'iple X cipher to be deciphered by recipient only. Would ou be a good chap and put it on the printer?"

"Of course." Muir looked at his watch. "Two-thirty .M. Hell of a time to wake the old man up. But that's our business. Here, come into the cockpit, so to speak." Ie walked across to the book-lined wall, took out a book nd fiddled. There was a click and a small door swung open. Mind your head," said Muir. "Old disused lavatory. Just 1e right size. Gets a bit stuffy when there's a lot of traffic oming or going, but that can't be helped. We can afford leave the door open." He bent down to a safe on the oor, worked the combination and brought out what looked ke a portable typewriter. He set it on the shelf next to 1e bulky teleprinter, sat down and clacked off the prefix nd routing instructions, winding a small handle at the ide of the machine at the end of each word. "O.K. Fire way!"

Bond leaned up against the wall. He had toyed with arious formulas on his journey down to Samaden. It ad to be something that would get through accurately M and yet keep Muir in the dark, keep his hands clean. ond said, "All right. Make it this, would you? REDOUBT ROPERLY FIXED STOP DETAILS LACKING AS EYE VENT SOLO AFTER THE OWNER WHO GREATLY EGRET GOT AWAY AND PROBABLY ITALICIZED Y NOW STOP FORWARDING FULL REPORT FROM TATION M THEN GRATEFULLY ACCEPTING TEN AYS LEAVE SIGNED 007."

Muir repeated the signal and then began putting it, 1 the five-figure groups that had come off the Triple X 1achine, on to the teleprinter.

Bond watched the message go, the end of another chapt of his duties, as Marc-Ange had put it, “On Her Majesty Secret Service.” What would Her Majesty think of th string of crimes committed in her name? God, it was stuf in the little room! Bond felt the cold sweat break out c his forehead. He put his hand up to his face, muttered som thing indistinctly about “that bloody mountain” and grac fully crumpled to the floor.

26 HAPPINESS WITHOUT A SHADOW?

Tracy gazed at him wide-eyed when she met him outsic Passport Control at Munich Airport, but she waited un they were inside the little Lancia before she burst in tears. “What have they been doing to you?” she said throug her sobs. “What have they been doing to you now?”

Bond took her in his arms. “It's all right, Tracy. I promi you. These are only cuts and bruises, like a bad ski-fa Now don't be a goose. They could happen to anyone He smoothed back her hair and took out his handkerchi and dabbed at her eyes.

She took the handkerchief from him and laughed throug her tears. “Now you've ruined my eye-black. And I put on so carefully for you.” She took out her pocket mirr and carefully wiped away the smudges. She said, “It's silly. But I knew you were up to no good. As soon you said you were going off for a few days to clean u something instead of coming to me, I knew you were goi to get into more trouble. And now Marc-Ange has telephon and asked me if I've seen you. He was very mysterio and sounded worried. And when I said I hadn't he ju rang off. And now there's this story in the papers abo Piz Gloria. And you were so guarded on the telephone th morning. And from Zürich. I knew it all tied up.” Sh put back her mirror and pressed the self-starter. “All righ I won't ask questions. And I'm sorry I cried.” She add fiercely, “But you *are* such an idiot! You don't seem think it matters to *anyone*. The way you go on playing R Indians. It's so—so selfish.”

Bond reached out and pressed her hand on the whe He hated “scenes.” But it was true what she said. I hadn't thought of her, only of the job. It never cross his mind that anybody really cared about him. A sha of the head from his friends when he went, a few caref lines in the obituary columns of *The Times*, a momenta ang in a few girls' hearts. But now, in three days' time, would no longer be alone. He would be a half of two eople. There wouldn't only be May and Mary Goodnight ho would tut-tut over him when he came back from some b as a hospital case. Now, if he got himself killed, there ould be Tracy who would at any rate partially die with m.

The little car wove expertly through the traffic. Bond id, "I'm sorry, Tracy. It was something that had to be one. You know how it is. I just couldn't back out of it. really wouldn't have been happy here, as I am now, if d shirked it. You do see that, don't you?"

She reached out and touched his cheek. "I wouldn't love ou if you weren't a pirate. I expect it's in the blood. I'll t used to it. Don't change. I don't want to draw your eth like women do with their men. I want to live with *ou*, not with somebody else. But don't mind if I howl e a dog every now and then. Or rather like a bitch. It's ly love." She gave him a fleeting smile. "*Die Welt*, ith the story in it, is behind the seat on the floor."

Bond laughed at her mind-reading. "Damn you, Tracy." e reached for the paper. He had been aching to see hat it said, how much had come out.

There it was, down the central gutter between the first ad, inevitably on Berlin, and the second, equally inevitably, the miracle of the latest German export figures. All it id, "from our correspondent," date-lined St Moritz, was IYSTERIOUS EXPLOSIONS ON PIZ GLORIA. Cable ailway to Millionaires' Resort Destroyed.' And then a few es repeating the content of the headings and saying that e police would investigate by helicopter at first light in the orning. The next headline caught Bond's eye: 'IN ENG-AND, POLIO SCARE.' And then, date-lined the day before om London, a brief Reuter dispatch: "The nine girls held various British airports on suspicion of having had con-ct with a possible polio carrier at Zürich Airport, also an nglish girl, are still being held in quarantine. A Ministry of ealth representative said that this was purely a routine pre-ution. A tenth girl, the origin of the scare, a Miss Violet 'Neill, is under observation at Shannon Hospital. She is native of Eire."

Bond smiled to himself. When they were pushed, the itish could do this sort of thing supremely well. How uch co-ordination had this brief report required? To gin with, M. Then the C.I.D., M.I.5, Ag. and Fish., H.M. istoms, Passport Control, the Ministry of Health and e Government of Eire. All had contributed, and with tremendous speed and efficiency. And the end produc put out to the world, had been through the Press Associatic to Reuter. Bond tossed the paper over his shoulder ar watched the Kaiser Yellow buildings of what had on been one of the most beautiful towns in Europe, now slow being rebuilt in the same old Kaiser Yellow, file by their post-war drabness. So the case was closed, the assignme over!

But still The Big One had got away!

They got to the hotel at about three o'clock. There w a message for Tracy to call Marc-Ange at the Maison Rou at Strasbourg. They went up to her room and got throug Tracy said, "Here he is, Papa, and almost in one piece She handed the receiver to Bond.

Marc-Ange said, "Did you get him?"

"No, damn it. He's in Italy now. At least I think is. That was the way he went. How did you get on? looked fine from down below."

"Satisfactory. All accounted for."

"Gone?"

"Yes. Gone for good. There was no trace of your ma from Zürich. I lost two. Our friend had left a surprise his filing-cabinet. That accounted for Ché-Ché. Anoth one wasn't quick enough. That is all. The trip back w entertaining. I will give you the details tomorrow. I sha travel tonight in my sleeping-car. You know?"

"Yes. By the way, what about the girl friend, Irma?"

"There was no sign of her. Just as well. It would ha been difficult to send her away like the others."

"Yes. Well, thanks, Marc-Ange. And the news from Englar is also good. See you tomorrow."

Bond put down the receiver. Tracy had discreetly retir to the bathroom and locked the door. She now calle "Can I come out?"

"Two minutes, darling." Bond got on to Station His call was expected. He arranged to visit the Head Station, a man he knew slightly called Lieutenant-Command Savage, in an hour's time. He released Tracy and th made plans for the evening, then he went along to his room.

His suitcase had been unpacked and there was a bo of crocuses beside his bed. Bond smiled, picked up t bowl and placed it firmly on the window-sill. Then had a quick shower, complicated by having to keep h dressings dry, changed out of his stinking ski clothes in the warmer of the two dark-blue suits he had brought wi him, sat down at the writing-desk and jotted down the headin of what he would have to put on the teleprinter to M. Th he put on his dark-blue raincoat and went down into the street and along to the Odeons Platz.

(If he had not been thinking of other things, he might have noticed the woman on the other side of the street, a squat, toad-like figure in a frowsty dark-green Loden cloak, who gave a start of surprise when she saw him sauntering along, hustled across the street through the traffic and got on his tail. She was expert at what she was doing, and, when he went into the newish apartment house on the Odeons Platz, she didn't go near the door to verify the address, but waited on the far side of the square until he came out. Then she tailed him back to the Vier Jahreszeiten, took a taxi back to her flat and put in a long-distance call to the Metropole Hotel on Lake Como.)

Bond went up to his room. On the writing-desk an impressive array of dressings and medicaments had been laid out. He got on to Tracy and said, "What the hell is this? Have you got a pass-key or something?"

She laughed. "The maid on this floor has become a friend. She understands people who are in love. Which is more than you do. What do you mean by moving those flowers?"

"They're lovely. I thought they looked prettier by the window and they will get some sun there. Now I'll make a deal. If you'll come along and change my dressings, I'll take you down and buy you a drink. Just one. And three for me. That's the right ratio between men and women. All right?"

"Wilco." Her receiver went down.

It hurt like hell and Bond couldn't prevent the tears of pain from squeezing out of his eyes. She kissed them away. She looked pale at what she had seen. "You're sure you oughtn't to see a doctor?"

"I'm just seeing one. You did it beautifully. What worries me is how we're going to make love. In the proper fashion, elbows are rather important for the man."

"Then we'll do it in an improper fashion. But not tonight, or tomorrow. Only when we're married. Till then I am going to pretend I'm a virgin." She looked at him seriously. "I wish I was, James. I am in a way, you know. People can make love without loving."

"Drinks," said Bond firmly. "We've got all the time in the world to talk about love."

"You *are* a pig," she said indignantly. "We've got so much to talk about and all you think about is drink."

Bond laughed. He put an arm gingerly round her neck and kissed her long and passionately. He broke away.

"There, that's just the beginning of my conversation. We'll go on with the duller bits in the bar. Then we'll have a wonderful dinner in Walterspiel's and talk about rings and whether we'll sleep in twin beds or one, and whether I've got enough sheets and pillows for two and other exciting things to do with being married."

And it was in that way that the evening passed and Bond's head reeled with all the practical feminine problems she raised, in high seriousness, but he was surprised to find that all this nest-building gave him a curious pleasure, a feeling that he had at last come to rest and that life would now be fuller, have more meaning, for having someone to share it with. Togetherness! What a curiously valid cliché it was!

The next day was occupied with hilarious meals with Marc-Ange, whose giant trailer had come during the night to take up most of the parking space behind the hotel, and with searching the antique shops for an engagement and a wedding-ring. The latter was easy, the traditional plain gold band, but Tracy couldn't make up her mind about the engagement ring and finally dispatched Bond to find something he liked himself while she had her last fitting for her "going-away" dress. Bond hired a taxi, and he and the taxi-man, who had been a Luftwaffe pilot during the war and was proud of it, tore round the town together until, at an antique shop near the Nymphenburg Palace, Bond found what he wanted—a baroque ring in white gold with two diamond hands clasped. It was graceful and simple and the taxi-man was also in favour, so the deal was done and the two men went off to celebrate at the Franziskaner Keller, where they ate mounds of Weisswurst and drank four steins of beer each and swore they wouldn't ever fight each other again. Then, happy with his last bachelor party, Bond returned tipsily to the hotel, avoided being embraced by the taxi-man and went straight up to Tracy's room and put the ring on her finger.

She burst into tears, sobbing that it was the most beautiful ring in the world, but when he took her in his arms she began to giggle. "Oh, James, you are bad. You stink like a pig of beer and sausages. Where *have* you been?"

When Bond told her, she laughed at the picture he painted of his last fling and then paraded happily up and down the room, making exaggeratedly gracious gestures with her hand to show off the ring and for the diamonds to catch the light. Then the telephone rang and it was Marc-Ange saying that he wanted to talk to Bond in the bar, and would Tracy kindly keep out of the way for half an hour?

Bond went down and, after careful consideration, decided that schnapps would go with his beer and ordered a double Steinhäger. Marc-Ange's face was serious. "Now listen, James. We have not had a proper talk. It is very wrong. I am about to become your father-in-law and I insist. Many months ago, I made you a serious offer. You declined it. But now you have accepted it. What is the name of your bank?"

Bond said angrily, "Shut up, Marc-Ange. If you think I'll accept a million pounds from you or from anyone else you're mistaken. I don't want my life to be ruined. Too much money is the worst curse you can lay on anyone's head. I have enough. Tracy has enough. It will be fun saving up to buy something we want but can't quite afford. That is the only kind of money to have—not quite enough."

Marc-Ange said furiously, "You have been drinking. You are drunk. You don't understand what you are saying. What I am giving you is only a fifth of my fortune. You understand? It means nothing to me. Tracy is used to having whatever she wants. I wish it to remain so. She is my only child. You cannot possibly keep her on a civil servant's pay. You have got to accept!"

"If you give me any money, I swear I will pass it on to charity. You want to give your money away to a dogs' home? All right. Go ahead!"

"But James"—Marc-Ange was now pleading—"what will you accept from me? Then a trust fund for any children you may have. Yes?"

"Even worse. If we have children, I will not have this noose hung round their heads. I didn't have any money and I haven't needed it. I've loved winning money gambling because that is found money, money that comes out of the air like a great surprise. If I'd inherited money, I'd have gone the way of all those playboy friends of Tracy's you complained about so much. No, Marc-Ange." Bond drained his Steinhäger decisively. "It's no good."

Marc-Ange looked as if he would burst into tears, Bond relented. He said, "It's very kind of you, Marc-Ange, and I appreciate it from the heart. I'll tell you what. If I swear to come to you if either of us ever needs help, will that do? There may be illnesses and things. Perhaps it would be nice if we had a cottage in the country somewhere. We may need help if we have children. Now. How about that? Is it a bargain?"

Marc-Ange turned doubtful, dogs' eyes on Bond. "You promise? You would not cheat me of helping you, adding to your happiness when you allow me to?"

Bond reached over and took Marc-Ange's right hand and pressed it. "My word on it. Now come on, pull yourself together. Here comes Tracy. She'll think we've been having a fight."

"So we have," said Marc-Ange gloomily. "And it is the first fight I have ever lost."

27 ALL THE TIME IN THE WORLD

I do.

James Bond said the words at ten-thirty in the morning of a crystal-clear New Year's Day in the British Consul General's drawing-room.

And he meant them.

The Consul General had proved himself, as British Consuls so often do, to be a man of efficiency and a man with a heart. It was a holiday for him and, as he confessed, he should have been recovering from a New Year's Eve hangover. And he had shaved many days off the formal period of notice, but that, he explained, he had occasionally, and improperly, risked in his career if there were exceptional circumstances such as the imminent death of either party. "You both look healthy enough," he had said when they first visited him together, "but that's a nasty cut on your head, Commander Bond, and the Countess is perhaps looking a little pale. And I have taken the precaution of obtaining special dispensation from the Foreign Secretary, which I may say, to my surprise, was immediately forthcoming. So let's make it New Year's Day. And come to my home. My wife is hopelessly sentimental about these occasional jobs I have to do, and I know she'd love to meet you both."

The papers were signed, and Head of Station M, who had agreed to act as Bond's best man and who was secretly longing to write a sensational note to the head of his London Section about all this, produced a handful of confetti and threw most of it over Marc-Ange, who had turned up in a "cylindre" and a full suit of very French tails with, surprisingly, two rows of medals of which the last, to Bond's astonishment, was the King's Medal for foreign resistance-fighters.

"I will tell you all about it one day, my dear James,"

he had said in answer to Bond's admiring inquiry. "It was tremendous fun. I had myself what the Americans call 'a ball.' And"—his voice sank to a whisper and he put one finger along his brown, sensitive nose—"I confess that I profited by the occasion to lay my hands on the secret funds of a certain section of the Abwehr. But Herkos Odonton, my dear James! Herkos Odonton! Medals are so often just the badges of good luck. If I am a hero, it is for things for which no medals are awarded. And"—he drew lines with his fingers across his chest—"there is hardly room on the breast of this 'frac,' which, by the way, is by courtesy of the excellent Galeries Barbès in Marseilles, for all that I am due under that heading."

The farewells were said and Bond submitted himself, he swore for the last time, to Marc-Ange's embraces and they went down the steps to the waiting Lancia. Someone, Bond suspected the Consul's wife, had tied white ribbons from the corners of the wind-screen to the grill of the radiator, and there was a small group of bystanders, passers-by, who had stopped, as they do all over the world, to see who it was, what they looked like.

The Consul General shook Bond by the hand. "I'm afraid we haven't managed to keep this as private as you'd have liked. A woman reporter came on from the *Münchener Illustrierte* this morning. Wouldn't say who she was. Gossip-writer, I suppose. I had to give her the bare facts. She particularly wanted to know the time of the ceremony, if you can call it that, so that they could send a camera-man along. At least you've been spared that. All still tight, I suppose. Well, so long and the best of luck."

Tracy, who had elected to "go away" in a dark-grey Tyroler outfit with the traditional dark-green trimmings and stag's-horn buttons, threw her saucy mountaineer's hat with its gay chamois' beard cockade into the back seat, climbed in and pressed the starter. The engine purred and then roared softly as she went through the gears down the empty street. They both waved one hand out of a window and Bond, looking back, saw Marc-Ange's "cylindre" whirling up into the air. There was a small flutter of answering hands from the pavement and then they were round the corner and away.

When they found the Autobahn exit for Salzburg and Kufstein, Bond said, "Be an angel and pull in to the side, Tracy. I've got two things to do."

She pulled in on to the grass verge. The brown grass of winter showed through the thin snow. Bond reached for her and took her in his arms. He kissed her tenderly. "That's the first thing, and I just wanted to say that I'll look after you, Tracy. Will you mind being looked after?"

She held him away from her and looked at him. She smiled. Her eyes were introspective. "That's what it means being Mr and Mrs, doesn't it? They don't say Mrs and Mr. But *you* need looking after too. Let's just look after each other."

"All right. But I'd rather have my job than yours. Now. I simply must get out and take down those ribbons. I can't stand looking like a coronation. D'you mind?"

She laughed. "You like being anonymous. I want everyone to cheer as we go by. I know you're going to have this car sprayed grey or black as soon as you get a chance. That's all right. But nothing's going to stop me wearing you like a flag from now on. Will you sometimes feel like wearing me like a flag?"

"On all holidays and feast days." Bond got out and removed the ribbons. He looked up at the cloudless sky. The sun felt warm on his face. He said, "Do you think we'd be too cold if we took the roof down?"

"No, let's. We can only see half the world with it up. And it's a lovely drive from here to Kitzbühel. We can always put it up again if we want to."

Bond unscrewed the two butterfly nuts and folded the canvas top back behind the seats. He had a look up and down the Autobahn. There was plenty of traffic. At the big Shell station on the roundabout they had just passed, his eye was caught by a bright-red open Maserati being tanked up. Fast job. And a typical sporty couple, a man and a woman in the driving-seat—white dust-coats and linen helmets buttoned under the chin. Big dark-green talc goggles that obscured most of the rest of the faces. Usual German speedsters' uniform. Too far away to see if they were good-looking enough for the car, but the silhouette of the woman wasn't promising. Bond got in beside Tracy and they set off again down the beautifully landscaped road.

They didn't talk much. Tracy kept at about eighty and there was wind-roar. That was the trouble about open cars. Bond glanced at his watch. 11.45. They would get to Kufstein at about one. There was a splendid Gasthaus up the winding streets towards the great castle. Here was a tiny lane of pleasure, full of the heart-plucking whine of zither music and the gentle melancholy of Tyrolean yodellers. It was here that the German tourist traditionally stopped after his day's outing into cheap Austria, just outside the German frontier, for a last giant meal of Austrian food and wine. Bond put his mouth up close to Tracy's ear and told her about it and about the other attraction at Kufstein—the most imaginative war memorial, for the 1914-18 war, ever devised. Punctually at midday every day, the windows of the castle are thrown open and a voluntary is played on the great organ inside. It can be heard for kilometres down the valley between the giant mountain ranges for which Kufstein provides the gateway. "But we shall miss it. It's coming up for twelve now."

"Never mind," said Tracy, "I'll make do with the zithers while you guzzle your beer and schnapps." She turned in to the right-hand fork leading to the underpass for Kufstein, and they were at once through Rosenheim and the great white peaks were immediately ahead.

The traffic was much sparser now and there were kilometres where theirs was the only car on the road that arrowed away between white meadows and larch copses, towards the glittering barrier where blood had been shed between warring armies for centuries. Bond glanced behind him. Miles away down the great highway was a speck of red. The Maserati? They certainly hadn't got much competitive spirit if they couldn't catch the Lancia at eighty! No good having a car like that if you didn't drive it so as to lose all other traffic in your mirror. Perhaps he was doing them an injustice. Perhaps they too only wanted to motor quietly along and enjoy the day.

Ten minutes later, Tracy said, "There's a red car coming up fast behind. Do you want me to lose him?" "No," said Bond. "Let him go. We've got all the time in the world."

Now he could hear the rasping whine of the eight cylinders. He leaned over to the left and jerked a laconic thumb forwards, waving the Maserati past.

The whine changed to a shattering roar. The windscreen of the Lancia disappeared as if hit by a monster fist. Bond caught a glimpse of a taut, snarling mouth under a syphilitic nose, the flash-eliminator of some automatic gun being withdrawn, and then the red car was past and the Lancia was going like hell off the verge across a stretch of snow and smashing a path through a young copse. Then Bond's head crashed into the wind-screen frame and he was out.

When he came to, a man in the khaki uniform of the Autobahn Patrol was shaking him. The young face was stark with horror. "Was ist denn geschehen? Was ist denn geschehen?"

Bond turned towards Tracy. She was lying forward with her face buried in the ruins of the steering-wheel. Her pink handkerchief had come off and the bell of golden hair hung down and hid her face. Bond put his arm around her shoulders, across which the dark patches had begun to flower.

He pressed her against him. He looked up at the young man and smiled his reassurance.

"It's all right," he said in a clear voice as if explaining something to a child. "It's quite all right. She's having a rest. We'll be going on soon. There's no hurry. You see"—Bond's head sank down against hers and he whispered into her hair—"you see, we've got all the time in the world."

The young patrolman took a last scared look at the motionless couple, hurried over to his motor-cycle, picked up the hand-microphone and began talking urgently to the rescue headquarters.

Other SIGNET Novels of Suspense